THE JANUARY WISH

JULIET MADISON

To Mum and Dad, for helping me create a new beginning.

CHAPTER ONE

D r Sylvia Greene had never done anything like this before in her life. She wasn't one for succumbing to fanfare or superstitious traditions. She didn't knock on wood or cross her fingers, and couldn't care less if she happened to walk under a ladder. But somehow, she'd found herself lining up to take part in the annual Tarrin's Bay Wishing Festival.

What on earth am I doing here? People I know might see me!

Sylvia glanced around surreptitiously through the lenses of her Dior sunglasses. There were a few familiar faces, but most of the people wandering around and standing in line were tourists. Probably because the locals knew that wishes made by tossing a coin into the historic four metre tall fountain certainly didn't come true. If they did, the local newspaper would be all over it. Not once had Sylvia read any proof that someone's wish had come true. But every year on the 4th of January, the anniversary of the fountain's construction, people came from far and wide to make their wish.

She only meant to wander around the market stalls in Miracle Park, soak up the delicious summer sunshine, and pick up a jar of her favourite chilli and tomato relish from the

'Homemade for You' stall, but as Sylvia walked past the huge line near the fountain, her legs had other ideas.

I should just go home.

She turned to the growing crowd behind her. To leave, she'd have to excuse herself past about fifty people in line, making herself *more* conspicuous. Plus, she spotted one of her patients in the queue. A particularly loud and talkative patient, Mr Benson. Damn it! She'd have to stay or get noticed backing out.

When she was a hospital intern it had been easy to get out of difficult situations by simply pretending to be on call and rushing off to deal with a fake emergency. It certainly came in handy during many a disastrous date. Now, though, she worked nine to five... well, to six or seven some nights, and was never on call. Sylvia loved her familiar routine. She'd been keen to get into general practice as soon as possible after receiving her qualifications, never having been able to cope with hospital shift work.

The coin in Sylvia's pocket cooled her warm fingers as she fiddled with it impatiently. At least this was all for charity. That would be her excuse if anyone asked why she, Dr Sylvia Greene, sceptic and all-round party-pooper, was making a wish. She had a great life; an interesting career, a best friend, good health, a nice house, and even a new boyfriend. What else could she possibly wish for? What *was* she doing here?

Distracted by her thoughts, she jumped when the person behind tapped her shoulder and flicked a hand towards the front of the line. Sylvia took a step forward. Only one person to go, then it would be her turn. A teenage girl stepped forward and threw her coin joyously into the fountain, a hopeful smile on her face. Probably wishing for the boy she liked to notice her, Sylvia thought. The girl walked around the fountain three times, before exiting the cordoned area framing it and running off to hug her friends waiting nearby.

Legend says on the day of its completed construction in 1907, a young woman tossed in a coin to make a wish and walked around the fountain three times. That evening, her missing husband returned safe and sound. Another woman made a wish that day and not even a week later was cured of a potentially fatal disease. Or so the legend says. Again, there had been *no* proof.

'Step right up, ma'am,' said the guy with the microphone, whose non-stop commentating brought more people to the line by the minute.

No turning back now.

With her wish in mind, Sylvia tossed the coin. A gentle plop sounded and circular ripples spread outward through the water. Tiny bubbles rose to the surface as the coin joined the others that had gone before. She walked quickly around the fountain three times, adjusting her sunglasses and dipping her head on the way. The process seemed to take forever; she was conscious that all eyes were on her.

Relief greeted her as she merged back into the crowd, but only for a moment.

'Doc! Who'da thought we'd see you here today, huh?'

Sylvia's patient waved as he waited his turn in line.

'So, what did you wish for, Doc? Wait! Don't tell me.' He covered his ears. 'If you tell someone your wish, it won't come true, will it?'

'I'm, er... just doing my bit for charity,' Sylvia said in her best doctor-like voice.

'Good on ya, Doc. Oh, I'll see you next week. First patient for the year I am, 9am sharp Mondee mornin'. Been waitin' patiently for you to resume work. Ya see, my constipation's returned, and geez, this prostate of mine, whoa! I tell ya, the nasty little bugger's givin' me such a hard time!'

Mr Benson would quite likely be perfectly okay with Sylvia doing a consultation and examination as he waited in line.

'...And don't get me started on me arthritis, let me tell ya—' The person behind him, gesturing to move forward, politely cut off Mr Benson. 'Oh, anyway, we'll discuss all the details next week. See ya then, Doc!'

Sylvia waved, thinking she should have wished for Mr Benson to switch doctors.

The sun warmed her skin as she walked out of Miracle Park, past the historic terrace shops with their homewares, boutique clothing and unique gifts, and up the road towards her house. The afternoon ocean breeze ran like fingers through her hair as Sylvia thought about her wish. Eighteen years had passed since the day that changed her life forever, the memory playing on her mind more and more lately. She lived a satisfying life, but a part of her, deep inside, needed to fill the void that sat there.

Sylvia came to an abrupt stop and shook her head. What was she thinking? She should try to forget about that day, just like she did before. Why dredge up the past? The chance of her wish coming true was unlikely anyway. After all, wishes don't come true. Do they?

CHAPTER TWO

'Twins?' Sylvia looked at the ultrasound photo that was thrust in front of her.

'I know, can you believe it?' Samantha Roseford circled a palm over her belly. 'Here I was thinking I might never be able to have children, and now I've got two on the way!'

'What does your husband think about two babies?'

'Mike's over the moon. A tad anxious, but very excited.'

Sylvia wrapped a cuff around Samantha's arm and pumped the inflator. 'He's not the only one who's excited, your blood pressure's slightly higher than last time.'

'It is?' Samantha glanced at the numbers on the blood pressure monitor. 'Not even halfway through the pregnancy and these little munchkins are already causing havoc.'

'I wouldn't be too concerned yet, but I'll make a note in your referral letter to Dr Engelstein. You've booked an appointment to see him soon, I hope?' Sylvia looked up with raised eyebrows after typing notes into the computer.

'Yep. Two weeks time,' replied Samantha.

'Great. You can be confident in him to take over your prenatal care.'

'I hope so. He's not an old fuddy-duddy, is he?'

Sylvia chuckled. 'He's been around for a while, but he's one of the best obstetricians on the coast. Not that there's many of them around. You'll be in good hands.'

Samantha leaned back in her chair, clasping her hands over her belly and looking down as though her babies had just been placed in her lap. 'I'm *so* looking forward to being a mother.'

Sylvia placed a hand on her patient's forearm and smiled. 'These twins will be lucky to have you, Samantha.'

'Thanks, Dr Greene.' A tear dribbled down Samantha's cheek. 'I'm sorry, these hormones are making me cry at the slightest things.'

'That's normal.' Sylvia smiled. 'Good luck. I look forward to seeing you down the track.'

After Samantha left, Sylvia sat for a moment and imagined what she must be going through. The joy, the shock, the anticipation, maybe even fear. In a few months she'd be a mother, and her life would change completely.

The phone beeped. 'I have Mr Benson on the line, do you have time to speak with him about his results?' Joyce, the receptionist, asked.

Sylvia sunk in her chair and sighed. 'Sure, put him through.'

Sylvia arrived home from work over an hour later, but after a quick clean of the fridge, a vacuum throughout the house, and a cup of coffee, she went out the door again.

'Hi, Sylv,' Richard said, pecking her on the cheek and lifting the Louis Vuitton suitcase from her hands.

'Perfect timing!' Sylvia smiled as she angled into the front seat of Richard's BMW, grateful for a chance to sit still for a couple of hours. Richard slid into the driver's seat and drove towards the highway. She would have taken the train, but jumped at Richard's offer to drive her to the airport.

'Thanks again for this. I'm sure you'd rather be spending your day off doing something else,' Sylvia said.

'It's my pleasure, hun, gives us a chance to spend time together.'

His lips curved into a smile, and the muscles in his forearm bulged through his olive skin as he switched gears.

'You look nice,' she said, only realising she'd spoken aloud once the words had left her mouth.

After five weeks, their relationship was still in the early stages where hormones had the first say. Wearing black pants and a charcoal grey shirt with the faintest silver pinstripes, even though his shirtsleeves were rolled up, Richard was dressed a little fancily for a drive to and from the airport. Not that she minded; nor did she mind the hint of cinnamon and spice circulating through the car with the help of the air conditioning.

'Thanks,' he replied. 'I have a birthday party to go to in the city tonight, an old mate from my uni days.'

So he wasn't just doing this as a favour to her.

It didn't matter, she always made efficient use of her time as well. No harm in killing two birds with one stone.

'Oh, well I chose the right day to catch a plane didn't I?' Sylvia said.

'Sure did.' Richard smiled. 'Sorry I can't pick you up when you return on Wednesday though.'

'It doesn't matter.' She flicked a hand in the air. 'I know you're busy at work.'

'I'm free next Thursday night, should we schedule dinner then?'

Sylvia's cheeks flushed with warmth. 'How's seven-thirty?'

'Perfect, shall we eat in at your place this time?'

Sylvia nodded, then added a reminder into her iPhone. Not

that she'd forget, but she liked to be organised. 'What's your schedule like after that?' she asked.

'Doing nights from Friday, then afternoon shifts, and I'll be on call the following weekend. What about the Monday after that?'

That was a little over two weeks away. 'Sure, I'll mark it in my calendar.'

Sylvia tapped away on her phone. She'd have liked to see him sooner, but understood his hectic work schedule came first. The life of a cardiovascular surgeon did not allow for much time off. If she worked at the hospital too there'd be more opportunities to see him. They'd pass each other in the halls, or collaborate on a patient's care, but she'd grown used to working in general practice and wouldn't leave it for anything, or anyone. Besides, her days were busy and went by quickly, and before long she'd see him again.

By the time they pulled up in front of the airport, they'd discussed Richard's recent surgeries, Sylvia's clinical success rate with a new hypertension drug, and had arranged to set three more dates in the coming month, based on Richard's schedule. He warned her that sometimes he may have to cancel at the last minute if the hospital needed him, or a surgery took longer than expected. But, of course, she understood. A small part of her, though, wished he could join her in Melbourne for the conference so they could spend five nights together. Oh well, at least she'd get to catch up with some old friends from medical school.

'Have a good flight, see you next Thursday.' Richard effortlessly lifted the suitcase from the boot, extending the handle and rolling it towards her with surgical precision.

'Thanks, enjoy the birthday party.' Sylvia curved her hand around the back of his neck, pulling him in for a kiss. Short thick curls slid between her fingers as she moved her hand through the back of his hair.

Beep beep!

A car behind was waiting to take Richard's spot, the driver motioning with his hand as if to say, 'Are you going anytime soon?' Richard nodded towards the driver, kissed Sylvia quickly on the lips, and returned to the car before driving off.

Check-in was relatively quick, and despite setting off the alarm at the security screening point with the metal in her shoes, Sylvia had forty-five minutes to spare before boarding her flight. The aroma of roasted coffee beans enticed her to the café next to the newsagent. She picked up a copy of *Healthy Cooking* magazine first, then ordered a large cappuccino, opting for takeaway so she could wander around, keeping the blood circulating in her legs after the car trip and before the upcoming ninety-minute flight.

It was nice to be among the crowd, nobody knowing who she was. Sylvia loved the homely feel of Tarrin's Bay, but sometimes it was nice to be anonymous. Almost everyone in town knew her, and as a respected member of the community she made sure she always gave a good impression, and never lost her cool while waiting in a queue or stuck in traffic. Sylvia valued her reputation highly, and felt a responsibility to set a good example and be a respected role model. It was easy anyway. She wasn't a 'party-girl' or an outgoing eccentric, but a sensible, independent, thirty-four-year-old woman who had worked hard to get to where she was.

After checking the time, Sylvia sat in a seat at gate eighteen to await the boarding call. The plane arrived outside the window and, almost hypnotised, her eyes followed the luggage handlers heaving the bags from the plane to the carts. Passengers filtered into the airport through the doorways, and those waiting for the flight shuffled in their seats, pulling out boarding passes from their pockets. Some stood, preparing to line up for the boarding announcement. Sylvia remained still. No rush. She didn't understand why people always tried to get in first. Everyone would get to their seat eventually. Plus, having chosen an aisle seat, there'd be no point rushing, as the passengers allocated seats next to hers would only have to clamber over her.

The herd of people filtering in from the plane dissolved gradually into the crowd, some walking quickly, others stopping to yawn and stretch. Sylvia wondered what each was doing in Sydney. She amused herself by trying to guess who might be arriving home and who was simply visiting. Perhaps some had bought a one-way ticket and were staying.

Then her heart skipped a beat.

A young woman entered the airport, placing earbuds into her ears, the thin white cords trailing down to her pocket. She smiled at the flight attendant as she walked past, and stopped to glance around, as if wondering which direction to go. The woman had a youthful radiance about her, a sense of excitement, like she was stepping into the world for the first time. She resumed walking, her head bobbing rhythmically to whatever music she was listening to, curly tendrils of hair bouncing happily about her face. Red curls, not orangey-red, but warm russet-like red curls...

Just like hers.

It was as though Sylvia was looking into a mirror, a younger image of herself reflected back. Like seeing her own ghost.

As if connected by the similarities in their appearance, Sylvia stood and followed the young woman. She walked behind her in the crowd, until the woman stopped to admire a dress in a shop window; a long, floaty summer dress, with large pink and purple flowers printed on it. Not Sylvia's style at all, but the woman seemed inspired by it. She took out her phone and snapped a picture of it.

Strange.

A smile growing on her face, the woman entered the shop, walking out a few minutes later with a large plastic bag in her hand. Sylvia couldn't remember the last time she'd bought an outfit on a whim like that. Her purchases were always planned with purpose; crisp plain shirts, sensible heels, black, navy, or cream tailored pants for work, and casual jeans, t-shirts, and knit tops for weekends.

She continued following the woman and waited again while she stopped to sample hand cream at a beauty shop.

Should she approach her?

But what would she say?

Sylvia now felt incredibly silly, following a complete stranger. It was just her mind playing tricks. They weren't really *that* similar. Their hair was practically identical, but the woman lacked Sylvia's height, although her build was the same: small-chested and big-hipped.

'Final boarding call for Dr Sylvia Greene. Dr Sylvia Greene to gate eighteen please.' The voice beamed through the airport speaker system and Sylvia's eyes jumped wide open.

Oh God, my flight!

How could she not have heard the first boarding call? She spun around and headed in the direction of gate eighteen, then turned back around.

The woman was gone.

Part of her wanted to continue through to the baggage terminal but that would be crazy. She had to go. Shaking the moment of insanity from her head, Sylvia ran in as dignified a way as possible to the boarding gate where an attendant was just about to block off the entrance with rope.

A minute later she sat puffing in her seat on the plane.

'Hi there, I'm Wayne,' the elderly man next to her said as he held out his hand. 'What do you do for a living, love?'

'I'm a doctor,' Sylvia replied.

'Oh, really?' The man twisted in his seat, sidling up close to her. 'I might have to pick your brain then, you see, I've got this problem with...'

Sylvia released a gentle sigh as Wayne told her his medical history and current symptoms. He was probably a relative of Mr Benson's.

This was going to be a dreadfully long ninety minutes.

When the man seated on the other side of Wayne got involved in the conversation after mentioning that he too had suffered with unrelenting tinea for years, Wayne twisted to face him and they proceeded to discuss the fungal infection in detail. Sylvia took the golden opportunity to close her eyes and pretend to be asleep. She'd flip through the *Healthy Cooking* magazine on the flight home next week instead.

Her mind drifted back to that woman's face, and the way her hair stood out from the crowd like a sunset on the horizon. Then she saw herself back at the Wishing Festival, tossing a coin into the fountain.

Making a wish one day, stalking a stranger the next — what had gotten into her? Maybe she was working too hard. Maybe the ten days she took off over Christmas weren't enough. Or maybe a hidden part of her was surfacing, trying to come to terms with what she did all those years ago.

CHAPTER THREE

The medical conference was a welcome distraction; immersed in technical data and surrounded by other doctors, Sylvia almost forgot about her life back home and the crazy things she'd been doing. But time flew by. Thursday morning soon arrived and she was back at work.

'Welcome back, how was the conference?' asked Joyce.

'Not bad, a little depressing though, which is kind of ironic considering it was a mental health conference,' replied Sylvia. 'But it was interesting, and nice to catch up with old friends.'

'Well, we're glad you're back. Dr Bronovski has been worked to the grindstone without you here. We've had an influx of sick children lately.'

'Oh dear.' Sylvia's shoulders sunk. 'Well, I better get started.' She turned towards her room.

'Oh, Sylvia, before you disappear, management called. They've decided on a new practitioner for the spare room, he'll be starting next week.'

Tarrin's Bay Medical Clinic had just the two doctors, along with a physiotherapist, but the other room had become available when the dermatologist left three months ago.

'Please tell me it's a paediatrician? It has to be a paediatrician.' Sylvia leaned forward onto the reception desk.

It's not that she didn't like children, she just felt… uncomfortable working with them. She preferred patients you could reason with, who kept still, and didn't have bodily fluids escaping out of various orifices without warning. Plus, as the only female general practitioner in town, parents flocked to her, probably expecting that her supposedly inbuilt maternal instinct would somehow make her a better doctor for their children.

'Nope, no paediatrician I'm afraid,' said Joyce. 'A naturopath and acupuncturist will be joining the team.'

'A what?'

'A naturopath and acupuncturist. Mark Bastian, he'll be in tomorrow to set up the room.'

'You've got to be kidding!' Sylvia looked at Joyce's unblinking eyes and knew she wasn't. 'A paediatrician would have been *so* good, or even a psychologist, but a *naturopath*? I thought this was a medical centre.'

'C'mon, Sylvia, you've got to get with the times! And anyway, I hear he gets great results with his patients. He'll be an asset to the centre.'

Sylvia grumbled under her breath, shuffling off to her room and grabbing her mail on the way through.

Just as she feared, her day was filled with sick children, anxious parents, and the odd minor injury and infected boil. Three quarters of her time was spent with existing patients, the rest were newcomers. If work kept betting busier she'd have to close her books for a while, or work longer hours, something she wasn't keen on. Sylvia loved her job, but some days were a challenge. Though the thought of seeing Richard tonight kept her going. She should be able to get home with enough time to prepare a simple salmon and dill pasta dish before he arrived.

One of her regular weekday meals. Quick, easy, and tasty. Plus Richard was a big fan of seafood.

Having had only ten minutes to scoff down lunch, and a couple of coffees in between patients, Sylvia was yawning by the time she finished off the paperwork and phone calls at the end of the day. Joyce and the other practitioners had already left, so she turned off the lights and air conditioning, switched on the alarm, and locked the door behind her as she left the refurbished weatherboard cottage that was as historic as the Wishing Fountain in Miracle Park.

Although just after six-thirty, the sun shone as brightly as it did at midday. Not that she'd been able to enjoy it. She'd been indoors all day and only managed a quick glance out the window at lunchtime. Its golden glow sat low on the horizon, preparing to surrender to the night in another hour or so. Sylvia closed her eyes, savouring the refreshing breeze that whooshed past her.

She opened her eyes and caught sight of a young woman nearby, her pink and purple floral dress billowing in the breeze.

It was her.

The woman from the airport with the russet-coloured curls... *just like hers.*

Their green eyes locked, and a faint smile touched the woman's face, just before her skin paled and she collapsed onto the grass next to the footpath.

Sylvia rushed to her side and patted her cheeks. 'Can you hear me? Are you okay?'

'What happened?' the woman asked as her eyes opened.

'It's okay, I think you just fainted. Here, have a sip of this.' Sylvia threaded her arm under the woman's shoulder and around her back, helping her sit up as she pulled a water bottle from her bag with the other hand and held it to the woman's mouth. 'How about I take you inside and check you out? I'm a doctor.'

'Oh, no, it's okay, I'm okay... really.' Shakily, the woman stood, holding onto Sylvia's arm for support. 'I'll be fine.'

'You sure? Maybe you need something to eat. Hang on, I think I've got something in my bag.' Sylvia rummaged through it.

'Seriously, I'll be fine. I was just a bit... overwhelmed, that's all.'

Sylvia looked up from her bag and into the young woman's eyes and knew she'd seen them before. Not just at the airport, but long ago.

The woman straightened and drew a deep breath, holding her own hands together as if for support. 'My name is Grace. I'm your daughter.'

CHAPTER FOUR

Although Sylvia guessed the truth before she heard it, Grace's revelation sparked a sharp gasp in Sylvia's throat. The ground appeared to soften beneath her, and she wished she had something to hold on to for fear of fainting herself.

'How... how did you find me?' Her voice shaking, she clutched at her bag awkwardly.

'I've been looking for you for a few months. The internet is a wonderful thing. Once I found out you were a doctor, it was easy,' Grace explained, while Sylvia's eyes wandered over her features, noticing how her nose twitched as she spoke, and how her chin had a slight dimple — like her father's.

'So, you're eighteen now?' The question escaped Sylvia's mouth just as she realised how stupid it sounded. Was that all she could do? Ask how Grace found her and state the obvious? Heat rose up the back of her neck and she rubbed her sweaty palm against it.

Grace nodded. 'Just.'

At only sixteen years of age, Sylvia had given birth to a baby girl on the first of January. New Year's Day. Had she been a *normal* mother she may have made the evening news or the local newspaper, but Sylvia didn't want to broadcast the hardest day of her life to the world.

'I'm sorry to turn up out of the blue. I wasn't even planning to introduce myself today. I just wanted to... see you.' Grace's soft eyes glistened.

'But then I recognised you,' Sylvia said softly.

'And what do I do? I go and faint, how pathetic!' A high-pitched giggle bubbled up from Grace's lips.

'That's one sure way to get my attention!' Sylvia smiled.

Grace paused for a moment and pursed her lips to one side. 'How could you recognise me? I mean, I guess our hair is the same.' She pulled at a curl, extending it to twice its length in front of her face. 'Was it my hair that gave me away?'

'Partly. But, well, I actually saw you at the airport last week.'

Grace's curl bounced up like a spring as she let it go. 'The airport? You were there?'

Sylvia nodded. 'But I didn't know it was you, I mean, there was something about you that made me take a second look, and I did wonder, but I had to catch my flight.' She didn't want to mention how she'd followed her halfway across the airport and saw her buy the dress she was now wearing.

'Wow.' Grace looked up at the sky. 'What a coincidence.'

It sure was.

Or was it?

Maybe there *was* something to that Wishing Fountain legend.

Nah, there couldn't be. Sylvia shook the thought from her mind. It was scientifically impossible.

'So, have you been here in Tarrin's Bay since then, or did you spend some time in Sydney first?'

'I've been here since the day I flew in. I'm staying over there at the caravan park.' Grace pointed up the hill. 'I rang your clinic to ask which days you worked, and the lady said you were away but due back on Thursday. So, here I am.'

Grace lifted her palms in the air as if to show she'd suddenly appeared out of nowhere, and Sylvia's heart lurched forward as she noticed Grace's long slender fingers and was reminded of how soft her baby's hands had been.

Like a feather.

If she focused hard, she could still feel the gentle warmth of Grace's little hand wrapped around her finger. So fragile, so tiny. She'd only had a brief moment with her daughter before they took her away. They said it was better not to hold her for too long, so Sylvia drank in the moment as best as she could, trying to imprint the memory in her mind.

And later, trying her best to forget it.

Sylvia swallowed the lump in her throat in effort to regain her composure. 'So, how long are you here for?'

'Don't know yet. I just finished high school last year, and I'm taking a break this year till I figure out what I want to do. I have some money saved, so I'll see how things go here for a bit — that's if you're okay with me being here? I mean, I can go if you want, I just wanted to meet you, I don't expect—'

'Stay as long as you want,' Sylvia found herself saying. 'I'm sure you have a lot of questions, and well... I'd like to spend some time getting to know you.'

Was this really happening? Sylvia's stomach flitted this way and that, her nerves tingled, and she felt... awake. Here she was, standing on the footpath talking to her own daughter after all these years! She'd never even imagined her baby as a grown woman, just kind of expected she'd stay as small as when she left her at the hospital. She'd kept that image of her baby girl in her mind for years, even after two years had passed, then three, then four. Sylvia knew her daughter would be growing bigger and heading off to school, but she'd tried not to think about those things. Somehow, the baby she'd given up was now a woman, standing right in front of her.

Grace's face glowed, in stark contrast to the paleness that had struck her down a few minutes ago. She was obviously pleased by Sylvia's agreement to see her again.

'Well, I'd better leave you to it, you're probably tired after work.' Grace twirled and extended a curl again. 'Would it be okay if we met up again sometime?'

'Of course.' This both scared and delighted Sylvia. 'I could meet you after work tomorrow evening. We could grab a bite to eat in town, if you like?'

'I'd love that.' Grace grinned from ear to ear. 'So I'll see you here, same time?'

Sylvia nodded. 'Sure.'

'Oh, and I'll try not to faint this time!' Grace turned around and floated up the hill towards the caravan park, snapping photos with her phone as she went. Sylvia's heart beat at twice its normal speed as she stood there watching Grace's figure become smaller and smaller in the distance until she could see her no more.

Soft pink hues coloured the sky as Sylvia walked to the lookout just up from Miracle Park. Some locals walked their dogs, while others sat on the rocky ledge eating fish and chips, and a few leaned over the railing of the lookout, staring out at the endless ocean. When she reached the top, Sylvia took hold of the railing and her shoulders softened, relieved to have something to steady her. She gazed trance-like at the deep blue water for a long time, until the sudden reality of her past crashed up against her heart like the waves against the rocky cliff below.

Warm salty air filled her lungs as she inhaled deeply. Her life would be different now. She couldn't keep the memory of her daughter locked away any longer. Sylvia's baby was all grown up, and she was right here in Tarrin's Bay, where it all began.

A brief melodic sound startled her. It was a reminder message on her phone.

Damn! She'd forgotten about dinner with Richard. It was seven-thirty already, and he'd be arriving any minute. She let go of the railing and ran down the hill, trying to send a text message at the same time. What should have been 'running late, almost there' turned into 'summing kate, bumost tgere'. Hopefully he'd know what she meant.

The last thing Sylvia felt like doing now was cooking, and she didn't want to waste any time with Richard so she picked up a couple of ready-to-go containers of food from the Thai restaurant opposite the park. That and a bottle of wine should be sufficient. She hoped Richard wouldn't mind the last-minute dinner change.

Her house came into view, and Richard sat on the doorstep, his thumbs tapping away at his phone. A subtle swish of the curtain in the house next door proved that Nancy Dillinger was spying as usual, probably wondering why Sylvia was late and a man was sitting on her doorstep.

'I'm so sorry, it's been a hectic day,' Sylvia apologised, panting when she reached Richard. Her face was flushed with warmth and sweat dampened her armpits. 'Someone needed my assistance after work, and I lost track of time.'

'I thought as much.' Richard slipped his phone into his pocket. 'Doesn't matter, after being on my feet all day yesterday it's good to sit for a while.'

Sylvia breathed relief into her lungs as they headed inside where she served up the Thai food on to her best plates and poured a glass of wine each. After placing the plates on the table, she ducked into the bathroom and gave her armpits a quick spray of deodorant. She couldn't be rude and have a shower, so hopefully the deodorant would do the trick for a couple of hours. She wondered if she should tell Richard about Grace, but decided the best thing to do was simply enjoy their dinner, and if it felt right later, she would bring it up then.

'So, how was your day?' she asked, as she sat opposite him at the dining table.

An hour and a half and two wines later, Sylvia motioned for Richard to join her on the couch where she kicked off her shoes and tucked her feet under her thighs, one arm on the back of the couch behind Richard. He leaned in and pressed his lips to hers, tucking a strand of hair behind her ear and caressing her cheek. He wrapped his arms around her, pulling her closer, but she stiffened. Suddenly, the fuzzy but unforgettable memory of the night Grace was conceived came rushing to the front of her mind.

'What's wrong?' Richard asked.

'Nothing, nothing's wrong,' she blurted.

'Yes there is, you've been distracted all night, and something happened just now. What is it?'

'It's been a long day, that's all, and I haven't had much time to wind down after the conference.'

Richard drew her closer for another kiss, then slowly backed away. He studied her face for a moment as though probing a patient for the cause of her problem. 'Talk to me.'

Sylvia sighed and looked down at her hands, and Richard lifted her chin with his finger.

She placed her feet back on the floor and looked him in the eye. 'Richard, there's something I should tell you.'

CHAPTER FIVE

'You're a mother?' The leather cushions made an awkward squelchy sound as Richard stood up from the couch. 'But when we met you said you didn't have any kids!'

'I know, but this is different.' Sylvia stood too. 'It's not like I *have* Grace, and I hadn't even met her until today.'

'Yes but you *had* Grace. You should have told me. This is big, Sylvia, you can't pretend it never happened.' He ran a hand through his hair, his chest rising sharply as he took a breath. 'Geez, I told you straight out I'd left a bad relationship where kids were involved, and I didn't want to get into another relationship with someone else who had kids. I was honest, and you should have been too.' He walked over to the dining table and leaned his hands onto it.

'I'm sorry, Richard, I didn't think telling you about the adoption was relevant at the time. I never thought I'd ever meet her.' Sylvia's voice weakened and the lump in her throat resurfaced. She wanted him to walk back to her, gather her in his arms and say it was okay, that he didn't mind she had a daughter. That he would even be happy to meet her, and they could continue with their relationship. But he didn't. He picked up his keys and phone and walked towards the door.

'Wait! Where are you going?' Sylvia rushed after him.

'Home,' he replied, frowning.

'But we should talk about this,' Sylvia pleaded.

'We should have talked about this six weeks ago, Sylvia.' He slipped the phone into his pocket. 'Look, you know I care about you, and I've enjoyed the past few weeks, but you have a child. I didn't sign up for this. I just can't take on anything complicated right now.'

Sign up for this? What was she, a difficult patient with a rare disease or something?

He stepped closer to her, his hand hesitating near her shoulder for a moment, then dropping back to his side. 'I'm sorry.' He turned and walked out, the bang of the closing door sending a painful jolt through Sylvia's body.

She went to turn the doorknob, but stopped. Tears of disbelief stung her eyes. So that was it? Had he really just broken it off with her? Their relationship was — *had been* — in the 'getting to know each other' stage, but she'd already developed strong feelings for him, and the possibility of something special had been yanked from her grasp before she'd had a chance to hold on. She slumped her shoulders in disappointment and pushed an irritating tear away with the heel of her hand.

He could have been the one, and now he was gone.

Grace put the takeaway food container in the garbage bin, and went inside the caravan to change into her pyjamas. Warmth filled her metal home, so all she needed was a thin cotton nightie. She picked up her phone as soon as it rang.

'Hi, Dad.' Grace flopped on the small bed. 'Yep, I met her this afternoon.'

'Was she shocked?' her father asked.

'I think so at first, but not more than me. I fainted, can you believe it?'

'You fainted? Are you okay, sweetheart?'

'Yeah I'm fine, don't worry. Anyway, next thing I knew she was by my side helping me up.'

'So what's she like?'

'She seems nice. I mean, we only talked for a bit, but... wow, I can't believe how much we look alike, it feels so weird!'

Silence followed.

'Dad?'

'Yeah, I'm still here.'

'Good. So anyway, we're going to meet up tomorrow night for dinner. That'll give us more of a chance to talk. And Dad?'

'Yeah, sweetie?'

'I have a feeling I might be staying here a while.'

Stay as long as you want. I'd be happy to spend some time getting to know you. That's what Sylvia had said. Her original, biological mother.

Grace had so many questions she wanted to ask Sylvia, and so much had happened in her short eighteen years on earth that she could probably write one of those bestselling memoirs. Maybe one day she would. But for now, Grace wondered, how much should she tell her?

After finishing the phone conversation with her dad, Grace opened the lid on her water bottle, tipped a small container upside down into her hand, and swallowed the tablets she took every night.

CHAPTER SIX

When she'd finally processed what had happened, Sylvia went to the bathroom and dabbed at her face with a cold cloth. Suddenly she was wide awake, even though it was ten o'clock and she would normally head to bed about now, read for an hour, then fall asleep. But there was no chance of that tonight.

She patted make-up from her powder compact over her cheeks, swept a dash of eye shadow across her eyelids, and followed with a light coat of lip gloss. Needing fresh air, she grabbed her handbag and went outside. Café Lagoon would be open till eleven tonight. A frothy cup of coffee and a piece of cake would make her feel better. As Sylvia headed towards the town, a light flickered in the house next door as Nancy Dillinger's curtains swayed against the window.

'Dr Greene, what brings you here so late at night?' asked Jonah, the young barista.

'It's been a long day and I'd kill for a cup of your best coffee.'

'Coming right up.' He winked.

Jonah knew how she liked her coffee. She'd been coming here regularly for several years, ever since his parents opened up the café, which was about the same time she started general practice at Tarrin's Bay Medical Clinic.

'Oh, and a big slice of hummingbird cake, please.'

Jonah widened his eyes. 'Must have been a tough day.'

'You could say that.' She took a seat on one of only two remaining bar stools near the counter. The café was surprisingly busy, mostly filled with twenty-somethings who alternated between chatting, laughing, and texting. She felt quite old and pathetic, and considered asking Jonah to make it a takeaway coffee until the man next to her spoke.

'Coffee, huh? You know, that stuff'll keep you up all night.'

She turned to face a stunning man with skin the colour of, well, warm velvety coffee, in latte form, and eyes a striking blue.

'So I've heard. But with the day I've had, I think I'll be up most of the night anyway so I might as well indulge.'

As if on cue, Jonah placed the steaming coffee in front of her. The rich, welcoming scent instantly put her at ease. The cake arrived next, a dollop of cream by its side.

'What are you drinking, is that decaf?' Sylvia asked the man.

'No, it's dandelion chai,' he said, before taking a long slow sip from the mug.

'Dandy what?' Sylvia furrowed her eyebrows.

'Dandelion chai, it's a type of tea.' He took another sip. 'You should try it sometime.'

Sylvia leaned back, cautiously eyeing his unfamiliar concoction. 'I think I'll stick to coffee, thanks.' She took a sip then dove a fork into the hummingbird cake with gusto, wiping a smudge of cream from her lip with the heel of her hand. She could easily devour two slices.

'Fair enough.' His lips formed a gentle smile, and for a

moment Sylvia forgot about Richard and their argument. Forgot how only hours ago she'd met her grown daughter for the first time, and how, amazingly, the wish she'd made had come true. Well, part of it anyway. Even if it *was* only coincidence. But right now, in this moment, she was entranced by the smile of a stranger, the taste of warm thick coffee relaxing her throat, and the sweet softness of the cake as it danced around her tastebuds.

'Did you go to the Jazz Festival last weekend?' The man widened his eyes, raising his voice and slowing his speech.

She mustn't have heard him the first time. 'Oh, um, no I didn't. I was away,' Sylvia replied.

'You missed out, it was brilliant! The whole town was alive, music everywhere, and the weather was perfect.' He took another sip of his seemingly endless cup of dandy-whatever.

'I'm sure it was. Anyway, the markets are on this Sunday, they're always good too.'

'Maybe I'll see you there.' The man smiled his charming smile again.

'Maybe.' Sylvia found herself twisting a curl of her hair, just like Grace had done today.

Getting only five hours of sleep didn't deter Sylvia from following her usual morning routine the next day. She rose at seven when the beep of her alarm clock hijacked a dream in which she was back at hospital as a sixteen-year-old, and her baby was too heavy to lift. Everyone laughed as she tried with all her might to lift Grace up, and as the alarm sounded, she thought it was meant to warn everyone in the hospital that she was unequipped to be a mother.

Sylvia shook the absurd dream from her mind as she got out of bed and changed into her swimsuit before swimming thirty laps in her backyard pool.

This morning ritual started when she moved into the house a few years ago, and every day, bar heavy rain or freezing weather, she'd swim laps. Sylvia loved the feeling of the cool water enveloping her skin, the gentle silky pressure as her hands pushed through the water, and the repetition that helped her mind prepare for the day ahead.

Afterwards, she'd take a quick shower, eat breakfast, do her hair and make-up and get dressed in one of her ten work outfits. Friday's combination was a burgundy short-sleeved cotton shirt teamed with cream-coloured wide-leg pants. Next Friday would be slightly different. She'd wear the same pants but with a navy version of the same shirt.

Sylvia liked that she never had to wonder what to wear each day. Five different outfits were washed, ironed, and ready to wear by Monday morning, hanging on wooden hangers labelled with a day of the week. She estimated that other women who weren't as organised as her probably wasted an average of 60.66 hours per year deciding what to wear. That was enough time for a solid week of work, or a relaxing holiday!

At precisely eight-fifteen, she'd lock the house, wave to Nancy Dillinger peering through her window, and walk to work. Fifteen minutes there and back each day, combined with her morning swim, was enough exercise to maintain her figure. Although she'd probably have to add in a session at the gym to counteract last night's cake and coffee. But she was making up for last night's binge by eating a healthy, albeit a little overripe, banana while walking to work.

'Good morning,' said a bright-eyed Joyce when Sylvia opened the door to the clinic.

It always seemed as if Joyce was a permanent fixture behind the reception desk, or at least on her chair, which rolled here and there as she manoeuvred her way around the desks and filing cabinets without needing to stand.

Ironically, Joyce chose that moment to stand. 'Here's your mail.' She placed the envelopes into Sylvia's unoccupied hand and followed her towards the hallway. 'And I'd like you to meet our new practitioner, Mark Bastian.' Joyce gestured towards the spare room where a man was kneeling, opening a cardboard box on the floor. Sylvia had forgotten the new guy was settling in today.

At Joyce's introduction, he stood and turned, his blue eyes meeting Sylvia's, the halogen lights adding a glow to his warm latte-coloured skin.

Oh God! Sylvia's face flushed with warmth.

'We meet again,' Mark said, holding out his hand and grinning.

All Sylvia could do was nod, tucking the envelopes under her armpit in order to give a limp shake of his hand. If she hadn't gone out last night in her moment of heartbreak, she wouldn't have met him, and they would have been introduced today without any fuss. But she'd let her professional guard down and somehow she felt... exposed.

'You two know each other?' Joyce glanced from Sylvia's face to Mark's and back again, waiting for a response.

CHAPTER SEVEN

'Well, not really, but—' Sylvia began, until the awkward introduction was gratefully interrupted by a knocking on the front door. The clinic wasn't due to open for another twenty minutes or so, but a frantic looking mother holding a screaming baby begged to be let in.

The screaming amplified when Joyce unlocked the door, putting an arm around the mother and ushering her towards Sylvia's room. It was Marisa, a single mother Sylvia had been treating since she got pregnant unexpectedly a year ago.

So much for a relaxing coffee before the onslaught of patient arrivals.

'I don't know what's wrong, he won't stop crying!' Marisa said above the screaming. 'I've fed him, changed him, and cuddled him. Can you help?' Marisa's eyes were moist and her chin quivered.

Sylvia did her best to examine the little one as he squirmed around. 'When was his last bowel movement?' She palpated his abdomen.

'A couple of hours ago I think, and last night.'

'But no diarrhoea?'

'No.'

The baby winced as Sylvia placed the cold stethoscope on his abdomen. Nothing wrong there, although his little stomach muscles pulsed in and out from the crying. She placed a hand on his warm forehead, his face and neck red as he wailed. 'I'll check his temperature,' Sylvia said, turning to get the digital thermometer. She instructed Marisa to hold him still while she tugged his ear backwards and inserted the end of the thermometer. It wouldn't go through all the way, so she pulled it out and shone a pen light into the baby's ear.

'I know why your baby is crying, Marisa.' Sylvia turned the pen light off momentarily and smiled. Marisa looked at her hopefully. 'He has a bug of some kind trapped in his ear canal.'

'Oh my God! Can you get it out?' Marisa forced a look into her baby's ear, then turned away, scrunching up her nose.

'Shouldn't be a problem, as long as we keep him as still as possible.' Sylvia looked at Marisa in a way that said, 'Are you ready for this?' Marisa held one hand tightly around the boy's head, and the other around his wriggly legs. Sylvia placed a headlight cap on her head to light the area, and moved in for the kill with a pair of tweezers. Screams engulfed the room, and Sylvia's eardrums vibrated. She worked quickly, removing pieces of what looked like a beetle, until the canal was clear.

'All done.' Sylvia disposed of the remains and had one last look in his ear. 'There's a bit of redness, but the eardrum is still intact so he shouldn't need antibiotics. I'll give you a prescription for some ear drops though.'

Marisa nodded as her baby's cries turned into whimpers. He took a few quick breaths in sharp succession before breathing out a heavy sigh, the corners of his mouth turned upside down. She patted the side of his face and kissed his forehead. 'It's all over, pumpkin.'

Marisa thanked Sylvia profusely, and apologised for barging

in early without an appointment. Sylvia waved her apologies away. 'That's what I'm here for, and if he has any more trouble, let me know.'

Marisa walked out just as the first patient of the day walked in.

By one o'clock Sylvia was able to retreat to the staff kitchen and unwrap a sandwich she'd brought for lunch. Her time alone was brief, as Joyce walked in.

'Your next patient cancelled, so you can take a few more minutes break if you like.'

'Oh, thank goodness.' Sylvia ran her fingers through her thick curls. 'Thanks for letting me know, Joyce.'

Joyce walked out, then popped her head back in. 'Are you okay?'

'Me? I'm fine, why do you ask?'

'You look a bit tired that's all, and you've seemed a little... distracted today.'

Sylvia fiddled with the collar on her shirt. 'I have?'

Joyce's eyes looked inquisitively at hers.

'I am a bit tired I guess, coming straight back to work after the conference.' She looked down at her sandwich. 'And Richard and I broke up.'

'Oh, Sylvia, I'm so sorry!' Joyce walked to the table and placed a comforting hand on Sylvia's arm. 'Do you want to talk about it?'

'No, thanks. I better keep focused on work today.' Sylvia straightened and took a bite of her sandwich.

'Right then.' Joyce went to the door. 'But if you need a chat, I'm all ears.'

Sylvia erupted in laughter, crumbs bursting from her mouth onto the floor like missiles.

'What's so funny?'

'Sorry, it's just that I've had enough of *ears* today.'

She relayed the story about the beetle incident. Normally she wouldn't discuss a patient with anyone, but somehow this didn't seem like a big deal, and she doubted Marisa would sue for revealing the details of her son's bug predicament. Joyce wasn't a gossip anyway. She was the type of person you could trust with your life. Although Sylvia tried to keep a strictly professional relationship with her since they began working together, she couldn't help but become friends with her.

'Oh, I can hear Karen. I better go and let her know what I'm up to with things.' Joyce turned on her heel and left the room. Karen was the other receptionist who came in the afternoons, allowing Joyce an hour for lunch, and making the build-up of work in the second half of the day more efficient.

Sylvia finished the last of her sandwich just as Mark walked in. She surreptitiously wiped her mouth to remove any remnants of the missile launch from moments before. Was she going to be devouring food *every* time they crossed paths?

'How's the set up going?' she managed to ask.

'All done. How's your day so far, better than yesterday?'

Sylvia thought back to yesterday's events. In less than twenty-four hours she'd met her daughter, been dumped by her boyfriend, and met a charming stranger only to discover she'd be working alongside him every day. What would be next?

'So far so good,' she replied, throwing the plastic wrap from her sandwich into the garbage bin and missing. Why had she suddenly become a complete slob and klutz all rolled into one?

'Good to hear.' Mark smiled. 'Well, it was nice to meet you… *again*.' He gave a polite nod in her direction. 'I guess I'll be seeing you.'

'I guess you will.' Sylvia smiled awkwardly, aware of her heart beating a little faster than it had been a few moments ago.

As Mark left the room, she realised that he wasn't what she expected the new practitioner to look like. She didn't think he *looked* like a naturopath, although she also wasn't sure what a naturopath was supposed to look like. A vision of an old bearded man with an oversized multicoloured shirt popped into her mind until she shook it out. Sylvia's father had warned against following any form of health care except the standard medical system. He'd heard stories of some healer who'd caused the death of one of his patients, and had sworn against *those sorts of people* ever since. But he *was* the world's most paranoid person and had also sworn against Butterman's Breads after discovering an uncooked lump of flour in a loaf he'd bought.

Sylvia returned to her room, but not before sneaking a peek into Mark's office. As soon as she opened the door she wanted to swap rooms with him. Was he an interior decorator as well?

The desks had been rearranged so they no longer cut the room in half, and he'd brought in his own chair — an upholstered suede armchair, obviously for the patient's comfort. Sylvia's patients didn't sit in her room long enough to get comfortable, but she'd heard naturopaths spent way more time with theirs. There was a massage table against the far wall, and above it hung a sign reassuring the patients that all the acupuncture needles were disposable and only used once. Funny that people shied away from needles in her room yet paid for them willingly in Mark's. There was also an odd-shaped lamp in the corner, one of those crystal salt lamps, and a gorgeously framed print of a sunset over the ocean hung on the far wall. It added a welcoming touch as you entered the room.

Displayed on the wall over Mark's desk were several framed certificates of his qualifications, and even a mission statement. *A mission statement.* She began reading it, and almost fell backwards as Mark suddenly came into the room.

'Oh, sorry, I was just—'

'Having a stickybeak?' He grinned. 'That's okay, I checked out your room too, before you arrived. You know, you should really move your desk into a different position, it'd be much better Feng Shui,' he said, picking up some envelopes from his desk.

'Foong what?' Why did he always use words she'd never heard before? Hang on... 'Oh, you mean that Chinese design thing?'

'Yes, that Chinese design thing.'

And why was he always grinning?

'It's all about the flow of energy in the environment; it can make a huge difference to how you feel and what happens in your life.'

How desk placement could affect her personal life she had no idea, but she nodded anyway.

'I should lend you a book about it, it's really quite interesting.'

Hmmm... He seemed... *nice,* and so... *cultured.* But he looked every bit the rugged, masculine man.

'Anyway, I just came back to get these.' He raised the pile of envelopes he'd picked up from his desk. 'I almost forgot. I have to get these change-of-practice forms sent.'

'Oh, Karen can put them in today's outgoing mail if you like,' Sylvia offered.

'No, it's okay. I'm going down the street anyway, might as well do it myself.'

Sylvia stepped out of the room first, and Mark followed. 'Hope the rest of your day is slightly better than *so far so good,*' he said, before turning and walking out of the clinic.

Sylvia hoped so too.

After lining-up for ten minutes, Mark bought a set of stamps for his mail. Why they didn't have stamp vending machines, he didn't know. It would be so much easier for people who needed stamps and nothing else. It seemed post offices were a catch-all for all sorts of merchandise these days. Whatever happened to the simple go in, buy a stamp, maybe some envelopes, and post a letter or parcel? Now you could pay bills, get passports, buy gifts, and send money overseas.

Tarrin's Bay was a small town compared to where he lived before, but the line-up in the post office belied the fact. It was just like his father's pharmacy. They stocked all sorts of bits and pieces nowadays. Every opportunity to increase sales was taken advantage of, and the business could no longer function simply as a place to get your medicines.

If only life was as simple as it used to be.

Mark had grown increasingly weary with modern life and the twenty-four hour lifestyle that many people lived, which was part of the reason he'd moved from fast-paced Welston to Tarrin's Bay. *The Town of New Beginnings*, the tourist brochures said. It had all the conveniences of modern life, but they were nestled among a beautiful landscape of lush green hills on the outskirts of town which gave way to rugged headlands and beautiful beaches in the heart of town. There was something about being near the ocean that made you remember the simple pleasures in life, the things you often took for granted. Mark needed this place. Most of all, he needed to try to get his life back on track, without living in the shadow of his past. But as he found himself irritated by the smallest things whenever he was alone, and craving the kind of company he'd had with Sylvia last night, he knew that was easier said than done.

CHAPTER EIGHT

As promised, Grace was waiting outside the clinic when Sylvia finished work. A denim mini-skirt hugged her thighs, and she wore a red three-quarter sleeved top, hardly noticeable for the sparkling silver scarf wrapped twice around her neck, yet still hanging to her knees. All teenagers seemed to dress like that these days, summer outfits meshed with winter accessories; a juxtaposition of seasonal fashion. And in winter they'd wear woolly tops that exposed their midriffs, while complaining the weather was too cold.

'Hi, Grace, you ready?' Sylvia smiled.

'Yep, where should we go?'

'I was thinking Bayside, it's just around the corner.' Sylvia pointed. 'On Friday nights they have a beautiful buffet. I wasn't sure what type of food you like, and they have a bit of everything.' Sylvia wondered what Grace's favourite food was, and what she'd liked to eat as a child. Maybe she'd been a fussy eater and gave her parents grief, or maybe she was adventurous and ate anything at least once.

'Sounds perfect,' Grace replied as she turned and began walking.

Sylvia's head buzzed with curiosity. There were so many questions she wanted to ask her daughter. It seemed strange to be calling Grace *her daughter*, but she *was* her daughter, biologically at least. She wanted to know so much about her — what her childhood was like, which school subjects had been her favourite, whether she had a boyfriend, and whether the couple Sylvia had entrusted her daughter's life to had done a good job of raising her. First impressions suggested they did: she didn't look like a wayward youth or drug dealer or anything. She appeared a happy, healthy young woman. Anyway, there'd be plenty of time for questions, and Grace was sure to have plenty of her own.

'Welcome ladies,' a waiter said as they stepped into the air-conditioned comfort of the restaurant. 'There's a table for two over there.' He pointed to the far wall. 'And you can help yourself to the many delicious choices at the buffet.' He then pointed in the other direction. 'Non-alcoholic drinks are self-serve too, unless I can interest you in a wine perhaps?' He tipped his head forward in a kind of bow, as if the wine choices would topple from his head.

'Thanks,' Sylvia replied, wondering whether it was appropriate to drink or not. Grace was eighteen; she was old enough to drink. Weird to imagine your little girl having alcohol though. 'Um, no wine for me tonight,' Sylvia said, before glancing at Grace.

'Oh, none for me either.'

They made their way along the buffet table, ladling food onto their plates. Surprisingly, Grace went for the opposite of what Sylvia chose. While Sylvia loved the look of the chicken cacciatore and Mediterranean vegetables with a crusty bread roll, Grace opted for the barramundi in coconut sauce and a risotto, among other things.

They sat at a corner table and Sylvia clinked her glass against Grace's.

'Cheers,' they said at the same time.

'So, Grace, where are you from?' Easy enough first question. One down, several thousand to go.

'Northern suburbs of Sydney originally. Then we moved to Melbourne when I started school and Dad got a new job.'

Sydney. Sylvia remembered her time in Sydney. Although born and bred in Tarrin's Bay, her parents had moved her to Sydney when they discovered she was pregnant. Her father had been offered a new position at a private boys school, originally turning it down so as not to uproot Sylvia from school in Tarrin's Bay. But when she told them her news not long after, he saw it as an opportunity. Not only for his career, but for taking her away from the ridicule and embarrassment that was bound to bombard a pregnant sixteen-year-old in a small town. Sylvia often wondered if he really did it to save face himself. After all, as a school principal he was a well-respected member of the community. Having *any* pregnant teenager at the school, let alone his own daughter, could have ruined his reputation.

And so no one ever knew, except Sylvia's best friend, Larissa. As soon as they moved into their new house in Sydney, Sylvia enrolled into distance education and completed Year Eleven at home. Grace was born conveniently at the start of the following year, allowing Sylvia to return to regular school for Year Twelve. She didn't make many friends at her new school. Didn't want to. Her only aims were to achieve the marks needed to get into medicine at university, and to keep busy to avoid thinking about what she'd been through. It was amazing she'd been able to endure it all, but luckily there hadn't been much morning sickness, and by the last month of pregnancy school had finished for the year.

'I lived in Sydney a while myself after you were born, and that's where I got my medical education. After that, the ocean drew me back here I guess.' Sylvia poked a piece of chicken with her fork, but it rebelled and slid off the plate onto the floor. 'Oops.' She leaned over discreetly to retrieve it, wrapping it in a serviette and putting it to one side.

Grace chuckled. 'I'm usually the type of person that does that!'

Like mother like daughter.

Sylvia paused for a moment. 'I just realised I don't know your last name.'

'It's Forrester,' Grace replied proudly.

Grace Forrester. Sounded good. Although, she probably would have chosen a different name had she kept her. Maybe Lily, or Christina, or Daniella, but she'd never let herself consider it. Whenever she'd hear a nice name, she'd force the idea out of her mind before getting carried away. The less she bonded with the being growing inside her the better... so she was told. But Grace, Grace was a good name. She was glad her parents had chosen it for her.

'So, your parents... um,' Sylvia said, searching her overflowing mind for the right words.

'Were they good to me?' Grace interjected.

'Well, yes, I guess that's what I'm trying to ask!' Sylvia tried to hide her awkwardness by taking a sip of water.

Grace's eyes became shiny, and she blinked a few times. 'They were. They are. I mean...' Now Grace was the one taking a sip of water and looking awkward. 'I have a wonderful father, and I had a wonderful mother.'

Had? Sylvia stopped chewing momentarily.

'My mum died last year,' Grace explained, fiddling with the napkin on her lap. 'She'd had heart problems for a few years, and well, they eventually caught up with her.' She wiped at the corners of her eyes with the napkin, blinking tears away.

Sylvia's heart dropped into her stomach with a big plop. 'Grace, I'm *so* sorry.' Instinctively she touched Grace's hand, which was holding a spoon loaded with risotto. 'I don't know what to say. I can't imagine what that must have been like — *is* like, for you.'

'It's okay, things are getting better slowly, and Dad is my rock. He's always kept the family together. We've been through a lot, but we're a strong bunch, and I know my mum would have wanted me to get on with life and make the most of it,' Grace said.

My mum. Strange to hear your daughter calling someone else Mum.

'Well, I'm glad you have a supportive father in your life, and I'm sure you have many special memories of your mum.' Sylvia swallowed the lump that was becoming a permanent resident in her throat.

'I do. In fact, I'm making an album to give to Dad at Christmas.' Grace shuffled in her seat and rounded her shoulders. 'I know we've had Christmas barely a month ago, but at the next one I want to give Dad something special to remember Mum by. So, I'm putting together an album of photographs and memories. The first half will be of happy times when Mum was alive, the second half I'm going to fill with new memories I'll be creating this year. Kinda like, to show Mum what I'm doing now, to show her that I'm making the most of my life.' Grace took that moment to whip out her phone, and took a picture of the restaurant. 'No time like the present!'

Sylvia smiled, touched by Grace's thoughtfulness and amused by her spontaneity. 'I'm sure your dad will love it.'

'I hope so. I mean, I don't want it to upset him with all the memories and that, but I think as time goes by it'll be something he'll look at again and again. And hopefully the photos of *my* life will remind him there's always hope for the future.' Grace leaned forward in her chair and took a mouthful of risotto.

I can't believe she's my daughter. Sylvia silently acknowledged her gratefulness for the couple who took her daughter home as their own. The couple who cared for her, fed her, taught her, and obviously loved her. She wondered how Grace would have turned out had she taken the responsibility of bringing her up herself. Would she be the same girl that sat here now? Would she dress the same, speak the same, and like the same food? Would she be making a memory album of *her* if she'd been the one who'd died?

A few quiet moments followed while they ate their meals, and the restaurant became busier with groups of people coming in and lining-up for the buffet. Did people think they were mother and daughter? Or perhaps aunt and niece? It was strange to be having dinner out with an eighteen-year-old girl. Sylvia only ever went out with Larissa, a current boyfriend, or colleagues for a work function. And occasionally her parents on the rare occasions they came to visit, or when she visited them. Since her father's retirement a year ago, Sylvia thought they might visit more often now they had more time on their hands, but it seemed they'd filled their spare time with golf, day trips with friends, and nights at the theatre. Not to mention the adult education courses they had enrolled in. She couldn't understand why after a lifetime of working in schools her father would want to become a student himself, let alone study the oriental horticultural art of Bonsai. Her mother, yes, but she was happy to go along with anything.

After more conversations about general topics and a dessert of lemon meringue pie, Sylvia wondered when she should see

Grace next. Should she be taking her under her wing and inviting her to stay at her house? Would a parent want their daughter staying in a caravan by themselves? She couldn't decide the right thing to do. Deciding on a course of action with a patient was relatively easy. You assess the priorities and target each issue step by step. But she wasn't trained for this.

'You know, I'm loving the caravan park, everyone is so nice and friendly, and the bathrooms are actually quite decent. I've put up a few pictures in the caravan too, just to make it more homely,' Grace said.

'That's great,' replied Sylvia. *Phew.* Decision made. Looks like it was probably best to leave things the way they were for now. Besides, she barely knew her daughter. It would be utterly strange to have her under the same roof.

'Oh, I've heard the monthly markets are on this Sunday, are they any good?' Grace asked, resting her elbows on the table.

Yes! That would be the perfect 'next meet-up', plenty of distractions around to get them talking. Sitting one on one at a table felt slightly awkward. Although Grace was showing herself to be quite the talker. Sylvia found it easy and fascinating to listen to her.

'They're fantastic. Many people come down from Sydney for the day. There are food stalls, art, craft, jewellery, live entertainment... it's a great day out. Even though I've been to more than I can remember, I still enjoy wandering around the park on market day.' Sylvia dabbed at her lips with a napkin, then straightened in her chair as she adjusted her shirt.

'Sounds awesome, I'll definitely check them out.' Grace fiddled with her phone.

Sensing that Grace was waiting for her to say something, Sylvia leaned forward slightly. 'Would you like to meet there?'

Grace's cheeks warmed with a pink glow. 'I'd love to. I

mean, that is, if you don't have other things to do,' she said feebly.

'No, I'd love to join you for the day,' Sylvia replied. 'How about we meet at eleven?'

'Sure, whereabouts?'

Sylvia thought for a moment and smiled softly at the irony. 'At the Wishing Fountain in Miracle Park.'

CHAPTER NINE

'All ready for tonight, Syl?' asked Larissa.

With all that had been going on lately, and an uncharacteristic sleep-in this morning, Sylvia had momentarily forgotten about her best friend's hen-do tonight. As the more responsible of the bridesmaids, she was to be the designated driver, which meant no drinking, or at the very least, one glass of wine early in the evening. Sylvia and alcohol didn't mix well. She did drink here and there, but never more than one or two at the most; not after that night back in high school when she'd had four or five drinks, resulting in a night she could only just remember and a baby nine months later.

'Yes, of course,' replied Sylvia, while opening her wardrobe to check which outfit she would be wearing, and gulping in horror when she realised she hadn't yet prepared it on the clothes hanger labelled 'special events'.

'What's that noise?' Larissa enquired curiously into the phone.

'What noise?' Sylvia rebutted, as hangers slid and clothes swooshed along the railing until she found the outfit she planned on wearing. It was clean, but a little crumpled from being sandwiched between the hardly-worn funeral outfit and the often-worn conference suit.

'Don't tell me you're rifling through your wardrobe figuring out what to wear, Sylvia Greene?'

'Um, I already know what I'm wearing, don't you worry.' Sylvia yanked the long black dress with ruffled chiffon neckline out from its hanger, almost ripping the shoulder seam on the way. She placed it on the bed then reached up to remove the strappy heels from the front-opening transparent shoe boxes stacked neatly from floor to ceiling, organised by colour, type, and purpose. Not that there were many different colours, only black, cream, and one pair of white sandals. Flats lived at the bottom, and heels towered above, gradually increasing in heel height by the time they reached the top.

'Good, so I'll see you at my place at 2pm?'

'Absolutely, see you then.' Sylvia ended the call and carried the dress to the laundry to iron it, making a mental note to tighten the threads on the shoulder seam.

A few hours later she'd picked up Larissa in the van they'd hired for the night, and driven her and the three other bridesmaids, plus some other friends, to a classy day spa in the city of Welston, about a half hour's drive from Tarrin's Bay. Going there always reminded her of times gone by. She'd had placements at Welston hospital during her training. Sadly, it now also reminded her of Richard, as this was where he worked and lived.

Each woman was to get a facial, foot massage, and their hair and make-up done, before heading over to The Rooftop Restaurant and Bar. When Sylvia had been put in charge of organising the night, she immediately booked the *actual* rooftop of the restaurant, aware of how quickly it booked out to group functions. She'd had her thirtieth birthday party there, and the atmosphere, food, and service was impeccable. Despite her birthday being in autumn, the weather had been mild, and the chimineas on the rooftop kept the surroundings comfortably warm. Today, though, was a steamy thirty-three degrees, so she doubted the chimineas would be in action tonight.

Sylvia slipped out of her dress and into the robe provided by the day spa, and rang the tiny bell to indicate she was ready for her pampering session. Well, ready at least, but pampering she was not used to. She always felt she should be doing something productive, instead of wasting time having her skin rubbed, massaged, and slathered with creams containing God knows what *miracle ingredient* sourced from some exotic country or an obscure part of an amphibian's anatomy. But heck, she may as well try to enjoy it. It could take her mind off Richard. She still couldn't believe he'd been so inflexible and heartless. Okay, so she didn't tell him she had a daughter, but she wasn't exactly expecting to bump into her, at least not yet.

'Okay, Sylvia, close your eyes and try to relax...' the beautician's soft voice permeated the room as she floated in.

Why was it that whenever someone said, 'try to relax' she'd end up becoming more tense? It was like at work when she'd say to patients, 'try to think of something nice', while shoving a hypodermic needle into their deltoid muscle.

As the beautician rhythmically lathered a thick cleansing cream over her neck and cheeks in soft upward movements, she somehow got a mental image of slopping a heap of cream onto Richard's face, in a kind of 'take that!' gesture. Like they did with a cream pie in old movies. The bastard, he didn't even stay to *talk* about the issue that night, he simply left. Just like that. Oh well, maybe she'd be better off without him, if he was the type to run at the first hint of commitment. Besides, once, when he helped load the dishwasher, he put the forks and spoons together in the same segment of the cutlery holder. *Unforgiveable.*

As the Richard in her mind tried to wipe the cream away from his face, so he could breathe again, gluggy droplets of cream bobbed up and down and side to side as he cried, 'What the hell do you think you're doing!'

Laughter burst out of Sylvia's throat, as the image of Richard looking like a cross between a melting vampire and the marshmallow man from *Ghostbusters* was too much to bear.

'Oh.' The beautician stopped lathering. 'Are you okay, Sylvia?' She hovered above, a curious half-smile on her face.

Sylvia cleared her throat, trying to eradicate the image of Richard from her mind. 'Yes, sorry about that, it's just, er... I'm a little ticklish that's all,' she reasoned.

'No problem, I'll adjust the pressure, shall I?'

The beautician resumed lathering but slowed the pace, exerting a firmer, more definite pressure. Then, somehow, Sylvia got a mental image of lathering shaving cream onto *Mark's* face, in an 'I want you' kind of gesture. Spreading the cream from the base of his neck, over his Adam's apple, up over his chin, the side of his cheeks, and around his lips.

Sylvia sprung from the table to a sitting position and gasped, sending clumps of cream cleanser onto her lap and almost knocking over the beautician.

What the hell am I thinking?

Creases of annoyance and perhaps a little fear formed in the beautician's forehead as she edged backwards. She probably wasn't used to clients having spontaneous fits of laughter or Tourette's Syndrome-like jack-in-the-box behaviour.

'Er, Sylvia, is there something wrong?' she asked tentatively, slinking further backwards, and probably trying to grab the nearest sharp implement or hot tub of wax to use as a weapon should her client turn into a psychotic beautician-killer.

'Oh no, I'm *so* sorry, you must think I'm a complete nutcase!' Sylvia bowed her head. 'I've just got a lot on my mind that's all. I've had more drama in the past few days than an episode of *Desperate Housewives.*' She managed a weak laugh, and to her surprise, the beautician, whose nametag said Katie, sat next to her on the table.

'Tell me all about it,' Katie insisted, rubbing the cleanser through her fingertips in anticipation.

Sylvia wasn't the type to enthusiastically hug people she barely knew, let alone people she knew, but an hour later as she walked out of Katie's treatment room all glossy-faced and glowing, she welcomed Katie's embrace.

'Now go on, make the most of this night. You need to let your hair down. And remember, that guy is not worth it. Focus your energy on getting to know Grace. Oh, and don't discount that other guy, he sounds gorgeous.' Katie winked, and Sylvia slightly regretted telling her about the shaving cream fantasy.

But it *was* nice to let out everything that was piling up in her head, even if it was with a complete stranger. She hadn't even told Larissa yet about Richard leaving, or about Grace turning up, for that matter. She didn't want to bring any of it up now. This was Larissa's night, her night to celebrate.

Another hour or so later, Sylvia emerged from the day spa with the others feeling like a new woman. She certainly didn't look like the mother of an eighteen-year-old, and tonight she planned on simply being herself. Not Dr Greene, not Richard's ex-girlfriend, not the pregnant sixteen-year-old who chickened out of motherhood, and not Sylvia the woman who was strangely attracted to a man she'd only just met and now worked with. She was Sylvia Greene — an attractive, exciting woman in her prime. Well, perhaps exciting wasn't the right choice of word for her personality. Pleasant, yes, that's what she was — pleasant. But maybe tonight she'd try to be just a little bit exciting. It *was* a hen night after all.

A *little bit* exciting was an understatement. Sylvia hadn't partied this way in years, and there's no way she would have had the hen night been in Tarrin's Bay. While out, Sylvia would always do a routine glance around the premises to ensure no patients were there. She could never shake the feeling that she shouldn't be out enjoying herself in public, and that she was supposed to live a quiet, studious life, always on her best behaviour. And she always was, but tonight she went so far as to join the other bridesmaids, dancing on a table in the bar section of the restaurant. Granted, they'd had a few glasses of champagne, and Sylvia only one, but when Aretha Franklin's song *Respect* came on there was no stopping them. She even agreed to sing karaoke for the first time in her life, but only as a duet with Larissa. *The Final Countdown* never sounded so good!

Before dancing, they'd enjoyed a sumptuous dinner on the rooftop, with stimulating conversation and the odd explosion of laughter. Sylvia made sure to involve all the women in the 'How well do you know Larissa?' quiz she'd created before they got to know the champagne too well. Even Larissa had to answer the questions but, surprisingly, only scored ninety-four percent! Larissa's younger sister won the quiz, scoring herself a framed photo of the subject in question. The night was enjoyable, and Sylvia somehow managed to deflect any questions aimed at her regarding her personal life, mostly by saying, 'More champagne, anyone?' and lifting the bottle up in the air.

As designated driver, Sylvia delivered everyone to their respective homes at the end of the night, and lastly, Larissa. Her fiancé, Luke, was at his buck's night. Larissa said he'd be crashing at a mate's house, and hoped he wouldn't end up tied to a tree in the middle of nowhere with his eyebrows shaved and wearing nothing but an adult nappy.

'Thanks for driving us all, Hun,' Larissa said as Sylvia walked her inside. 'And thanks for not letting me overdo the champers!'

Despite Sylvia's persistent asking if anyone wanted a refill, she managed to keep Larissa from having too much bubbly after Larissa had stressed how she didn't want a repeat of her engagement party, where she'd thrown up during her father's speech. It was the alcohol, of course, but as the embarrassing event occurred right when he'd got talking about Larissa and Luke producing a Toyota Tarago full of grandchildren, who could really be sure?

'I hope you enjoyed the night, Riss. I did,' said Sylvia.

'I *know* you did! Who are you and what have you done with my friend?' She forced open Sylvia's jaw and peered inside. 'Hello! Sylvia, are you in there?'

'Stop it, you!' Sylvia gently slapped her on the arm.

'Can I take off this God-awful thing now?' Larissa tugged at her Bride-To-Be tiara, trapped in her hair-sprayed hair. 'Ouch!' When she finally pulled it from the top of her head, her hair looked like Cameron Diaz's in the movie *There's Something About Mary*.

Sylvia covered her mouth but laughter escaped, and only intensified when she led Larissa to the hall mirror to show her the post-tiara hairdo. They both sunk to the floor, Sylvia's belly aching from laughing so much. Then something surprising happened. Sylvia felt her stomach muscles contracting again, but not from laughter. Bubbles of emotion fizzed up inside, finally reaching her eyes which stung like she'd accidentally squirted them with lemon juice. Tears flooded her face, and sobs replaced the laughter.

Larissa's laughter subsided, and she looked at Sylvia with concern. 'Are you... crying?'

Sylvia nodded, as more tears joined the deluge.

'What... what's wrong?' Larissa shuffled along the floor to sit next to Sylvia.

Sylvia tried to speak, but every time she opened her mouth the sobs got a head start. She forced a breath of composure, not sure how long it would last, and blurted out everything that was on her mind. 'I met her! I met Grace and she fainted and we had dinner but before that Richard found out and dumped me so I went out and I met Mark and I ate too much cake and now we work together and I'm so upset about Richard but then I started thinking of Mark and shaving cream and tomorrow I'm seeing Grace again but—'

'Whoa! Sylvia, slow down!' Larissa placed her hands over Sylvia's cheeks. 'Take a breath... good,' she said while demonstrating a deep breath. 'Okay now, who's Mark, who's Grace, and... oh my God, Richard dumped you? Why didn't you say anything before?'

'I didn't want to spoil your night,' Sylvia said, sniffing.

'Hey, you shouldn't have worried about that; you should have called me as soon as it happened, I would have come over.' Larissa pulled Sylvia close to her. 'So what happened, why did he break up with you?'

'He didn't want to be with someone who had children,' Sylvia replied.

'But you don't have... hang on, what, you mean he found out what happened all those years ago and held that against you?'

'Not exactly, sort of, um...' Sylvia took another deep breath and turned her body to face Larissa. 'Grace. She's my daughter.

She found me two days ago. And we had dinner last night.' A lone tear dribbled down to join the moist gloss over Sylvia's cheeks. 'I met my baby.'

'Oh my God. Sylvia, I can't believe it.' Larissa slumped against the wall. 'What's she like?'

Sylvia smiled. 'She's beautiful.'

They spoke for a long time, reminiscing about their high school days, and Sylvia shared everything she'd learned about Grace so far. Larissa convinced Sylvia to stay at her place for the night, since it was technically morning anyway, and set her alarm to make sure Sylvia would have time to dash home and get showered and ready for her day with Grace.

'Oh hey, you didn't say who Mark was.' Larissa looked quizzically at Sylvia.

'Oh yeah, I met him at Café Lagoon the night Richard and I broke up, and the next day he turned up at work.'

'As a patient?'

'No, a colleague. He does alternative medicine,' Sylvia stated.

'Cool.'

'Cool?'

'Yeah, I might book in for an appointment. Maybe he can give me something to keep calm on the big day.'

'I doubt it.' Sylvia crossed her arms.

'Do you have something against this guy?'

'No, I just prefer my system of medicine, that's all. Plus, there's something about him that irritates me, he seems so perfect and together, I don't know,' Sylvia said.

'Is he nice to you?'

'Well, yes, but—'

'Does Joyce seem to like him?'

'Yes, but—'

'Is he hot?'

Sylvia stared at Larissa for a moment, aware of her sneaky game. Then she licked her finger and touched it to her arm, making a sizzling sound with her tongue.

'So you like him, hey?' Larissa poked Sylvia's ribs.

'No, of course not. Just because he's hot doesn't mean I like him.' Heat flushed Sylvia's face.

'Okay, fair enough. I won't pry any further. C'mon, let me set you up in the spare room.' Larissa linked her arm under Sylvia's and helped her up.

Sylvia wouldn't be hungover in the morning, but she felt the thick fog of exhaustion seeping through her body.

Larissa turned over the sheets on the spare bed and fluffed the pillow, then paused. 'So, what was that thing you mentioned, about... shaving cream?'

Sylvia's flush returned. 'Don't ask.' She smiled as she hopped into the bed and pulled the sheet over her face.

CHAPTER TEN

A glorious summer morning greeted Grace through the window of the caravan. Lush green leaves danced about in the breeze, the sky an intense cobalt, and the salty smell of the ocean enticed her to the beach for a swim. Well, if you could call it that. She wasn't used to swimming in the ocean; growing up in the heart of Melbourne meant she was limited to the occasional seaside holiday with her parents. But she enjoyed it nonetheless, wading into the water, feeling the pull of the wave as it receded to its source, and relishing the cool caress of the water on her hot sun-kissed skin.

She giggled along with some children nearby when each new wave approached. They would try to run away from it, but she walked into it, each splash enlivening her, waking her. *What would it be like to live here all the time?* If she did, she'd probably come to the beach every morning; it was a great way to wake up and start the day.

Grace's eyes soaked up the vast expanse of blue surrounding her, and she wasn't sure where the ocean finished and the sky began. It was all connected. Up to her right, the famous 'Tarrin' sat proudly on the headland. The brochure she'd read said the town was named after the unique 'Earth Man' rock formation, which naturally resembled a man's face. Years of waves gone before had sculpted cheekbones, a strong jawline, and a protrusion that looked like a nose. It was amazing, actually, that a random natural phenomenon could produce something that appeared to be sculpted on purpose.

After a few minutes, Grace walked back up the hill to the caravan park, took a quick shower and got dressed into denim shorts and a white t-shirt. Now that it looked like she might be here for a while yet, she'd have to buy more clothes. Hopefully the markets would have some inexpensive options.

By eleven, Grace stood at the Wishing Fountain in Miracle Park, reading the plaque nearby.

'Hi Grace.' Sylvia approached; her eyes slightly bloodshot.

'Oh hi, I wish I'd known about this Wishing Festival thing, I could have come here earlier for that and made a wish!'

'Not to worry, maybe next year, huh?'

'Yeah, maybe,' she replied.

'Hey, I was thinking we should probably exchange phone numbers,' Sylvia said, scratching her ear and alternating her stance to her other foot.

'Sure.' Grace whipped out her phone from the canvas satchel strapped diagonally across her chest. She punched in Sylvia's number, and Sylvia did the same on her phone.

'So, is there anything in particular you'd like to look at, or will we just wander around?' asked Sylvia, turning her head from one side to the other.

She's probably seen all these stalls a million times. I hope she doesn't mind being here.

'I'm happy to wander, although I'd love to get some new clothes somewhere.'

'There's a lot of bargains here, let's see what we can find, shall we?' Sylvia smiled, and Grace's heart warmed. Here she was, enjoying the summery ambience of the markets, and shopping with her biological mother.

She remembered shopping with Maria, the only mother she'd known and loved all her life, and buying her first bra. Her mother had to fight back tears when the shop assistant rang it up and handed Grace the plastic shopping bag. Grace couldn't wait to get home and put it on, so much so, she even took a raincheck on her mother's offer of taking her to her favourite dress shop. At that stage, Grace knew she was adopted, but it didn't concern her all that much as she'd grown up knowing the truth since she was little. In fact, when she was younger she assumed that all children were adopted, and that parents simply picked the kids they wanted from an orphanage. After asking just about every child in her kindergarten class when they were adopted, David and Maria Forrester were advised by teachers to explain the situation a little better to their daughter.

As she got older, Grace of course wanted to know if they knew anything about her birth mother, and why she'd given her up. Her parents said that she was too young to be able to care for her properly and give her a good life, and she loved Grace enough to give her to a couple who couldn't have children of their own.

Our special little angel, they'd called Grace since she was little.

'Oh, those tops are awesome!' Grace seemed pulled to one of the clothing stalls like a paperclip to a magnet. She lifted and turned the tops on the rack, and held some up to her body in front of a mirror. 'Only ten bucks each, wow!'

In no way concerned with passers-by, she lifted her t-shirt off right there, revealing a spaghetti-strap singlet beneath. Grace pulled a top over her head and turned side to side in the mirror. 'What do you think?' she asked Sylvia.

Sylvia seemed taken aback. 'I um, I think... it suits you,' she replied.

'Good. I'll have four of these,' she said to the salesperson, while lifting the top over her head and replacing it with her own. The tops were cotton, with an over-layer of mesh sewn haphazardly in different angles across the front. Grace chose the pink, blue, white, and silver tops, and handed forty dollars to the sales person.

'Listen, if there's anything else you want, or need, I'm happy to buy it for you,' Sylvia said quietly.

Grace flicked her hand. 'Oh, you don't have to do that. Thanks though, I appreciate it.'

'Well, if you ever do need anything, don't hesitate to ask, okay?'

'Okay.' Grace smiled, and they walked to the next stall, a homemade food stall, where Sylvia picked up four bottles of chilli and tomato relish.

They wandered for another half hour or so, grabbed a bite to eat, then Grace found another stall she wanted to check out.

'How cool, I'm going to do it!' Grace said, as she eyed the fancy equipment and saw a person walk away thanking the stallholder, grasping a large photo. 'I've always wanted to try iridology! Do you mind?' Grace's eyes queried Sylvia's.

'Um sure, go ahead. But while you're doing that, I might just take a look at this stall over here,' Sylvia said, walking awkwardly towards the next stall displaying knitted baby clothes and toys.

Why would she want to look at baby items? 'Er... okay then.' Grace eyed her curiously, until Sylvia looked at the baby items and her face became red.

'Oops, I meant that stall... over there,' she said, pointing to a handmade jewellery display.

'Sylvia, long time no see.' Grace turned around to see the

man behind the iridology equipment winking in Sylvia's direction.

'Oh, hi, Mark,' Sylvia said, in what seemed to be a fake tone of surprise.

'So you've been to this stall before, Sylvia?' Grace asked.

'Me? No, no, Mark and I work at the same clinic.'

'Oh, right. Cool.' Grace smiled and walked up to Mark, holding out her hand. 'I'm Grace. I'd love to see what my eyes tell you.'

'Sure, just take a seat, and rest your chin here.' Mark pointed to something protruding from the equipment, and she settled her chin on it while he took a photo of her eyes.

'I, ah, I'll just be over here.' Sylvia was obviously anxious to check out the jewellery.

'No worries, I'll fill you in on the secrets of my soul later!' Grace replied. Sylvia nodded and scuttled away.

Mark fiddled with a laptop computer, and soon the irises of her eyes appeared enlarged on the screen.

'Whoa! How weird is that?' Grace had no idea her eyes contained that much detail. There were colours woven through her irises that she didn't even realise were there.

Mark smiled, and examined the photo. 'Okay, first of all, this tells me that your circulation isn't as good as it could be. Are you prone to dizziness or fainting spells?'

Grace chuckled, nodding her head.

'And what about cold hands and feet?' Mark asked.

'How did you know?'

Mark ran a finger around the dark outer rim of Grace's irises on the computer screen. 'This here is called a scurf rim. Most people who have this sign have poor circulation. And see these other markings,' he moved his finger over what looked like cracks of some kind, 'I'd say you're also prone to muscle cramps and spasms. Do you get any leg cramps or eyelid twitches?'

Grace thought she could feel her eyelid twitching as he spoke, and then found herself rubbing her calf muscles. 'Wow, you're good. I always get those eyelid twitches, and once they start they're hard to stop. What does it mean?'

'Sometimes it's due to eyestrain, but often it's a simple magnesium deficiency. Do you have trouble winding down, or falling asleep at night?'

'Definitely trouble winding down, I can't seem to switch my mind off sometimes. But I can also find it hard to get going in the morning, especially now I'm not at school anymore. It's easy to sleep in.' Grace went off on a tangent, as she often did. 'I'm also really tired in the afternoons, but as soon as I've had dinner I'm wide awake!'

Mark nodded. 'That's common with magnesium deficiency. It can make it hard to relax, but also contribute to fatigue. But if you're tired often, that's not great for someone as young as you, so if it concerns you it might be good to come in for an appointment so I can assess your diet and lifestyle.'

'Sure, I'd like to, actually.' Grace picked up one of Mark's business cards, then looked at the computer screen. 'What's that ugly spot thing?' She pointed to a dark patch on the lower part of her right eye.

'That's a psoric spot. They usually appear over areas that have a genetic inefficiency of some kind. Are there any kidney problems in your family history?'

Family history was one thing Grace had no idea about. Maybe she should bring it up with Sylvia? 'Um, I'm not exactly sure,' Grace replied, twisting her lips to one side. 'But I have had a problem with my kidneys once. Actually, there's something I should probably tell you...' Grace filled him in briefly on her medical history and left the stall with a photo of her irises, an appointment booking for Wednesday morning, and a questionnaire she was to fill out and bring to the appointment.

Thank God, here she comes. Sylvia had just about memorised the entire display of jewellery and their prices, as she tried to look interested while waiting for Grace. The stallholder must have presumed she was concocting a tactical strategy for stealing the pieces, as she hovered back and forth wherever Sylvia was standing. She asked 'Can I help you?' and 'Is there anything in particular you're looking for?' and 'You're sure there's nothing I can help you with?' several times, and each time Sylvia replied, 'No thanks I'm just looking.'

'Thanks for waiting, what did you get?' Grace asked as she approached.

'Er, nothing,' said Sylvia.

'Oh, I thought you must have wanted to get something, you seemed keen.'

'Nothing really caught my eye.'

'Oh well. Hang on... unless you weren't trying to avoid talking to *him* were you?' Grace's eyes glanced in the direction of Mark, who was now busy talking to another interested customer.

'Huh? What do you mean?' Sylvia said, trying to shut out the shaving cream fantasy from her mind again, and most likely turning a deep shade of crimson. Now that she worked with Mark, it would be best to keep a professional distance. Plus she didn't want him to know Grace was her daughter, didn't want to give off a false impression or be judged in any way.

'You two, you haven't been... *involved* or anything, have you?'

'Oh no, definitely not!'

'Oh good, I wouldn't want to cause any awkwardness between you. I've booked in for an appointment with him, he's going to assess my diet and give me some health tips. Look at the picture of my eyes!' Grace showed Sylvia the print-out.

'Hmm, interesting. Well, I'm glad to see that you're health conscious,' Sylvia replied. But why did she have to believe all this hype about iridology; surely it wasn't an accurate way to assess someone's health?

'So, I take it you're not married,' Grace said, eyeing Sylvia's bare fingers. 'Do you have a boyfriend?'

Sylvia almost replied, 'Yes, his name's Richard,' but the memory of him storming out that night caught her words.

I didn't sign up for this.

I just can't take on anything complicated right now.

All of a sudden, she was classed as 'complicated', even though all her life she'd strived to be the reliable, consistent, successful, organised, and easy-going woman that any man would be happy to have in his life. Grace's arrival *had* complicated things. Part of her was so pleased to have met her and to be with her right now, and the other part was wondering whether it would have been best to leave the past in the past, and keep living the stable life she'd worked so hard to create. The life where no one knew what happened eighteen years ago, and her reputation could remain intact. So many people in town that she knew as a child still lived here today. They'd smile and wave as she passed them in the street, and some had even become patients. It would be a shock for them to find out the real reason she'd left town all those years ago.

'So, do you?' Grace nudged Sylvia's arm with her elbow.

'No, I'm single,' Sylvia replied coolly. She couldn't say, 'I did until you turned up.' It wasn't Grace's fault, and she didn't want to make her feel like she was intruding.

'Me too,' Grace said. 'Although I've seen a few cute guys around here!'

'I'm sure you'll find someone special when the time is right.'

'I hope so.' Grace glanced around. 'Oh, hey — do you mind if we check out the bookstore?'

'Sure.' Good idea. Sylvia had nearly finished the book she was currently reading and would need another one soon. She only ever bought one or two books at a time, refusing to buy any more until she'd read the others. Unlike Larissa, whose To-Be-Read-Pile resembled the Leaning Tower of Pisa.

'I'm a bit of a bookaholic,' Grace said as they walked across the road.

'Well, it's a good addiction to have, I guess.' Sylvia smiled.

'Wow, this isn't like any other bookstore I've seen, it's so... homely.' Grace's eyes widened as they entered Mrs May's Bookstore and wandered along the creaky timber floor aisles. Tall wooden shelves divided the shop into sections, and in the corner were a couple of old-fashioned velvet upholstered armchairs. There was even a separate room housing the children's books, complete with tables and chairs and a puppet theatre.

Sylvia always welcomed the warm, rich scent of timber and books, and each time it brought her back to her childhood. This store had been around for as long as she could remember. She'd come in here after school with her mother in the days when Mrs May herself worked in the store. Now in her eighties, Mrs May still owned the store but it was run by her daughter and granddaughter, although she still came in occasionally to check on things. Sometimes Sylvia saw her at the clinic, as she was a patient of Dr Bronovski, and always admired her strength of character and resilience. She'd had a few health challenges, but just as she'd start to look frail, she'd bounce back again. A penchant for hard work seemed to run in the family. Sylvia had gone to school with Mrs May's granddaughter, Olivia, who now seemed to work at the store every day while raising a daughter on her own.

Sylvia remembered flipping through books in the store with her mother and tugging on her skirt in hope of having one bought for her. Sometimes they'd sit at one of the chairs and read together. On Fridays, the children's room would be packed full of kids, waiting in anticipation for Mrs May's weekly puppet show.

'Yes, the store is definitely one of a kind,' Sylvia said.

'So, what sorts of books do you like reading?' Grace asked.

'Um... a bit of a mixture, I guess. I like suspense and mystery novels, but I also like real life stories — you know, people who have overcome difficult odds and survived, or have been through something major — that sort of thing.'

'So you like stories with a bit of *meat* in them?'

'Yeah I guess, but nothing too gruesome, more psychological and intellectual suspense than anything.'

'Oh! Have you read this one? It's totally amazing.' Grace shoved a copy of *A Difference of Opinion* in her face, and Sylvia had to lean back to be able to read the cover properly. God, she wasn't losing her perfect eyesight was she? She hoped it'd be a while before she'd have to wear glasses like both her parents, who had to lean back, squint, and extend something in front of them as far as their arm would reach in order to read it. She saw it all the time, people over the age of forty-five or fifty, whose ability to read and focus on things up close gradually diminished. There was a name for it: presbyopia. One of the most common eye problems affecting middle-aged people.

'No, I haven't.' Sylvia turned the book over to read the back cover.

'It's got everything — mystery, suspense, secrets, lies... and then, just when you think you have it worked out — bam!' Grace clapped her hands together. 'A twist appears that throws everything you ever thought out the window.'

Hmm... sounds like my life. Sylvia held the book close to her side. 'I'll take it then.'

'Great! You'll love it. Okay, now let's find you another goodie. Oh, here's one,' Grace said enthusiastically.

'Actually, I usually only buy one book at a time. When I've finished this one I'll come back and get another,' Sylvia stated.

'Really? Okay, well remember this for next time. This one's about a woman who travels to India in search of her missing husband. It's like the TV show 24 on steroids. There's fast-paced action, but also a lot of mind games and stuff that you'd probably like.'

Sylvia nodded, impressed by Grace's sales ability.

'And this book,' Grace said, holding up a copy of *The Stranger*, 'is more of an emotional mystery than suspense, but it totally hooks you in from the start and you really feel like you know the characters personally. The last few chapters were so intriguing I stayed up half the night to finish them!'

'I'll add it to my mental list.' Sylvia decided. And later she'd add it to her *actual* list, or more precisely, her 'Books I Want To Read' spreadsheet, with books listed in categories and in order of priority.

Grace had other ideas. *Click!* She took a photo of the two books. 'I'll give you a copy of the pic so you remember exactly what they look like when you come back to find them.' Grace ran a finger along the bookshelves. 'Do you have a favourite book? Like, a favourite book of all time?'

Sylvia rolled her eyes upward and thought for a moment. 'Actually, there's one book that stands out for me. It's a classic, written in the 1860s. *The Woman in White* by Wilkie Collins, have you heard of it?'

'Oh my God! I *so* want to read that one! I've heard of it but haven't got around to finding a copy yet.' Grace rubbed her hands together.

For a girl of eighteen Grace seemed quite 'literary-aware'.

'Tell you what, you can borrow my copy if you like.'

'Yeah? That'd be great, thanks!'

'If we walk to my place after we finish here, I'll give it to you.'

'Sounds good. I promise I'll get it back to you as soon as possible.'

'Take your time,' Sylvia replied. *But please don't have it for too long*, she thought. She hadn't lent many books to people over the years, but just in case, she'd made a special chart that had room to write the name of the book, the author, who had borrowed it, the date it was borrowed, and a reasonable time frame to allow before giving them their first reminder notice to return it. She would have made a kick-ass librarian.

Grace grabbed a book she wanted and took it to the counter.

'Here, let me buy this for you.' Sylvia held out her hand for the book.

'It's okay, you don't have to,' Grace replied.

'I'd like to, and since I'm buying a book too we might as well do it all at the same time,' Sylvia said.

'Well okay then, thanks, Sylvia.' Grace handed her the book and Olivia rang it up at the counter.

'Has it been busy at the markets?' Olivia asked Sylvia.

'Yeah, quite busy actually. How are things here at the store?'

'Despite the eBook surge in the marketplace, things are still going strong. In fact, I've been a bit overworked, hoping to cut down my hours so I can spend more time with Mia in the afternoons after school.'

Sylvia nodded. 'How old is she now?'

'Five. She's just started kindy and loving it, thank goodness.' Olivia seemed happy, but weary, her eyes sheltering dark shadows. 'You seem to know a lot about books,' she said to Grace. 'Sorry, I overheard you talking.'

'I'm an avid reader, always have been. If I could get paid to read books all day I would.'

'Would you settle for being *around* books all day?'

Grace eyed Olivia curiously.

'We need a casual assistant at the store. With me reducing my hours, and another staff member off on maternity leave as of tomorrow, we need someone as soon as possible. You interested in applying?'

Grace looked at Sylvia in surprise, then at Olivia. 'Um, I might be, I mean I am, I'm just not sure how long I'll be in town, that's all.'

'Will you be here at least the next two weeks?'

'Yes, I can't see myself leaving just yet.'

'And if you liked the job, could you see yourself hanging around a bit longer?'

'It's possible, I'm just getting to know the town, see where I want to be and what I want to do. I just finished high school last year, and I'm taking the year to figure out what to do next.'

'Would you have time right now to answer a few more questions, out back in our storeroom slash office?' Olivia gestured to the door behind the counter.

Grace looked at Sylvia with enquiring eyes. 'Go ahead,' Sylvia said, gesturing to the door as well. 'I'll wait out front.'

Olivia asked a very pregnant salesperson to take over the counter and led Grace to the office as Sylvia went to walk outside.

Then she stopped.

Why not?

She walked back to the shelf of books she'd been looking at before and picked up the two books Grace had recommended, taking them to the counter. 'I'll take these,' she said to the lady.

'Good choice,' she replied.

'First baby?' Sylvia asked.

'No, my fourth. I'm an old hand when it comes to having babies!'

Sylvia could barely get over having one, let alone four, and she didn't even keep hers! It was the most pain she'd ever experienced, such a shock to the system. She wouldn't go through it again in a hurry, but part of her ached for a second chance. A chance to do it right from day one. Be a proper mother. Which was why she'd also wished for that when she tossed the coin into the Wishing Fountain at the festival.

But maybe *this* was supposed to be her second chance — getting to know Grace and being some kind of mother-figure in her life. Sure she'd missed the early years, but mothering didn't stop when the child grew up. That's what her mother had said, when sixteen-year-old Sylvia briefly wondered, 'What if I *could* bring this baby up myself?'

'You'll never be able to become a doctor if you keep this baby,' her father had said, and he was right. Maybe she could have done it later on, but being a young single mother would have been hard enough. Although her heartbreak grew as her belly grew, Sylvia knew it was the best choice. The only choice. If she'd missed out on her dream she would have resented Grace, even though it wouldn't have been her fault.

A few minutes later, Grace walked victoriously out of the bookstore. 'Looks like I *will* be staying here for a while!'

'You got the job, already?'

Grace nodded and smiled. 'Like she said, they needed someone right away. They're going to start training me tomorrow.'

Even though her life had already changed in the few days since Grace's arrival, there was no doubt about it, Sylvia's life was about to change even more.

CHAPTER ELEVEN

'Nice house,' Grace commented as they walked up the steps to the front porch. 'Who's that?' She discreetly eyed the house next door.

'That's Nancy.' Sylvia chuckled as Nancy took up residence in her usual position. She tried to be inconspicuous, but was always visible through the slightly open curtain of her kitchen window.

'Bit of a stalker by the looks of it.'

'Ah, she's harmless,' Sylvia said.

'Do you ever speak to her?'

'Not really, we wave to each other sometimes, and I've tried to be nice when we've crossed paths out front, but she's pretty quiet. I think she's lonely. Doesn't get many visitors, although I can't be sure, because I'm not here during the day.'

'Maybe you should bring her a cake or something,' Grace suggested.

'Maybe.'

Sylvia let Grace through the door first, into the small entry foyer that merged with the modern kitchen to the left, and gave way to the open plan dining and living area on the right.

Neutral tones of beige with a hint of caramel unified the interior and there were accents of burgundy in the sofa cushions, a lamp, and a vase on the dining table. Sylvia loved that her place was easy to maintain, probably because she didn't have visitors very often, and certainly no kids. As an only child, she hadn't been subjected to visits from unruly nieces or nephews, and her three cousins and their kids lived interstate. She didn't even own a pet. Sylvia was used to living alone, but sometimes on a Sunday afternoon, or a Friday night, she wondered what it would be like to share her life with someone. She'd had a glimpse of that scenario with Richard, but had never really felt completely comfortable with anyone before. There was always this niggling feeling that she had to put on a performance, appear to be the model girlfriend. In a way, being single was a relief.

'Nice,' Grace said as she scanned the room. 'So tidy.'

'Thanks.' Sylvia pulled a book from her alphabetised collection in the bookcase near the dining table. 'Here's *The Woman in White.*'

Grace took hold of the book. 'Great, thanks! Wow, it even looks old. I love books that have that ancient appearance, makes you just want to curl up in front of a fireplace and read them.' Grace held the book to her chest.

'Although not in this weather!' Sylvia remarked. 'Can I get you a tea or coffee, or a cold drink?'

'A cold drink please. Whatever you have is fine.'

'Okay. First though, I just have to duck to the bathroom,' said Sylvia, pointing down the hall.

'Sure.' Grace slipped her sandals off with her toes and walked into the expansive living area. 'Oh wow, you have a piano?' Her eyes lit up like a child on Christmas morning.

'Oh, that old thing? It belongs to my mum, she used to teach. She and my father moved into a unit after Dad retired, but there was no room for it so they brought it here for storage. She couldn't bring herself to get rid of it.'

'May I?' Grace gestured towards the piano, raising her eyebrows.

'Sure, go for your life. I'll be back in a tick,' Sylvia said as she scurried down the hallway and into the bathroom.

So the day's gone well, she thought, apart from the encounter with Mark. No wonder he'd said he might see her there. He must have been trying to drum up business for his new start at the clinic. Why did she feel so awkward around him?

Sylvia flushed the toilet, and as the sound abated it was replaced with music. A beautiful melody filtered through the walls of the bathroom. *What the?* Was that really... *Grace* playing?

Sylvia opened the door quietly and edged out into the hall where she could see Grace sitting at the piano, playing the keys enthusiastically. *Oh my God. She's brilliant!* Sylvia stayed in the hall and listened until Grace finished playing and turned to look at Sylvia.

'Oh, I didn't know you were watching, hope you don't mind me giving it a good workout. If there's a piano in the vicinity I can't help myself.'

Sylvia seemed stuck to the floor.

'Are you okay?'

'Grace... that was amazing!' Sylvia walked slowly towards Grace, as if walking too fast would somehow destroy the memory of what she'd just heard. 'Why didn't you tell me you could play piano?'

'It didn't come up in conversation I guess. Anyway, it's just something I do for fun; we've got a piano back home. My mum plays — er, *played* too.' Grace stood.

'With that level of skill, you must have had many lessons over the years?' Sylvia asked.

'Not really. I had a few when I was about thirteen, but they got interrupted by...'

Sylvia nodded, waiting for her to continue.

'Um, never mind, I ah... just got out of the habit of going to lessons. Most of the time I taught myself, and Mum taught me a little too, but she was better at playing than teaching — too impatient!'

'Seriously, you should be doing something with that talent. You really are amazing.'

'I could go on one of those television talent shows but I'd get heaps nervous. I've never even performed in front of anyone before, except my parents, my cats — who aren't with us anymore, God rest their little souls — and now *you*.'

'Well, anytime you want to practise, feel free to come over and use it. It's just sitting there gathering dust.'

'Thanks, I'd love to,' Grace responded.

'Oh, let me get you that drink.' Sylvia poured two glasses of juice and plopped in a few ice cubes before handing a glass to Grace.

'Thanks.'

'You're welcome. And thank *you* for that little performance.' Sylvia clinked her glass to Grace's, and a smile of astonishment graced her face.

I don't think she has any idea how good she really is.

Sylvia had an idea, a great idea, but she'd bring it up with Grace at a later time. She didn't want to scare her off.

CHAPTER TWELVE

'Welcome to your first day, Mark,' Joyce chirped as Mark walked into the clinic on Monday morning carrying his equipment from yesterday. 'How did your stall at the markets go?'

'Really well, thanks. Got quite a few bookings out of it. Here are the adjustments to my appointment schedule,' Mark said, handing Joyce a sheet of paper.

'Thanks, I'll get these into the computer system now for you.'

'Thanks, Joyce, you're a gem.'

'Just doing my job.' She smiled. 'Morning, Sylvia,' she said as Sylvia walked into the clinic at precisely eight-thirty.

'Good morning, Joyce, Mark.'

'Sylvia.' Mark gave a quick nod of his head. 'Well I better get organised, first patient's at nine-thirty, right?'

'Right.' Joyce nodded.

Mark closed the door to the consultation room behind him. He set his iridology camera up on the desk, plugged in his laptop, and turned the power points on. He checked that his dark field microscope was working then laid out the small boxes containing glass slides and cover slips so they were within easy reach. He opened the filing cabinet and withdrew the files of existing patients who were coming today. Even though the old clinic at his father's pharmacy was about thirty minutes drive away, many of his patients had agreed to continue seeing him after he moved to Tarrin's Bay. This pleased Mark; although he was a proactive promoter of his business, he didn't want to have to start again completely from scratch.

He placed the files on the desk then added a few empty files to the pile, to be filled with the history, complaints and concerns of patients he had yet to meet. He always enjoyed seeing a new patient for the first time, finding out what they wanted help with and assessing their state of health before working out a treatment program. Sometimes he'd try to guess what they were coming to see him about as soon as they entered the room. Sometimes he was right, and sometimes he wasn't. Once he presumed that a young, slim woman entering his room was perhaps coming to him for help with headaches, or tiredness, but in fact she had breast cancer and was about to undergo aggressive treatment. She'd wanted to know if there was anything to support her body during the treatment, and had eagerly accepted an acupuncture treatment there and then to calm her nerves.

Mark had seen a huge range of complaints in his seven years of clinical practice. Some minor, some major, but each and every one fuelled his motivation to maintain an optimal state of health himself. Congruence was important in his profession. He had to practise what he preached and set a good example. He was a confident practitioner, and knew if his patients did what he said there was every chance they would improve in some way. But he also knew there were cases that just couldn't be fixed. He'd learned that the hard way two years ago.

Knock, knock.

Joyce popped her head into the room after Mark asked, 'Yes?'

'I'm just getting myself a coffee, can I get you anything?' she asked.

Unaccustomed to this sort of hospitality at work, Mark shifted his stance awkwardly. 'Oh, a peppermint tea would be great, thanks, Joyce.'

Minutes later she brought in a plain white mug, steam rising and curling as the peppermint scent reached his nose. He blew gently into the tea and it bubbled and rippled, then he took a few slow sips, before placing it on a coaster next to his penholder.

At a quarter past nine, he was ready and waiting for his first patient to arrive. He'd heard what appeared to be Sylvia's quick footsteps going down the hall twice already. He'd noticed her smart heeled shoes when she walked in this morning; beige coloured with a tiny pearl on the tip of each one. Sensible but sexy, in a classy way. She really should be in *this* room, he thought, as it was closest to the waiting room and she need only duck her head out the door to summon the next patient.

It had been nice to see Sylvia at the markets, even though she seemed to be trying to avoid him. The glow of her red hair in the sunlight had reminded him of rich red autumn leaves. He'd noticed that the girl, Grace, had similar hair. She must be Sylvia's niece or something, or even a young cousin perhaps. After what Grace had told him in confidence yesterday he was anxious for her appointment on Wednesday to come around. He enjoyed challenging cases and hoped he'd be able to help her. She certainly needed it.

Knowing he had time to spare, Mark closed his eyes and breathed deeply, visualising the day being a success. He'd tried to do this at the start of each day in the past, but some days had a life of their own and seemed to be one endless rush hour. Not anymore. Things were going to change, starting now. He was in a new town, with new people, and a new job. It was time to take control.

'Denise Fairweather?' Mark quietly called as he opened his door and peered into the waiting room which was now a bustling lobby. An overweight woman of about fifty rose from her chair, smiling as she walked towards him.

'Hi,' she said, as Mark led her to the consulting room.

'Nice to meet you, Denise, I'm Mark. How can I help you today?'

Denise settled in the armchair, sighing with a smile and commenting on how comfortable it was. 'Well, a friend of mine sees a naturopath in the next town and said I should see one too, and when I saw that you were starting at the clinic this week I thought I'd try it out. I'm a patient of Dr Greene's you see, so it makes sense to come here. With you two and my physio, it's now a one-stop-shop!'

Mark smiled and nodded, keeping quiet to allow her to continue.

'The thing is, I'm at risk for diabetes. Runs in my family. I've been diagnosed with insulin resistance and metabolic syndrome, and Dr Greene has had me on some medication as of two months ago, but the progress is slow and I'm feeling so tired. Can't lose weight either. I was wondering if there's anything to help boost my energy and speed up the results?'

'Sure, once I've assessed your overall health I'll have a better idea of where things stand, but I'm confident we can get some improvements happening.'

'Oh, that's good. I just hope I haven't left it too late.'

'Denise, it's never too late to make positive changes.'

Over the past few months, Mark had been trying to make a few of his own.

CHAPTER THIRTEEN

Inspired after her consultation with Mark Bastian, Grace stepped out the door of Tarrin's Bay Medical Clinic and took a deep breath of warm salty air. She hadn't seen Sylvia at the clinic. She'd obviously been in her room with a patient both when Grace had arrived and when she'd left. Not to worry, she wouldn't have had time to chat anyway, and they'd arranged to go to the movies together on the weekend.

This week the focus was on her new job at Mrs May's Bookstore, and giving her health some attention. Mark had spent about an hour with her, asking questions and performing various tests. She'd already had the iridology done, so that saved some time. She'd been amazed to see the photos of her eyes up close and to learn what each marking meant, but she was even more amazed when Mark took a tiny drop of blood from her fingertip and in an instant her blood cells were visible on the monitor. It was like a whole other universe. She could see cells floating around like bubbles and tiny white dots dancing on the screen. Mark explained what everything was, but she'd already forgotten. Anyway, it had been really cool to see.

He'd given her some initial recommendations and advised her to come back in a month or so to check how she was feeling, then he'd do further tests and move onto the next step. 'Health is a journey,' he'd told her, and rarely could everything be addressed in one consultation. He'd also said it might be a good idea to have some standard blood tests through a doctor's referral, but Grace didn't think she'd worry about that now. The fingertip blood sample hadn't hurt, but she didn't feel like having a proper one with the big needle. Besides, it was like she was on holiday here, even though she now had a job, and holidays shouldn't involve needles, should they?

As Grace walked down the road and around the corner to the main street, waving at Olivia as she passed the bookstore, she couldn't believe she'd been here for just under two weeks and already had a job. She'd worked the past two days, had today and tomorrow off, and would be back in on Friday and Saturday. The first day was taken up mostly with learning and watching, getting used to how the shop worked. She'd mastered the cash register and EFTPOS machine and was gradually learning about the computer system and how to order books for customers. On Friday, Olivia was getting her to help with a window display for new releases and she was looking forward to unleashing her creativity.

She passed Waves, the café where she'd eaten lunch yesterday, and Bob's Take Away, where she'd bought lunch on the Monday. Grace had planned to eat at a different place each day this week, to try out all the cafés in the main street. She probably wouldn't do it all the time as the cost piled up, but thought, *what the heck; it's my first week on the job!*

Today she was trying out Café Lagoon. Apparently it was open from early till late, whereas most of the other places closed at five. They had decadent looking cakes in the glass display out front, but she'd have to reduce food like that in her diet after speaking to Mark. He did say the occasional treat was okay though. *I wonder if giving into temptation ten minutes after the consultation is a total cop-out?* Maybe she could start the change in eating habits tomorrow. Grace thought she ate pretty well for an eighteen-year-old, but Mark pointed out some things in her diet that weren't as good as she'd thought. Anyway, she was here for lunch not cake. But if she had room in her stomach afterwards, maybe one slice wouldn't be too bad. The hummingbird cake looked good, and at least it had fruit in it. Whoever thought to put pineapple in a cake was a genius!

Grace took a photo of the café and walked in. By the looks of people holding little metal stands with numbers on them, this café did not have full table service. Grace went up to the counter and eyed the menu on the blackboard. Whispering the choices to herself, she decided on the roasted chicken and avocado salad. She was about to place her order when her gaze lowered to meet that of a totally delicious guy. Suddenly the hummingbird cake was bland in comparison.

'What can I get for you?' he asked, eyeing her with a soft smile.

'Um...' Grace forgot what she'd decided to order. She looked up again at the blackboard and thankfully retrieved the memory. 'I, ah, I'll have the roasted chicken and avocado salad, thanks. I mean, please.' Was that warmth on her cheeks from the hot weather or was she going red?

'Sure thing. Would you like a drink as well?' asked Mr Delicious, whose nametag read 'Jonah'.

'Yes, do you have squeshly freezed juice?'

Jonah grinned from ear to ear. 'Ah, yes, we do have *squeshly freezed* juice.'

'Oh God! Is that what I said?' Grace's hand rose to cover her mouth.

Jonah nodded. 'Don't worry, when I was training to be a

barista I had to get used to all the different types of coffee. By the end of the day I'd be saying "One shouble dot dinny decaf laramel latte coming right up!"'

Laughter burst from Grace's lips, and she felt instantly connected to Jonah. 'Well, I'll have a *squeshly freezed morange and ango* juice please,' she asked, totally shocked that she'd just said that.

'Sure. Oh, and do you want the sessing on the dide of the salad?'

'Sorry, I can't decipher that one!'

'Yeah, it was tricky. I said, do you want the dressing on the side of the salad?'

'Oh, yes please.' More warmth spread across Grace's cheeks.

'Take a seat and I'll bring it out for you,' Jonah said, handing her a number. Grace wished he'd handed her *his* number. 'You're number seven today.'

'Seven's a lucky number,' Grace replied, as she walked over to a table near the counter so she could keep an eye on him.

'Then today must be your lucky day.' Jonah smiled, then turned to serve another customer.

As she went to walk out of the café after eating her salad, and somehow not feeling like she needed the hummingbird cake after all, Jonah's eyes locked with hers and they both gravitated towards each other like magnets.

'Thanks for a nice lunch,' Grace said.

'Any time. Hey, I didn't get your name,' Jonah said quietly.

'Grace.'

'Hope to see you in here again, Grace.'

'Where else am I gonna get a squeshly freezed morange and ango juice as good as the one I just had?' Grace smiled and walked out of the café.

Maybe she wouldn't bother trying out the other cafés in the street. Café Lagoon suited her just fine.

CHAPTER FOURTEEN

Work going great, thx 4 asking. Should c
window display I did, looks awesome!

Sylvia smiled as she read Grace's reply to her text message on Friday afternoon. It was actually nice having her around. Although she'd felt awkward at first, she was beginning to loosen up around her and felt more like a friend than a mother. Unlike with Mark. It seemed every time she saw him that knot in her stomach pinched tighter and tighter. Especially after seeing Denise Fairweather today.

'What have you put my patient on?' Sylvia's words had shot from her tongue like a sting, as she'd joined Mark at the lunch table in the staffroom.

'Excuse me?' Mark looked up from whatever the colourful mixture was that he was eating.

'Denise Fairweather. I saw her today and she's taking all these extra supplements. I don't know what they are or how they might interfere with her medication.' Denise had given the okay for Sylvia to collaborate on her case with Mark.

'It's okay, I looked at what she's taking and there shouldn't be any problem. No known contraindications,' Mark assured her.

'*Shouldn't* be any problem, or won't be? Natural medicine is not really an exact science.'

'Look, as far as my training tells me, she'll be fine taking the supplements. Do you think all the different types of medications you prescribe have been tested in all the possible combinations? No, but they're prescribed anyway. Medicine is not always an exact science either, Sylvia.' Mark's usually cheerful expression was now one of seriousness.

He was right. Damn him! 'Well, I hope you know what you're doing with my patient.'

'She's my patient too, Sylvia. And, I'll have you know, I did one year of a pharmacy degree before I studied naturopathy. And even if I hadn't, I'd still be confident I'm doing the right thing.'

Sylvia held her arms out to the side. 'Fair enough. But what's this she tells me about you wanting her Metformin dosage reduced?'

'I've put her on some herbal insulin sensitisers. The particular formula she's taking has been shown in some studies to work just as well, actually, slightly better than medication. It's not as fast acting as drugs, so all I need is for her to be monitored more frequently so the dosage can be reduced if the herbs get her levels down further.'

'You bet I'll be monitoring her.' Sylvia stood from the table and took her lunch from the fridge. The knot in her stomach tightened further as she tried to pull the lid off the airtight plastic container. When it finally gave way, the container leapt from her hands and the tuna salad fell to the floor. 'Crap,' she said, bending over to scoop up the mess and put it in the bin.

'I've got an extra serving of my lunch in the fridge if you want some,' Mark said.

Sylvia peered into Mark's bowl and scrunched up her nose, then looked at the remnants of her lunch in the bin. 'Okay,' she said, resigned. She slid some of the colourful meal into a bowl, and took a mouthful.

'It's good, isn't it?' Mark said.

Sylvia curved her mouth downwards and tipped her head to one side. 'Not bad,' she replied. *Not bad?* It was bloody delicious.

CHAPTER FIFTEEN

Only four days since starting her new health regime and Grace was a little more energetic already. *Probably no need to worry about getting those blood tests,* she thought, as she downed a glass of a sweet orange tasting powder mixed with water that Mark had given her. She was to take it twice a day and report back next month. He'd also given her a couple of tablet formulas. It was no bother; she'd just take them alongside the Chinese herbal tablets she'd been taking for the past year. Mark said they wouldn't interfere.

Grace had risen early this morning to take a photo of the sunrise over the beach, so she was looking forward to a relaxing afternoon at the movies with Sylvia. It was hard to believe it was two o'clock already. Despite getting up early, the day seemed to fly. Or maybe it was because she'd spent most of the time daydreaming about Jonah. His warm brown eyes and chestnut hair, swooping diagonally across his face like some kind of artwork in itself. It didn't look girly or too 'done' though, but simply fell that way as if wanting to cradle his gorgeous face.

Grace had gone back to Café Lagoon for lunch on Friday, feeling fulfilled after helping set up the window display in the bookstore. Unfortunately, Jonah hadn't been there, so she ate lunch quickly and went for a walk to the lookout and back again. Things were so different here compared to Melbourne. No one seemed to be in a rush, and every second person wore bare feet, many guys without shirts on. *I could get used to this!* she'd thought.

Grace had gone back to Café Lagoon on Saturday as well, and luckily Jonah *was* there that time. 'You're back!' Jonah's eyes had lit up when she walked in, or was he like that with everyone? Many people called him by name when they entered the café. 'Hey Jonah,' 'Jonah, buddy, how are ya?' and 'Working hard, ay Jonah?' It should have been called Café Jonah.

On approaching the counter he'd asked, 'The usual?' to which she'd replied, 'The usual? I've only been here once before!' He needn't know she'd been in the day before too. The café was full, and Jonah moved about like a pro; taking orders, making coffee, and bringing meals out to tables, including hers. 'Booklover, huh?' he said, pointing to her nametag which read, Grace Forrester, Mrs May's Bookstore. 'Have you read *A Difference of Opinion*? It's an awesome thriller,' Jonah asked.

Mmmm... cute, and he reads! 'Have I ever, I totally loved it! Did you see that twist coming at the end?'

'No, it came out of nowhere! As good as the twist in *The Sixth Sense.*'

'I reckon. Hey did you know they're going to make a movie out of the book?'

'Really?' Jonah sat for a moment on the chair opposite Grace, his eyes widening with interest.

'Yep, my boss told me. They often hear about these things before the public. It helps to sell more of the books too, as people like to read the book before seeing the movie.'

'I can't wait for it.'

'Me neither.'

'Well, maybe we'll have to go and see it together.' Jonah smiled.

'Maybe we should,' Grace replied, her heart tingling.

Jonah nodded to someone to his left, and quickly got up. 'Better get back to work. Enjoy your meal, Grace.'

'Thanks, I will.'

And she did.

The crunch of car tyres on the gravel path outside alerted Grace to the present moment, and she took a quick look in the small mirror above the sink, dabbing on some lip gloss.

'Hi, Grace.' Sylvia appeared in the doorway to the caravan.

'Hi. I'll just lock up and then we'll go.'

Grace walked out, the bell she had hanging on the inside of the door jingling as she closed it, before twisting the key in the lock. Mr and Mrs Bennett from the adjacent caravan waved as she got into Sylvia's car, and she waved back. She'd struck up a conversation with them the day of her arrival, and they were always friendly. She felt safe knowing they were nearby. The first few nights at the caravan were a little scary for Grace, having never lived on her own before, but it didn't bother her now. Her father had made her bring a whistle and promise to keep it under her pillow at night, so she'd obliged, and even taken a photo of it to send to her dad so he wouldn't worry. He checked in with her daily, and she didn't mind, but some days she just wanted to do her own thing without having to give him a regular update.

'I've booked the tickets, so we can go straight to the counter to collect them and get some snacks, instead of having to wait in line,' Sylvia said, as she turned the car around and drove out of the caravan park.

'Thanks for that, I'm glad you're organised. I'd usually just turn up, pick a movie, and line up only to be told it's sold out,' Grace said.

Sylvia chuckled. 'Always pays to be organised, line-ups are such a pain.'

In the time Grace had known Sylvia, she could tell her mother was a reliable person. Punctual, neat, and well prepared for everything. While at her house, she'd noticed that Sylvia had stuck to her fridge the most comprehensive shopping list ever seen in the history of shopping lists. It had vertical columns for the days of the week, woven with horizontal columns, each representing one grocery item. Then, each item had a tick allocated on certain days of the week, so she knew when to buy that particular item. By the looks of it, she did most of her shopping on alternate Saturdays, with a few perishable items purchased more frequently during the week. That, and the fact that her bookshelves were more organised than those at the bookstore, gave Grace a giggle.

'How was your consultation with Mark, if you don't mind my asking?' Sylvia glanced briefly at Grace, before indicating left and turning the corner onto the main street.

'It was great, he's a goldmine of information,' Grace replied.

'Just out of curiosity, does he, ah... know about us?'

'Does he know I'm your daughter? No. I just told him we're related. I figured it might be easier for you, I didn't know whether you wanted people to know or not. And you're probably still getting used to the whole situation yourself.' Sylvia looked relieved, and Grace felt a twinge of disappointment. 'He did ask about my family medical history, but I said I didn't know much about it.' Grace looked at Sylvia who was keeping her eyes on the road. 'Is there anything I should know?'

'Let's see...' Sylvia began. 'I haven't had any significant

issues, I don't have any siblings, and my parents are still going strong.'

Sylvia's parents. *Her* grandparents. She wondered what they were like. Would they want to meet her?

'Although Dad has slightly high blood pressure, Mum a little arthritis. And Mum's sister, my aunt Mary, had lymphoma. That's a type of cancer. But she recovered and is doing well, and as far as I know, her two kids are well.' Sylvia turned onto the highway. The movie theatre was in the next town. 'I hardly speak to Dad's brother and his kids, so I don't really know about them. And my only living grandparent is Grandma Greene; she's in a nursing home in Sydney. My other grandparents all died between ages eighty and eighty-five; Nan had breast cancer, but the others had heart issues.'

'Thanks for sharing all that,' Grace said.

'Well, you're entitled to know.'

The fact that Sylvia's family all seemed to live to a ripe old age reassured Grace. When her adoptive mother had died, she'd almost forgotten that Maria wasn't related to her biologically and asked the doctor if she herself would be at risk of heart problems like her mother. She'd felt silly when he reminded her of the situation.

Half an hour later Grace and Sylvia sat in the movie theatre sharing a box of popcorn. The warm buttery smell and the rustling packets of crisps brought back childhood memories for Grace of going to the movies with her parents. Every time she went to the movies she felt somehow comforted, like she was at home.

As the movie began and the room fell quiet, Grace noticed Sylvia's chest rising gently up and down, and was strangely mesmerised. Long ago, those lungs had breathed oxygen into her mother's bloodstream, delivering it to a baby growing in her womb. Her. And now Grace was older than Sylvia had been when she'd had her. She couldn't imagine going through pregnancy and childbirth at such a young age, the thought of going through it now or anytime soon was too much to comprehend. One day, sure, but only when she was ready. When she met the right man, had travelled and experienced the world, and achieved her dreams. First, she had to figure out what those dreams were.

When everyone in the theatre laughed, Grace realised she'd missed the first scene of the movie, lost in her thoughts. Lost in a movie-worthy scene of her own life.

'The sky is so beautiful at this time of day, do you mind if we stop and take a few pictures?' Grace asked Sylvia as they drove back to Tarrin's Bay after the movie had finished.

'Sure, no problem,' Sylvia said, pulling into the parking area of the main beach, near the lookout.

They stepped out of the car and walked over to the sand, still warm from the slowly fading sun. A mother washed sand off her child under the tap, before drying her vigorously with a towel while yelling, 'C'mon Benjamin, time to go home!' to an older child who was still in the water. Grace wondered if these kids lived here. What would it have been like if she'd grown up here? Would she have turned out differently? Would the same things still have happened to her?

Click! Grace took a photo of the sky on the horizon, then took off her shoes and walked with Sylvia alongside the water's edge. 'You mentioned your parents before... do you see them often?'

Sylvia stopped for a moment, as though suddenly aware Grace would want to know about her grandparents. And of course she did. She was also curious about her real father, but thought it best not to broach that subject yet. He was probably just a guy who got Sylvia pregnant and didn't stick around. Anyway, she already had a great father.

'Actually, I don't. Not since I moved back here. We get together occasionally, but mostly we lead separate lives.' Sylvia resumed walking, kicking a piece of driftwood out of the way. 'Would you... like me to contact them and tell them you're here?' Sylvia asked feebly.

'Only if you want to, if you think it's a good idea. No rush though, with my new job I'm obviously going to stay for a little while at least,' Grace said, and Sylvia nodded. 'I'll leave it with you to decide.'

'Okay,' was all Sylvia said.

Was there something unresolved between Sylvia and her parents? Grace couldn't imagine not keeping in touch with her family. If her mum was still alive she'd be on the phone to her almost every day, as with her father. Both sets of her adoptive grandparents lived near the family home in Melbourne, so she saw them regularly, except her mum's mum who'd died when Grace was a child. She also had seven adoptive cousins; two girls and five boys. The girls were around Grace's age, so she grew up with them as though they were sisters. Now they all stayed connected online, through Facebook mostly. Grace's dad tried signing up and 'friending' her before she left for Tarrin's Bay, but Grace refused. 'Dad! That's just too weird!' she'd said.

Grace and Sylvia walked in silence for a while, the early evening breeze whooshing past them, weaving and tangling their curly hair. 'Hey, how about we get a photo together?' Grace asked suddenly.

Sylvia nodded, and Grace approached a woman nearby with her phone. She didn't look like the type to run off with something, two kids dawdling behind her, one hanging onto her leg as she walked.

'Smile!' the woman said, as Grace and Sylvia slipped an arm

around each other's back and tilted their heads together. *Click!* Another picture to add to the memory album — although, was it appropriate? Grace wasn't sure. She wanted to collect pictures that showed she was living her life to the full, but would a photo with Sylvia upset her father and dishonour her mother's memory? She'd sort it out later, at least now she had a photo of herself with her biological mother, and no matter what happened down the track, she could look back happily on this time they spent together.

Soon they came to the part of the beach that curved around into the headland, the shoreline edged with a rocky landscape. Waves washed over the rocks, before receding and weaving between them. Sylvia sat down on one of the rocks and Grace picked up a twig. She began drawing a shape in the sand. Moist sand squished between her toes as she drew a large circle, while Sylvia watched. Then she added arcs around the circle.

'A flower?' Sylvia asked.

'A sunflower,' Grace replied. 'My favourite. I know they don't look as nice as other flowers, but they have a special meaning for me. Every time I see one, I feel happy.' She smiled as she finished the drawing with a long line for the stem. She stood upright and placed her hands on her hips, admiring her spontaneous artwork. Then she took the phone from her bag and took a photo of it. And another. One close up, and one from higher up while she stood on a rock. 'Ahh!' she squealed as she just caught her balance on the rock, almost toppling off it. Sylvia stood quickly, then sat again as Grace steadied herself and giggled.

Sylvia looked awkward for a moment, as though she was about to speak but then stopped.

Grace pointed to her sand drawing. 'Maybe I should forget the piano and take up art, what do you think?'

Sylvia laughed. 'If you're as good an artist as you are a

pianist, then yes! I mean, don't give up the piano, but you could take up art as well,' Sylvia said, relaxing a little and leaning her elbows on her thighs. 'Actually, I wanted to ask you something,' she said.

Grace sat on the rock next to her.

'I know you said you've never played piano in public before, but I was wondering, well, there's an annual variety concert on at the local high school in June. The music teacher at the school, William Randleman, has been organising it for the past few years, and it's always a great night.'

'And you want me to consider performing?' Grace threaded her fingers together, and shifted as the rock beneath her suddenly felt pokey and uncomfortable.

Sylvia smiled hopefully. 'Well, you'd have to audition, but I don't see how they could refuse you.'

'I don't know... I'm just, it's just... I'd get so nervous. What if my fingers wouldn't co-operate and I messed it up?' Grace scrunched up her nose. 'I'd probably need intravenous sedation to calm me down!'

Sylvia laughed. 'That's what practise and dress rehearsal is for, and I'm sure you'd be fine. It'd be a great experience to include in your memory album,' Sylvia suggested.

Grace nodded. 'That's true... but I still don't know.'

'Anyway, have a think about it, and if you like I can take you to an audition.' Sylvia leaned back on the rock, and flicked her head back to remove a mop of curls from her face that the wind had placed there. 'It's also a charity event, to raise money for the children's oncology department at Welston hospital,' she added.

Grace sat up straight. How could she refuse? 'Okay I'll do it. On one condition — you come shopping with me to buy a new dress to wear on the night.'

The grooves of a smile etched their way into Sylvia's cheeks.

'It's a deal,' she said, holding out her hand. Grace shook it, and they both stood to walk to the car.

'I'll tell you what,' Sylvia said. 'How about I call my parents and see if they'd like to attend the concert?'

'Really? It would probably make me ten times more nervous, but it would be great to meet them,' Grace replied.

'Okay then, I'll get your audition organised first, then I'll give them a call.'

Why did Sylvia suddenly look as nervous as Grace felt?

CHAPTER SIXTEEN

That bloody woman! Mark's chest tightened as he walked out the door of the clinic on Friday. It was only lunchtime, and already his patience was wearing thin. He wished he could finish early and go for a long run on the beach but he had a full afternoon of patients to see. Since his run-in with Sylvia last week about Denise Fairweather's treatment, she'd been agitated and irritable around him. And now a few more of Sylvia's patients had come to see him, so their interactions lately were a constant exchange of 'why are you giving her this?' and 'what's your rationale for that?' and 'what kind of name for a medicine is *silybum marianum?*' and 'yes Sylvia, I know what I'm doing'. She obviously didn't like anyone stepping on her toes. *Control freak.*

As usual, Mark had packed his lunch to eat in the clinic, but there was no way he could stand another lunchtime debate. He'd grab something in town. But right now he couldn't eat. He needed to walk, merge into the lunchtime busyness of the main street and distract himself from work for a while.

People at tables spilled out of cafés and onto the footpath, umbrellas barely shielding them from the sun's insistent shining.

Waiters and waitresses weaved between the tables, carrying multiple plates and trays expertly in their hands. As Mark walked past Café Lagoon, a customer came close to knocking one over as he pushed his chair back and stood, but the waiter's reflexes were quick and he stopped the tray from crashing down onto the footpath. *Nice save*, he thought.

Mark stopped for a moment outside Mrs May's Bookstore, surveying the window display for *Dr Don's Weight Loss Revolution* book. No wonder it was a bestseller, it promised fast, easy weight loss in a matter of days. Sure, it worked, but Mark often saw patients who had tried it only to put the weight back on again later. Mark knew that real, sustained weight loss took time, but unfortunately that concept didn't sell books.

He entered the bookstore, taking in the expanse of books with a circular sweep of his eyes. As usual, he headed in the direction of the health section and scanned the books on the shelves.

'Don't you already know everything there is to know about health?' a voice asked.

Mark turned his head to see Grace Forrester smiling at him.

'Oh, hi Grace, I forgot you worked here. How's it going?'

'The job, or me?'

'Both.'

'Loving the job, it really doesn't feel like work at all, and as for me, I'm feeling good, like I have more energy,' Grace explained.

'That's good to hear, on both counts.' Mark smiled.

It always pleased him when patients began feeling better. But as he knew, it was at the two to three month mark after the first consultation that you could really tell how well they were doing. Some people got great results to begin with, but lost interest in their health regime after a while then wondered why their symptoms came back. That's when he had to switch to 'coach' mode, and use the interpersonal skills he'd been taught at university to work through each patient's emotional blockages and false beliefs that were subconsciously sabotaging their efforts. He'd found out not long after entering practice that achieving wellness was one quarter physical and three quarters emotional.

'So, is there anything I can help you with, Mark?' Grace eyed the bookshelves.

'Oh no, I'm just checking out what's popular in the health field,' he replied.

'Sure, well this one's been selling like hotcakes,' Grace said as she pointed to a book, and then another. 'And this one's been around for a long time but keeps selling steadily, so I'm told.'

Mark nodded, but didn't pick up either of the books. 'Do you ever have any books on sports health, or natural health for athletes?'

Grace's eyebrows furrowed as she quickly scanned the shelves. 'I don't think we usually carry that sort of stuff, but let me see what I can find.'

Grace went over to the counter and tapped at the keys on the computer. 'There doesn't seem to be much available in that area. Would you like me to show you a couple that are available to order in?'

'No, that's okay, thanks Grace. I don't need the book myself, I'm just... doing some research,' he said.

Grace paused for a moment. 'Oh, are you thinking of *writing* a book on that topic?'

Mark felt as though he was standing in quicksand. He'd never told anyone his dreams of being an author before, and all of a sudden he felt silly for some reason. 'Um, yeah, I mean... possibly.'

More than possibly, he'd already written half of it. But he hadn't touched the manuscript for almost two years. What if all his work led to nothing and the book was a complete flop? And anyway, was it really that important a topic? Perhaps he should write about more significant things like cancer, or Alzheimer's, or diabetes, or—'

'You should go for it!' Grace interrupted his thoughts. 'My friend's boyfriend is a swimmer hoping to try out for the Olympics, so I'm sure he'd like it. And, there must be a lot of up-and-coming athletes who would welcome anything to boost their performance,' Grace spoke quickly. 'Oh! And you could give talks at the Australian Institute of Sport, and promote your book to local sports clubs, schools, fitness centres...' Grace's eyes darted all over the place, as though searching her mind for more promotion opportunities for his unfinished book.

'If I become an author, remind me to make you my publicist!' Mark laughed, as a ripple of excitement spread through his body at her suggestions. Maybe he *should* dig the manuscript out of its digital cave and resume working on it.

Just then, Grace raised her index finger and clicked her tongue. Mark envisioned a light bulb appearing above her head.

'I know just the book for you!' She scurried over to the shelves in another section, and returned with a book in her hand, giving a flourished wave around it with her other hand as though she was on *The Price Is Right* television show.

'*Become An Author In Seven Easy Steps*, huh?' Mark picked up the book and turned it over. It looked good, but he did wonder if it was a *Dr Don's Weight Loss Revolution* for the aspiring author. Maybe he'd follow the program, get the book written, but nothing would come of it and he'd be back where he started.

'Apparently,' Grace said as she led Mark back to the health section and picked up a book, 'this author followed the program and now her book's a bestseller.'

'That's good to know.' Mark flipped briefly through the

book on becoming an author, then closed it with a decisive snap. 'Sold.' Mark smiled at Grace and followed her to the counter.

'You've got an awesome sales assistant here,' he told the other woman at the counter.

She smiled at Mark, then at Grace. 'We know.'

As he walked out of the bookstore, Mark realised he'd managed to keep Sylvia out of his mind completely for the last few minutes. Well, until. now. Thinking of how he'd stopped thinking of her, he was now thinking of her again! The way she tensed her shoulders around him, the way she raised her chin in the air when arguing her point, the way her soft curls swam around her face... *What?* He shook his head and decided he better eat some lunch. The low blood sugar was probably playing with his mind.

Five minutes later he was sitting on a bench in Miracle Park, eating a sushi roll. A swarm of seagulls leapt overhead, flying in the direction of the beach. *Lucky buggers.* When he finished eating, Mark tossed the plastic wrap into a bin and walked over to look at the Wishing Fountain. He read the plaque, and the story of the supposed 'miracles' that had occurred years ago.

'Hmmph,' he mumbled. *Where was my miracle when I needed one?*

'Bye, take care.' Mark farewelled his last patient for the week.

Back in his consulting room he slumped in the chair and exhaled slowly. Since returning from lunch he hadn't crossed paths with Sylvia and was hoping to keep it that way. Throughout the week he'd tried to either leave as early as possible, or leave later — after she'd left. He'd use the time to work on his marketing plan and check his emails.

He sat silently for a while; ears pricked in anticipation of the trademark scuttle of sensible heels along the hallway. Nothing. Maybe she'd already left. Sylvia had mentioned this morning that she 'didn't have time for arguments' as she had somewhere to be tonight and didn't want to run behind schedule with patients. Despite this, she'd managed to keep talking, reasoning her point of view. He couldn't keep avoiding her forever, though, and he hoped she'd eventually grow to like him and respect his work.

He filed documents away, turned off the equipment and power points, and headed towards the staff kitchen to get his uneaten lunch and car keys.

'Ouch!' Sylvia's voice surprised him as he pushed open the kitchen door and it collided with her head. She was obviously on her way out, and just about to open the door from the inside.

'Oops,' Mark said, shuffling past her. 'Sorry, I didn't know you were in here.'

'Oops, is that all you can say?' Sylvia rubbed her temple.

'I said sorry, too.'

'Right. Well, I'll be okay, it's just a little bump.' Sylvia straightened up, as Mark grabbed his car keys. 'You're not working late tonight?' she asked.

'Nope. It's Friday night, I have plans.'

'Good for you. So do I,' she replied.

'Oh yeah, what sort of plans?' Mark probed.

'You know... places to see, people to go.'

Mark grinned.

'What's funny?'

'Don't you mean: places to *go*, people to *see*?' he corrected.

'That's what I said,' she replied, rubbing her temple again.

'You sure it's just a *little* bump?' Mark asked, still grinning.

'It's nothing.' Sylvia looked confused, obviously unaware of her verbal slip. 'Anyway, I have to go. Enjoy your... plans,' she said, closing the door behind her.

Mark laughed. She may be irritating and narrow-minded, but she was also incredibly... cute. He withdrew his lunch container from the fridge, and went to open the kitchen door, when it opened for him. He held the door open as Sylvia slid past him.

'Forgot my jacket,' she said, picking it up off the chair before sliding past him again, leaving a subtle floral scent in her wake. He stood for a moment and watched her exit the clinic, then followed suit.

<h1 style="text-align:center">CHAPTER SEVENTEEN</h1>

'God, I'm an idiot!' Sylvia got into her car forty-five minutes later, and having realised her faux pas a little too late, shrunk in the seat and rested her head on the steering wheel. 'Ow!' She shot up, reminded of her little bump to the head courtesy of Mark. It'd been a long day, and her cognitive abilities had officially switched off. At least she had an enjoyable evening to look forward to at Larissa's wedding rehearsal dinner. She could eat, drink (just one), laugh, and forget about the past week.

Putting the gearstick in reverse, she backed out of her garage and onto the road, turning towards the highway. Out the corner of her eye she saw Nancy Dillinger's kitchen curtain move. Nothing new. The poor woman must lead a boring life if all she did was watch other people. She seemed perpetually at home, barring Sunday mornings when she'd walk to the end of her driveway to collect the newspaper, before scurrying back inside. No car was ever parked in her carport, and Sylvia occasionally saw her getting out of a taxi with grocery bags, never more than two or three at a time. Maybe she *should* bring her a cake and show some neighbourly courtesy, like Grace suggested. She'd have to buy one though. Baking and Sylvia didn't mix. She could whip up a fancy dinner easily enough, but for some reason, whenever she tried to bake a cake it would either burn to a crisp, crack like an earthquake, or sink in the middle like an old mattress.

Sylvia turned her head to check for oncoming traffic and veered onto the highway. Heavy grey clouds hovered anxiously above, as though waiting for the most opportune moment to spill their load — probably as soon as she got out of the car. She quickly swivelled her head to look towards the back seat. Phew, her expensive black umbrella was exactly where it always was, poking out of the pocket on the back of the front passenger seat, along with a small box of tissues, and a street directory. Always prepared. She liked knowing what was ahead of her, and that all contingencies were planned for. Surprises weren't often welcomed in her life, although meeting Grace was an exception. She still couldn't quite believe that her grown daughter was really here in town, spending time with her.

Sylvia glanced at her phone in its holder on the dashboard as it rang. Larissa. She'd be seeing her shortly, so why was she calling? Probably just checking that she'd left on time. Even though Sylvia was never late. Larissa had been getting anxious about the wedding, and kept repeating things like, 'Are you sure the band have been given the correct date?' and 'You'll be at my place 9am Saturday, right?' and 'Where on this bloody planet did I put my garter belt?' Sylvia let the call go to voicemail, it wasn't worth the risk to drive and talk on the phone at the same time, but she always liked to have it visible in case there was an emergency with a patient.

Before too long, Sylvia pulled into a parking spot just around the corner from the church at Welston. They'd be rehearsing the formal proceedings before walking a couple of blocks to a restaurant for dinner. She exhaled deeply as she got out of the car, releasing all tension from the day.

A high-pitched beep pierced the air as Sylvia pressed the central locking button on her key. She walked around to the front of the church and climbed the steps, and Larissa appeared at the doorway above.

'Sylvia, I tried to call to warn you, but—'

'What's *he* doing here?' The tension she'd released came hurtling back to her like a boomerang. The bump on her head throbbed as she reached the top of the steps and saw Mark inside the church, talking to Larissa's fiancé, Luke.

'He's one of the groomsmen, a uni friend of Luke's,' Larissa explained. 'I got talking to him before you arrived, and he said he'd moved to Tarrin's Bay. When he told me where he now worked, I realised he must be the Mark you mentioned the night of my hen party.'

'How did I not know this before?'

'You weren't at the engagement party, remember? You had that bad flu at the time.'

Sylvia tipped her head backwards. 'Holy crap. This will be... awkward.'

'Sylvia!' Larissa exclaimed, gesturing to the cross above the church doorway.

'What? At least I said *holy*,' she rebutted, attempting a laugh.

Larissa took hold of Sylvia's arm and leaned in close. 'Sylv, there's something you should probably know about...'

'Hey there, Doc!' Luke suddenly appeared behind Larissa. 'Right on time, we're just about to get started. Have you met Mark?'

Mark took position next to Luke, but kept his distance from her. By the unsurprised look on his face, Larissa must have already told him Sylvia was coming.

'We, ah, work together actually,' Sylvia replied. 'Evening, Mark.' She glanced briefly at him.

'Sylvia.' Mark gave a polite nod of his head.

'Well there you go! Small world. Good thing you two are partnered together for the ceremony, much easier if you already know each other.' Luke smiled, before ushering everyone inside.

Much easier my arse. Sylvia gritted her teeth and walked into the church foyer, her heels clicking on the floorboards and sending sharp jolts right up her legs to her throbbing temple. Larissa was whisked away by the maid of honour, who pretended to adjust her veil and train, while Larissa's mother, Judith, suddenly appeared and shoved Sylvia into position, ready to practise her walk down the aisle.

The flower girl skipped along the aisle, throwing pretend petals along the way, and Judith nodded sharply at Sylvia, mouthing 'Go!'

Sylvia made her entrance, while Luke, Mark, and the best man stood at the front of the church staring at her while she walked the length of the aisle.

'Slowly, Sylvia. Slowly!' Judith whispered insistently from the sidelines.

Could this get any more uncomfortable? After what seemed like an hour, she arrived at the front of the church, soon joined by the maid of honour. Larissa followed, delivered to the altar by her father, tears dribbling down her face.

'Oh, Riss, it's not even the real thing yet!' Luke leaned in and planted a kiss on his fiancée's forehead.

'Sorry! I can't help it. I can't believe we'll be doing this for real tomorrow.' Larissa clasped Luke's face in her hands and kissed his lips.

'No kissing until I pronounce you man and wife,' the priest said, grinning.

'Oops, sorry!' Larissa stepped aside and tucked her hands behind her back.

The priest proceeded to explain what would happen next, showing everyone where they should sit and stand at the appropriate times as though directing a play. Larissa kept getting confused and apologising, while Luke's ever-present smile softened the awkwardness. Mark kept quiet, his eyes distant, as though lost somewhere in his mind. As Sylvia linked her arm with his and walked down the aisle once the proceedings had been rehearsed, she felt his bicep muscle tense ever so slightly, almost making her flinch. They couldn't release their grip soon enough, stepping away from each other as soon as they reached the church doorway. By the time the happy couple exited the church, Larissa was crying again, Luke wrapping his arms tenderly around her. If she was like this now, Sylvia could only imagine the blubbering mess Larissa would be tomorrow.

Seemingly oblivious to anyone around them, Larissa and Luke began walking up the road towards the restaurant, followed by their loyal army of bridesmaids, groomsmen, parents, and friends. Sylvia picked up her pace, but Mark's easy stride caught up with her.

'We keep bumping into each other,' he said, his eyes straight ahead.

'So we do,' she replied.

'How long have you known Larissa?' he asked.

'Since primary school. We've kept in contact ever since. And you met Luke at uni?'

'Yep.'

Sylvia nodded, even though Mark wasn't looking at her. They walked the rest of the way in silence, as the maid of honour and best man were deep in conversation, and Judith kept trying to stop the flower girl from climbing the nearby trees.

The noise at the crowded restaurant provided a welcome distraction, and Judith directed everyone to their seats, Sylvia's wedged between Judith and the maid of honour. Mark took his seat opposite her and immediately filled his glass with water from the carafe in the centre of the table, before downing it in one deliberate gulp. Forget the water, Sylvia hoped a waiter would offer some wine as soon as possible. When he did, she downed half of it at once, the liquid warmth spreading throughout her throat.

'How's work, Sylvia?' Judith asked.

'Good, thanks. Busy as usual,' she replied.

'And are you still seeing that nice young surgeon?'

Judith had a way of getting down to the nitty gritty right away. When Sylvia and Larissa were teenagers, she'd grill them after a night out until she was satisfied they hadn't done anything dangerous, stupid or illegal. Most of the time her satisfaction was assured on the dangerous and illegal part. But stupid? Well, when you're fifteen, stupid decisions are as normal as wearing a bucketload of eyeliner just to walk to the shops in case cute boys were there. Sylvia's stupid decisions came to a halt, however, a few weeks after the night she was rewarded with a nine-month gift. From then on, she made it a priority to follow the rules and stick to her plans. Finish high school, go to medical school, become a general practitioner, and devote her life to helping the sick. It had all gone to plan, mostly, but she hadn't planned on meeting Grace again, or breaking up with Richard, or meeting Mark – who had inconveniently disrupted her sense of self-control and poise.

'Ah, no. We're not together anymore,' Sylvia replied quietly. She noticed Mark glancing in her direction.

'What? But you two were like peas in a pod — made for each other! What happened, love?'

'Nothing, it just didn't work out,' she replied, before

finishing her wine and gesturing to the waiter to refill her glass. Better make this one last, otherwise she wouldn't be able to drive home.

'Mum, I'm sure Sylvia doesn't want to discuss her personal life right now,' Larissa interjected, her eyes asking Sylvia if she was okay. Sylvia nodded a *thank you.* 'So, Mark, are you still playing soccer these days?' Larissa turned towards Mark and clasped her hands together on the table.

'Not at the moment, haven't joined a club since moving here, but I've started playing squash at the gym. Doesn't take up as much time.'

'Yeah, you must be busy, setting up a new business. How's it going?'

'Pretty well. Some of my patients followed me here, and I'm picking up new clients as well. Still plenty of room for more though, so I'm spending a fair bit of time on marketing,' Mark explained.

Sylvia never had to 'market' herself. Patients flocked to her, and she rarely had a free appointment slot. Thank goodness. She hated the thought of having to 'promote' herself, it seemed so desperate. But if Mark kept stealing her patients maybe she'd have to start. Out of concern for the health of the community of course.

'Good luck with it all, I'm happy to hand out your business cards to friends if you like. *After* the wedding, that is.' Larissa looked lovingly at Luke again, her eyes becoming red and shiny.

'Thanks, Larissa, that'd be great.'

'So, Mark,' Sylvia began, assuredness seeping into her nerves — halfway through her second glass of wine, she really should have waited for the food to arrive before drinking. 'Why did you give up a pharmacy degree for alternative medicine?'

Mark shifted in his seat. 'I prefer to call it *complementary* medicine. It's not an alternative but a complement to other forms of treatment.' He took a sip of water before continuing. 'While I was working as an assistant in my father's pharmacy, I'd see regular patients coming in; some getting their prescriptions, and others seeing the naturopath we'd hired. It seemed those seeing the naturopath were getting healthier while the others were getting sicker.'

'Really?' Sylvia crossed her arms over her chest.

Mark nodded. 'I got talking to the naturopath and realised how interested I was in it, and how much science there was behind it. Plus I'd been struggling with an old soccer injury, and the naturopath gave me some tablets and referred me to an acupuncturist. Haven't had a problem with it since.' He took another swig of water, while Sylvia tried to take only a small sip of her wine, before crossing her arms again.

'So, you just quit?'

'No. I changed paths. I realised what I *really* wanted to do — help people maximise their health, not just treat illness.' Mark sat back in his chair, his eyes looking confidently into hers.

Isn't that what *she* did? By treating illness she was maximising their health too.

'You see, by using nutrition and lifestyle strategies, along with natural medicine, the human body becomes better able to withstand any stress or illness. It's the body that does the healing, I just give it the tools it needs to do the work,' Mark elaborated.

Thankfully, Sylvia didn't need to respond as the food arrived and a symphony of 'ooohs' and 'ahhs' ensued. She quickly scooped up a few mouthfuls of risotto, hoping it would bind to whatever alcohol was left in her stomach and prevent her desire to further interrogate Mark.

Sylvia spent the rest of dinner chatting to Judith and Larissa, while the maid of honour seemed fascinated by Mark and his discussion of how a person comes to develop allergies.

After dessert, Larissa dabbed at the corners of her mouth with a napkin, then stood. 'If I could have your attention, please.'

'Oh my God, are you pregnant?' Sylvia blurted out, then covered her mouth in effort to hold in any further verbal mistakes.

Larissa laughed. 'Of course not! Not yet anyway... well, not as far as I know.' She looked at Luke who suddenly went as pale as his napkin. 'I'd like to ask my bridal party to follow me into the private room back there,' she said, pointing to a door in the far corner of the restaurant. 'It's a bit last minute, but I've taken the liberty of creating a little *routine* I'd like us to perform at the reception.'

Sylvia's hand dropped suddenly from her mouth to her dessert plate, propelling her spoon across the table and into Mark's lap. Mark flinched, then politely returned the spoon to its proper place, his lips holding back a grin. Sylvia couldn't help herself and let out a laugh, while the sleepy flower girl was now wide awake, giggling and pointing at Sylvia and Mark.

When she recovered her composure, Sylvia remembered what Larissa had just said. 'Do you mean routine as in a *dance* routine?' she asked cautiously.

'Uh-huh.' Larissa nodded.

Oh Dear Lord. Not only did she have to walk arm in arm with Mark down the aisle, she'd have to perform a dance routine with him too. This was getting beyond humiliating. How could Larissa do this to her?

'C'mon guys, let's go.' Larissa ushered the bridal party in to the private room. 'Now don't fret, it's just a bit of fun. I've made up a medley of songs, and the choreography is very simple.'

Simple? As a child, Larissa would make Sylvia learn complex dance routines and perform them for her parents. One routine had them twirling lengths of pink satin fabric around in the living room to Madonna's *Material Girl*. The only twirling

Sylvia wanted to do right now was with a swizzle stick in a cocktail, preferably on a beach in Hawaii, or somewhere else far away from here.

Mark looked just as terrified as Sylvia felt, while the maid of honour bounced up and down in excitement and the best man rubbed his palms together in anticipation. Larissa moved everyone into position, and demonstrated the first few moves. Not too bad so far, at least there was no touching anyone.

Yet.

The next sequence involved partnering up and dancing to Michael Jackson's *The Way You Make Me Feel*, followed by an energetic tribute to *Love Shack* by The B52's. Mark managed to step on Sylvia's toes twice, and she returned the favour by sharply whipping him in the face with her hair, mid-pirouette. Well, it wasn't exactly a pirouette, but more of a lop-sided-spin-and-grab-the-closest-thing-to-avoid-falling-over kind of move. After several run-throughs, surprisingly, they had all memorised the routine, and by the end of it were laughing together in a heap on the floor. Sylvia's belly ached, and just when she thought she'd recovered from laughing, she'd look at the best man grabbing his crotch and letting out a high-pitched Michael Jackson squeal, and the laughter would begin all over again. Even Mark was in hysterics, and he dabbed at his watery eyes with the edge of his shirtsleeve. Sylvia handed him a tissue she had tucked into her pants pocket, and took one for herself too. All the tension she'd felt today dissipated, and she forgot why she'd been so irritated with him. Trust Larissa to give everyone a night to remember. She was a bit overwhelming at times, but knew how to have fun.

Remnants of laughter hung on Sylvia's lips as she walked back to her car, Mark alongside her and the others trailing behind. It didn't remain for long. A loud metallic crushing sound broke the moment and the screeching of car tyres followed, as a car U-turned and sped off out of sight.

'No!' Sylvia lifted her hands to her face as she looked at her mangled car hugging the telegraph pole on the footpath near the church. The driver had obviously turned the corner too fast and rammed into her Mazda. Idiot! She ran towards the car but slipped as light rain trickled from the sky, adding a gloss to the footpath. Bracing herself for a painful bump to her backside, she shrieked as her fall was broken by the same arms she'd linked with in the church.

'Whoa, careful,' Mark said, helping her to her feet. 'Did anyone get the number plate of the car?' He turned to ask everyone who'd witnessed the accident. Heads shook. He walked with Sylvia to the car and scrunched up his face as he surveyed the damage, while droplets of rain stuck strands of hair to his forehead.

Sylvia plucked her phone from her handbag and dialled the number she'd stored in her contacts but hoped never to need. 'Hi, I need a tow at the corner of Church and Cobbler, in Welston,' she instructed. It would be a twenty minute wait, and Mark insisted on waiting with her under the shelter of the church porch, then driving her home, as they both lived in Tarrin's Bay. Sylvia shooed Larissa and Luke away, telling them they needed their rest for tomorrow, and once everyone realised Mark was staying they left too.

The rain grew stronger, and twenty-five minutes later the tow arrived. Sylvia told them to take it to her local smash repairs garage. She'd have to call them on Monday and drop the keys off before work. At least she didn't have to drive to work, and most things in Tarrin's Bay were in walking distance. Except decent clothing stores. She'd have to hire a car or take a bus with Grace to help her choose a dress for the charity concert. She'd also have to get public transport to Larissa's house tomorrow, and catch a cab home after the wedding. All these thoughts raced through Sylvia's mind in an instant. Her medical training had taught her to gather her thoughts quickly and work out solutions. In an emergency there was no time for hesitation. You make a decision and stick to it, then deal with the results.

Mark dashed through the rain to his car to open the passenger door, and Sylvia ducked in. 'So, where's the house of Dr Greene?' he asked, his hand poised on the ignition. She told him her address and promised to lead the way when they arrived back in Tarrin's Bay.

'I live in the hills. Not as close to town but great views,' Mark said. 'Have you always lived here, or did you move away for uni?'

'Moved to Sydney for a few years, but the Bay drew me back.'

'Sure is a beautiful place.'

'What about you, why Tarrin's Bay?' Sylvia asked.

'Why not?' Mark smiled.

'That's a good enough reason I suppose.' Sylvia smiled too, and they drove in silence for a while. Was she actually getting along with him now? Maybe it was just the wine, and the food, and the dancing, and things would go back to their uncomfortable normality at work on Monday.

'I'm sorry I interrogated you earlier, about why you switched university courses,' Sylvia said. 'I didn't mean any disrespect.'

'I know. Don't worry, I had to deal with my father's disapproval for a long time. He really wanted me to take over the family pharmacy.'

'Yeah, it's hard to disappoint parents,' Sylvia commented. 'But in the end you've got to do what's right for you.'

'I've realised that,' Mark replied.

Their conversation dwindled, as thunder sounded and

water lashed loudly at the windscreen, the wipers working overtime yet not doing a good enough job at maintaining a clear view of the road.

'Geez, this is bad,' Mark said loudly above the roar of the rain. 'Do you want me to pull over somewhere?' A jagged spear of lightning lit up the sky for a split second.

'We're close to my place, but it's up to you,' Sylvia yelled back.

'We'll keep going then.'

She instructed him to take the next left turn, and led him towards her house, just as the rain transformed into hard clumps of ice, pelting on the roof of the car like a thousand angry fists.

'You can park in my garage till it passes,' Sylvia said, gesturing towards the final turn into her street. She bit the corner of her bottom lip, realising that the hail would probably be adding to her car's damage, and she didn't think the tow truck driver would be concerned with finding shelter for it.

A wedge of light from Nancy's window signalled Sylvia's arrival home. A beacon in the night. She pressed the remote on her key ring and the garage door rolled upwards. They pulled into the garage, the roar of the hailstorm suddenly abating. Sylvia closed the garage door behind them and got out of the car, shaking water from her hair and clothes. 'Would you like a cup of tea or something?' she asked.

'Love one,' Mark replied, ruffling his wet hair.

They entered the door that led through the laundry into the kitchen, taking off their shoes on the way. Sylvia flicked on the lights.

'Nice place,' Mark said as his eyes scanned the room.

'Thanks.' Sylvia thought so too. She prided herself on keeping a tidy and clutter-free house. A person's home was a representation of themselves. She turned the kettle on and a deep rumble grew, escalating gradually, until suddenly it stopped and darkness overtook the house. 'Oh man! Two more minutes and we would've had boiling water. Can I interest you in a juice, or a glass of milk?' Sylvia said into the darkness.

'Juice will be fine,' Mark's voice replied.

Sylvia ran her fingers along the bench towards the corner drawer, where she kept a torch and matches. 'That's better,' she said, pressing the rubber 'on' button. The torchlight gave an eerie glow to the kitchen, as she shone it into the fridge and withdrew the juice. 'I better light some candles first.' Sylvia carried the torch in one hand and the matches in the other, lighting various candles she had positioned around the house. They were for decoration mostly, she rarely lit them, but the warm glow and delicate scent surrounding them had her thinking she must do this more often.

Sylvia poured the juice into two glasses. 'Here you go.' She handed one to Mark. He walked into the living room and sat on the lounge, while Sylvia brought over a bowl of pretzels and joined him. Not so long ago she was sitting here with Richard, and now she was sitting here with Mark. Who would've thought? Hail tumbled from the sky as they munched on pretzels and drank juice.

'You play piano?' Mark pointed behind her.

'Me? No, I'm just keeping it here for my mother. No room at her place.'

'I don't have a musical bone in my body,' Mark confessed.

'Although you did pretty well on the dance floor tonight.' Sylvia smiled, and they both laughed.

'I was terrified. Luke didn't tell me anything about having to dance, but I think it'll be fun. At least we're performing after dessert when everyone's already had a few drinks.'

'Larissa better not put it on YouTube, the last thing I want is my patients seeing me make a fool of myself.'

'They might start calling you "Dr Dance",' Mark joked. 'Or "The Dancing Doctor".'

Sylvia hid her face with her hands. 'Oh, what a night this has been!'

'Tell me about it.' Mark sipped his juice, and placed it on a coaster on the coffee table. 'Do you have a competitive streak?' he asked, pointing to the television cabinet where a collection of board games lay stacked on one of the shelves.

'If there's a competition, I'm in it,' she replied. 'I can't pass up a challenge.'

'Fancy a game of candlelit scrabble then?'

'I can't say I've ever experienced candlelit scrabble. How can I refuse?' Sylvia put down her glass and took the game from the shelf. The last time she'd played was after her birthday dinner last year, when her parents came to stay. The weather was miserable, and forced interaction through a board game was the least painful way of spending time with her parents, whose conversation usually revolved around politics and the latest current affairs, something she had no interest in.

Mark set up the board while Sylvia lit a couple of tea light candles and placed them on the coffee table. They each picked a tile to decide who would start.

'Ha! Me first,' Sylvia said, wriggling into a comfortable position and selecting seven tiles from the velvet pouch. She studied her letters and immediately formed the word: RIPPLE. 'Twenty points for me!' She jotted down her score onto a notepad.

'Twenty?'

'Yeah, when you go first you get a double word score,' Sylvia explained.

'Well, enjoy your temporary lead, because it ain't gonna last long,' Mark said, eyes of determination directed to his tiles as he shuffled them around in different combinations. 'Hey, do I get a double word score too if I add to your word?'

Sylvia shook her head side to side. 'Nope, and now I know you've got an 'S',' she replied.

'Not anymore,' Mark revealed, adding six tiles to the board and hijacking a 'P' from RIPPLE to form the word: SPECIAL.

'That's only fourteen points,' Sylvia remarked. 'What was that you said about my lead not lasting long?'

'Just you wait, I'll be ahead of you in no time.'

And soon he was. Sixty-two points ahead to be exact, thanks to a convenient triple word score and a venereal disease called SYPHILIS. If Sylvia hadn't put TY on the end of SPECIAL, he wouldn't have got it, so it wasn't as if it was due to any skill on his part, just pure luck. Plus, since he used up all seven of his tiles in one go he scored a bonus fifty points. Damn Scrabble rules.

Soon random words littered the scrabble board, and to add to their own amusement they tried making up sentences with as many of the words included as possible. Sylvia tried unsuccessfully to hold back a snort of laughter when Mark came up with, 'Ripples of syphilis waltzed downhill among moaning tigers'. It was so ridiculous it was funny, and Sylvia even managed to rearrange it into her own version, 'Moaning tigers waltzed downhill among ripples of syphilis'. Twice in one night she'd had a good old belly laugh. She'd forgotten what that was like. With Richard everything was so serious, and she couldn't imagine him ever mucking around for fun like she was with Mark right now. She didn't miss him anymore.

'You have a good vocabulary,' Mark said.

'You know a lot of big words yourself,' Sylvia responded.

'We're vocabuliferous,' he said with a grin.

'Since when is vocabuliferous a word?' Sylvia teased, lightly touching Mark's forearm.

'Since when is "moaning tigers waltzed downhill among ripples of syphilis" an acceptable sentence to say out loud, *ever?*'

Sylvia laughed again. 'Since tonight I guess.'

She shook her head at the ridiculousness that was this evening yet marvelled at how relaxed and at ease she felt right now. Somehow, Mark had inched closer without her noticing, and before she could process what was happening, he leaned forward, his eyes staring into her heart, his lips seeking hers. She tilted her chin ever so slightly, then jerked back in surprise as light flooded the room.

'Power's back on,' she blurted out.

'So it is.' Mark looked around the room, as though seeing it for the first time. The moment now gone, he picked up the two glasses and took them to the sink.

Sylvia wondered when the hail had stopped; only silence filled the air now.

'It's late, I better get going,' Mark said, turning his wrist to look at his watch.

Sylvia nodded in agreement, in conflict with the part of her that wanted him to stay.

'I guess I'll be seeing you at the church tomorrow,' he said with a gentle smile, as he put his shoes back on.

'Guess so.' She walked him into the garage and opened the automatic door. 'Thanks for driving me home.' She raised her hand in a royal-like wave as he slid into the driver's seat.

'My pleasure.' Mark closed the car door and reversed out, and she watched him drive away until the lights of his car faded into the night.

CHAPTER EIGHTEEN

After huddling under a blanket last night and most of Saturday morning, Grace finally opened the caravan door to check for any damage from the hailstorm. She'd fallen asleep about ten o'clock last night, *The Woman In White* book lying open on her chest, only to be woken soon after by the thundering downpour on her roof. She'd covered her head with a pillow, from fear of the roof caving in and showering her with a million shards of ice.

Apart from a few puddles and wayward branches on the ground, Grace could see no sign of damage. She even climbed a nearby tree to peer onto the roof just to make sure, and Mr Bennett, who was coming back from the bathrooms, a towel in hand, asked if she was alright. *I really should get a life,* she thought.

Inspired by the unexpected arrival of hot sun and cloud-free skies, Grace decided to take advantage of the weather and go for a bike ride. It would be a good way to explore the town further, and get some exercise. Apart from walking, she didn't do much physical activity, and despite her slim figure she wanted to tone up and look as attractive as possible. Like Jonah. He obviously worked out or something, arm muscles like his didn't just grow themselves. For a moment she imagined those arms wrapped around her, could almost feel their warmth and strength.

She walked the short distance to the bike hire shed before heading towards the riding track near the beach. Her mother used to take her riding on weekends through the large parks in Melbourne, and sometimes along the riverbank. Whenever she rode she'd feel free and powerful, and couldn't believe it'd been years since she'd gotten on a bike.

A skirt of curly hair escaped from the bottom of her helmet, lifting gently off the back of her neck as she picked up speed. Breath quickening and calf muscles burning as she pedalled up the steep incline, Grace kept her eyes on the top of the hill as it drew closer. Placing one foot on the ground in relief when she reached the top, she took a sip of water from the bottle in her knapsack, then stared in awe at the view. She took four photos of the wide expanse of sea and sky, and zoomed in to take one of 'Tarrin', whose earthy face commanded the headland on the other side of the beach. She then turned the camera on herself, smiled, and clicked. She'd cut off the top off her helmet, and was positioned a little too far on the right of the shot, but it would be the sort of photo her mother would have liked. Natural and in the moment.

Grace continued riding and smiled at a woman on a bike who passed her in the other direction. A baby about nine months or so sat strapped into a child seat on the back, his eyes squinting and mouth open wide in delight. As the track curved around and began declining, children swinging back and forth on the swings came into view, while others climbed a mesh of rope and slid down the slide. She slowed a little and swerved around as she neared the park, where a child on a tricycle pedalled as fast as his little legs could go, but only moved at the speed of a tortoise.

Then she saw them. The arms. Jonah's arms, bending up and down, veins pulsing atop his muscles as he did push-up after push-up on the sandy ground next to the park. Was she imagining this? Not long before, the image of those arms had popped into her mind and now here they were. The vision of those arms entwined around her body came to the forefront of her mind again, and she sighed.

She swerved again, but not in time to stop her bike colliding with one of the wooden stumps that formed a rather pathetic barrier from the riding track to the sand. The back wheel of the bike lifted up suddenly, and as it came back down the bike toppled sideways, Grace landing half on the concrete track and half on the sand. She looked up just in time to see The Arms pause mid push-up, their owner staring right at her. As if laughing at her predicament, the loud cackle of a kookaburra shook the air around her and an uncomfortable flush of heat rushed through her face.

'Are you okay, Grace?' Jonah asked as he approached, holding out a hand to help her up.

'Oh hi, I didn't see you there.' Lie of the century. 'I'm okay.' Apart from the burning graze on her knee competing with the burning embarrassment on her cheeks.

'What happened?' Jonah smiled, as he picked up the bike for her.

'The sun got in my eyes and, er... well you saw what happened.' That was the best she could come up with. What was she supposed to say? I was mesmerised by your biceps pumping up and down and lost my balance? She was dying to hold her sore knee but didn't want to seem like a wimp.

He must have read her mind. 'You should give that graze a wash in the salt water, c'mon.' He held out his hand again and led her towards the shore. They both walked knee-deep into the ocean, and Grace splashed the water around her knee, holding back a wince that tried to burst onto her face.

'Do you ride often?' he asked.

Was that a polite way of saying she must be a complete amateur? 'I used to, but this is the first time in years,' she said. 'As you can tell!'

He smiled again, but didn't laugh. 'So, how long have you been working at the bookstore?'

'About two weeks,' she replied.

'Are you new in town? I haven't seen you before, apart from those times at the café,' he asked.

'Yep, I am a newbie.'

'Thought so. Did you move here with your family?'

'No, just me. It might be temporary, but I'll see what happens.' Grace now had another reason to stay.

'Where did you live before?'

Grace laughed. 'I feel like I'm on a game show!'

'Sorry for the grilling, I'm not known for being shy!'

'I gathered that. I'm from Melbourne,' she replied, as they walked to where Jonah had propped the bike against a tree.

'Never been there before,' he said.

'Really? It's a great place, never boring.'

'Unlike Tarrin's Bay?'

'No, I love it here!' Grace smiled. 'Everyone is so friendly, and I love how you can walk everywhere.'

'Or cycle,' Jonah added.

'Well, try to.' Grace gestured to the scene of her tumble. 'So... you're not working at the café today?' *Duh!*

'I'm working tonight, actually. My parents own Café Lagoon so my shifts are pretty flexible. There's an awesome local singer and guitarist performing from eight tonight, so it should make for a good night.'

Grace nodded. 'Cool.'

'You should come.' Jonah touched her forearm lightly, and so briefly, that Grace wondered if she imagined it. 'A few of my friends will be there, and I can introduce you to them if you like.'

Grace's heart beat faster, as though it may lose balance and tumble over at any moment too. She couldn't stop the smile that tickled her cheeks. 'Sounds good, I'll be there.'

'Great, see you tonight then.' Jonah stepped aside as Grace straddled her bike, willing her legs to stop shaking and start pedalling. Although tempted, she didn't dare look back at him. She'd already fallen twice today. Head over heels on the pavement, and head over heels for him.

Larissa managed to keep herself together for most of the day, until she and Luke walked down the aisle and out of the church after the ceremony. By the time Sylvia and Mark reached the church porch, Larissa was red-eyed and crying with happiness, Luke cradling her in his arms. The maid of honour pulled a tissue from the bust of her dress and dabbed at Larissa's eyes. 'Hold it in, Larissa, you've got to keep your face nice for the photos!'

At this, Larissa found the strength to compose herself, and soon she was bombarded with guests filtering out of the church giving their congratulations.

'Nervous about tonight?' Mark asked Sylvia.

'Nervous?'

'About the dance routine,' Mark said.

'Oh that,' Sylvia replied, thinking he may have meant was she nervous about the two of *them*. 'Not so much, I'm sort of looking forward to it now.'

'Me too.' he smiled. 'Where else can you dance like Michael Jackson in public and get away with it?'

'Exactly. Weddings are good like that.' Sylvia smiled and held his gaze for a split second more than usual, before they were interrupted by Larissa's mother, ushering them towards the limousines so they could travel to the location where the photos were to be taken.

An hour and a half later, smiles permanently etched into their faces after the photo shoot, the bridal party arrived at the reception venue. Larissa broke down into tears again at the sight of the function room; silver helium balloons floating above each table, and silver bows on the back of each chair. Sylvia eyed the bridal party's table in the centre of the room. She wouldn't be sitting next to Mark, which for the first time she was unhappy about. Since last night and their 'almost kiss', she wanted nothing more than to be next to him. It didn't make sense. They were completely different people, and until last night couldn't stand being in the same room as each other, but somehow they'd connected. Sylvia wanted to talk to Larissa about Mark, about the feelings that were surfacing, but today was her friend's wedding day. Larissa had been completely preoccupied with getting ready and making sure everything was going to run smoothly, and Sylvia didn't want to distract her by bringing it up.

Occasionally, over dinner, Sylvia would pretend she was surveying the crowd and glance over in Mark's direction. He seemed to be doing the same, and more than once a subtle smile graced his lips.

Eventually, it was time for the dance performance, and they all ducked out for a quick run-through before taking their positions on the dance floor. Everything went quiet as the guests waited in anticipation, and the bridal party waited for the music to begin. The routine started off slowly, with the men on one side of the dance floor and the women on the other. When *The Way You Make Me Feel* came on, the men proceeded to 'woo' the women with their dance moves until they eventually gave in and entered the *Love Shack*. This was where things really amped up, the guests in the crowd laughing as the bridal party let loose to the music. The routine finished off with each of the men lifting the women and carrying them off, pretending to wobble and struggle with the weight of them, until they purposely fell on the floor in a heap. Sylvia and Mark cried with laughter, almost too weak to stand up. Mark hooked his arm around her shoulders to help her up, and they all bowed to the clapping of the wedding guests. Besides Larissa's hen night, this was the most fun Sylvia had experienced in ages.

'Can I give you a lift home tonight?' Mark asked Sylvia, after Larissa and Luke had bid their farewells and drove off, 'just married' written on their car in lipstick.

'I was going to get a taxi, but if you're offering...' she replied.

'I'm offering.'

'Thanks. Hopefully there'll be no hail tonight.' Then again, it would be a good reason to invite him inside again.

'I think we're safe,' Mark said, looking up at the clear sky.

Sylvia watched Larissa's and Luke's car disappear around the corner, their horn tooting loudly into the night. She remembered that Larissa had tried to tell her something last night at the wedding rehearsal, before Luke had interrupted. *'There's something you should know about...'* she'd begun to say. About what? Did she mean something about Mark, or herself, or something else? Surely if it was important she would have mentioned it later that night, or today. Although, she *had* been preoccupied with the wedding, understandably. Maybe Larissa *was* pregnant, and just didn't want to announce it last night until after the wedding? Anyway, no point wondering about it now, it would have to wait until the happy couple returned from their honeymoon in another week.

Sylvia and Mark said goodbye to some of the guests, and walked to where Mark's car was parked. He waited for her to slip inside before walking around the front of the car and getting into the driver's seat.

'I think I'll be sleeping in tomorrow, weddings are exhausting,' Sylvia sighed, relaxing her head against the headrest.

'Wish *I* could, I'm helping my brother and his family move house.'

'Ah, moving house comes a close second to weddings I'd say, as far as exhaustion goes,' Sylvia said.

'So it's the double whammy for me this weekend.' Mark chuckled, as he turned onto the main road and increased speed.

'You might need Monday off then,' Sylvia suggested, slipping off a shoe and rubbing the ache from her toes.

'I'll be alright, if I just keep going I won't notice if I'm tired.'

'Maybe have a quiet Sunday next weekend then.'

'Sounds like a plan,' Mark agreed, glancing briefly at Sylvia before returning his concentration to the road.

They drove without talking for a while, music playing softly on the radio the only sound between them. A familiar tune came on. 'I love this song.' Sylvia reached for the knob to turn the volume up; at the exact moment Mark did the same. Their hands brushed together, his skin like soft velvet against hers, sending a warm rush up her arm.

'Sorry,' they both said awkwardly, retracting their hands.

'Great minds think alike,' Mark added.

As the song filled the car for the next three minutes, they were quiet, and still. The only movement were their chests rising up and down, in rhythm to the music. The car trip seemed longer than last night, but eventually they arrived at Sylvia's house.

'We never got to have that cup of tea last night,' Sylvia mentioned.

'Are you asking me in?'

'I guess I am, that is, if you *want* to come in.'

Mark got out of the car and followed Sylvia to the front door, indicating that he certainly did. Sylvia's fingers trembled as she fiddled with her keys, which fell to the ground with a jingling clatter. 'Oops.' She picked them up and tried again, her breath held high in her chest. The door opened and she let Mark in first before reaching around the door to switch on the light as she walked in too. Sylvia turned around to lock the door behind her, and when she turned back Mark was right in front of her, his body only an inch or so from hers. In an instant he wrapped his arms around her waist, planting his lips on hers with an urgency and passion that seemed to erupt from within. Sylvia's body softened and succumbed to his lead, the keys clattering on the floor again. She brought her hands up to his hair, through his hair, kissing him back with the same intensity he gave out. Her lips tingled with a desire she'd never felt before, and heat simmered between their chests pressed tightly together.

A few moments later they pulled back slightly, his breath warming her face, before starting all over again with even more passion. Sylvia couldn't tell how much time passed, but eventually they stopped.

Mark stepped back. 'Sorry,' he said. 'I don't know what came over me.' His cheeks were flushed and a light sweat shone on his forehead.

'Don't apologise.' Sylvia stepped towards him.

He ran the back of his hand along her cheekbone and

smiled, then took his car keys from his pocket. 'I should probably go. It's late, and I have an early start in the morning.'

An ache formed in Sylvia's chest as he moved to the door. *Please stay*.

'I had the best night I've had in a long time,' he said, leaning into her and commanding her lips one last time.

Me too. The words were there but couldn't come out.

Mark got into his car and waved, then reversed out onto the road. Sylvia glanced at Nancy's house, the light in the window suddenly going out.

A mixture of emotions welled up inside as Mark drove up into the lush, green Tarrin's Bay Hills, darkened by the night sky. He could still feel the tingling of Sylvia's soft lips on his, the satisfying release as her body surrendered to the moment, and the distinctive floral scent of her perfume. Man, she'd looked hot in that dress. He'd barely been able to keep his eyes off her all night.

His desire had been briefly satisfied by their kiss, but it took all his willpower to leave. He knew where it would lead had he stayed, and he couldn't let that happen. Not now.

He turned into his driveway and exhaled loudly, realising he'd almost been holding his breath the whole way home. His heart raced at what just happened with Sylvia, but a pang of guilt also shot through him. Even more so when he opened his front door and was met by the unblinking eyes of his wife staring back at him.

CHAPTER NINETEEN

On Monday morning Sylvia got up a half hour earlier than usual. She had to drop the car keys off at the smash repairs garage, and didn't want to forego her morning swim. She swam faster than usual, too, fuelled by the rush of excitement in her bloodstream after her encounter with Mark. They would both have to face each other at work today, and although she was sure this was heading somewhere, they'd probably keep it secret for now until they were sure. Kissing after a wedding was one thing, starting a relationship in regular daily life was another, let alone when two people worked together.

She didn't try calling him on Sunday, that would have seemed desperate, plus he said he'd be busy helping his brother move house. Sylvia tried to keep busy herself, distracted by reading books and watching movies. After a lively weekend, she'd wanted to stay home and relax.

When Sylvia arrived at work Mark wasn't yet there. She poured a coffee and got her room organised for the day ahead. She'd even brought in a small posy of flowers to put on her desk. With the medical equipment, papers, computer, printer, and books, it needed something organic to balance it out. She'd never brought flowers into work before, but after her swim she'd had the urge to pick some from her garden.

At five minutes to nine, she came out to the waiting room. 'What time is Mark's first patient?' she asked Joyce.

'Nine, but he's not here yet. I've just called but there's no answer. Maybe he's on his way.'

Just then he walked through the door. 'Sorry,' he mouthed. His first patient, who was already waiting, stood to greet him. 'Hi, Robert, I'll be with you in just a moment.' Mark turned towards his room, glancing at Sylvia on the way and offering an awkward smile. A few minutes later he came back out, and ushered Robert into his consultation room.

Damn. Sylvia had hoped to sneak a few moments with him before work. Once the onslaught of patients began it was difficult to stop. Oh well, perhaps they'd grab a coffee or some dinner together later on.

By lunchtime, Sylvia was actually running on schedule. Talk about efficient. The idea of finishing work earlier had nothing to do with it, of course. She caught Mark as he was finishing up his lunch, but was on his way back to his room. 'How was the house-moving?' she asked.

'Full on, but went well. Thanks for asking.' He seemed agitated.

'Are you fully booked today?' In other words, when do you finish work and can we get together tonight and kiss like we did on Saturday?

'I am... actually, I better get ready for my next patient.' He raised his eyebrows briefly and went back to his room.

Not exactly the warm exchange she'd imagined after what happened on the weekend. Maybe he was just feeling awkward being at work with her. Or maybe he just wanted to keep his mind on work right now.

Sylvia ate her lunch at a leisurely pace for a change, then

went to the reception desk to hand some documents to Joyce. She had ten minutes or so to spare until she was back on the clock. A couple of patients were chatting to each other in the waiting room, and Sylvia's ears pricked up when one of them mentioned Mark.

'I've been a patient of his for ages, he's great. Didn't think twice about following him here to Tarrin's Bay, it's only a half hour's drive. Are you a patient of his too?'

The other patient shook her head. 'No, I'm actually here for the physio, but I used to live in Welston. I met Mark and his wife a few years back through a family friend...'

Sylvia's skin burned as though she'd been dipped in hot oil. Did that patient really say, 'Mark and his *wife*'? The rest of their conversation was drowned out, as the revelation throbbed in her ears, over and over again. He has a wife? Heat spread through her body, then an icy sharpness took its place.

Mark has a wife.

'Sylvia, do you have time to take this call? It's Mr Benson, says the medication is upsetting his stomach.' Joyce looked over her shoulder, her hand covering the phone.

'Um, sure,' she replied, forcing composure and walking quickly to her room.

Sylvia had to force herself to concentrate the rest of the afternoon. While at work, patients were her top priority. She'd never let anything personal get in the way of patient care, so as she often did, she pushed her emotions to that place in her mind where all the bad feelings went. All the guilt, shame, regret, and heartache made room for her anger and disappointment. She closed the door to that place in her mind, until she'd finished with her last patient and had made some important phone calls. Anything else would have to wait until tomorrow.

As she gathered up her things, she realised that this must have been what Larissa was going to tell her. So why didn't she just blurt it out, or send a text message or something? If only she could call her now, but she couldn't disturb Larissa on her honeymoon.

It was a quarter to six, and Mark would probably be finishing up paperwork in his consulting room, so she took a deep breath and tapped on his door. Silence. She walked down the hallway to see that Joyce was still there, busily moving about following her end-of-workday routine.

'Where's Mark?' Sylvia asked with a little too much urgency.

'He just left, said he was in a hurry,' Joyce replied.

Sylvia bolted out the door and around back to the staff parking area she never used, almost colliding with Mark's car as he drove around the corner. His car came to an abrupt halt in front of her, and he got out of the driver's side door.

'Sylvia, are you okay?' he enquired.

'I'm fine.' Sylvia pushed the hair back from her face with both hands. 'Actually, I'm *not* fine. We need to talk.' Both hands were now planted rigidly on her hips.

A 'V' formed in Mark's forehead, as he cocked his head to one side. 'Is something wrong?'

'Don't look at me like you don't know what's wrong!' The engine hummed as she made her way around the door to face him. 'I can't believe I fell for your charm. Here I was, thinking you were this nice, caring guy, and as soon as I let my guard down I get slapped in the face with the truth!' The boiling anger she'd felt earlier made its way to the surface, burning cracks in the icy sharpness that had attempted to hold it prisoner.

'I don't know what you're talking about,' Mark replied, holding onto the top of the door as if for support.

'Oh really? Is that what you'd say to your *wife* if she accused you of having an affair?' Sylvia's eyes shone like lasers towards him, pinning him down.

Mark froze for a moment, then exhaled deeply as he sat on the edge of the car seat, looking down at the gravel driveway.

'So you don't deny it? You're married?' Sylvia maintained her stance and focus.

He looked up at her, all colour drained from his face. 'Sylvia, let me explain...'

'Explain? I overheard a patient talking about how she'd met you and your *wife*,' the word burned on her tongue, 'and this morning you seemed like you were trying to avoid me, and now, you try to drive off without saying a word to me before you leave — explain that!'

'My wife, she—'

'Aha, so you *do* have a wife. Straight from the horse's mouth! Does she know about me?'

'Sylvia—'

'Does she know her husband's throwing himself at other women? *Are* there other women? And how will she react when—'

'Sylvia, she died,' Mark said.

'Huh?'

'My wife died.' He turned off the engine, leaving a painful silence between them.

'She... *died?*'

Mark nodded. 'Eighteen months ago. Bacterial meningitis. One day she was fine, the next... well. It all happened so fast.'

'Oh, Mark.' Sylvia dropped to her knees and placed a hand on his thigh, not caring that the gravel was poking into her kneecaps. 'I'm *so* sorry. I wish I'd known. God, what an idiot I've been! I'm *so, so* sorry.' If she could have taken back the last few minutes she would have. She wished she'd gotten the facts straight before accusing him of being an unfaithful bastard.

'It doesn't matter. I should have told you, but we were having such a good time at the wedding, it didn't seem appropriate.' He placed a hand over Sylvia's.

She couldn't believe he wasn't upset with her.

'Anyway, you're right,' Mark said. 'I *was* trying to avoid you this morning. You see, I haven't dated anyone since... it happened. Haven't *wanted* to, until now. And after Saturday night I freaked out a bit, felt guilty, like I was betraying her.' He looked up at the sky.

'It's okay, I understand,' Sylvia whispered, her eyes strained with concern.

Mark looked down at her. 'This... *us* probably happened too fast. I think, well, I *obviously* need more time to deal with things. I don't want to mess you around.'

You're not messing me around. Let's start again. Now she knew the truth she wanted to be with him even more.

'Let's take a step back. We've only known each other for a short while, and I'm still getting settled in town. It's probably best if we're just friends for now, and see what happens down the track.' Mark removed his hand from hers.

Sylvia didn't want to see what would happen down the track, she wanted to see what would happen tomorrow, next weekend, next month. But 'down the track' implied months, years, or *never*. But he was right. Having a relationship with someone who's still grieving was destined for heartache, and there was enough of that tucked away in that little place within her mind.

'Yeah, it's probably best.' Sylvia removed her hand from his thigh and stood up, flicking away remnants of gravel stuck to her trousers. 'But listen, anytime you want to talk. I'm here.'

'Thanks.' Mark stood too, as Sylvia stepped back from the car. 'Sylvia,' he said. 'I really enjoyed the weekend.'

'Me too,' she said, leaning into him and giving him a friendly hug.

'I thought you guys had already left!' Joyce appeared from around the corner. 'Everything alright?'

Mark and Sylvia nodded. 'Everything's fine,' they both said, and Mark got back into his car, turned on the engine, and drove away.

'Can I give you a lift home, Sylvia?' Joyce asked.

'You know what? That'd be great.' All energy had drained from her body, and she wanted to get home, eat, and go to bed as soon as possible.

When Mark opened his front door, he stared for a moment at the picture of his wife on the wall, her eyes looking right at him as though she was really there. 'Oh, Cindy...' he ran a finger over her glossy, dark hair. 'How am I supposed to move on?' A slight trembling affected his chin and he looked away from the picture. He took a beer — usually only a once-a-week treat — from the fridge, and sat on the couch. He took a long gulp, and sighed.

Looking around the room he realised how much work was still to be done. He'd managed to hang pictures but still hadn't unpacked the wine glasses, or the good dinnerware, or the books. Not to mention the other boxes that needed to be dealt with. The boxes with *her* things in them. Cindy's whole life reduced to a few boxes of material possessions. As long as he had them it was like she still existed. Mark's brother had advised dealing with them before moving house, but he wasn't ready. 'I'll deal with them once I've settled in,' he'd replied. But he couldn't find the energy or desire to sort through them. He'd come here for a fresh start, but had only managed to bring the past with him.

Half the beer gone, and noticing the sun fading outside his living room window, he thought back to that horrible afternoon. *If only I hadn't gone into work that day. She might still be alive.* He took another gulp, swishing it around along with the memories.

Cindy had felt unwell for a day or so, and on that fateful Thursday morning he'd asked her if she was feeling any better. 'Not really,' she'd replied. 'It's just a bad flu. But you go off to work, I'll probably be much better by the time you get home.' She'd smiled weakly at him, and rolled over to face the bedside table where he'd left her phone, tissues, a water bottle, some food, and a liquid herbal medicine. 'Okay, but you'll let me know if you need me to come home or take you to the doctor?' She'd nodded.

Cindy, a fitness instructor, had been a tough nut to crack. Always with the attitude of 'I'll be right', she never complained, and rarely got sick. On the occasions she did, she always bounced back quickly, so Mark expected nothing less this time. But when he tried calling her twice that afternoon there'd been no answer. On the third try she'd picked up, but he only heard a sound like the phone dropping. He'd rushed home without a second thought to find her half conscious with a blotchy rash on her body that hadn't been there that morning. The dark colour of the rash didn't disappear when he pressed on it, and he knew immediately what it was.

Knowing he'd get to the hospital faster by driving than if he'd waited for an ambulance, he lifted her into the backseat of the car and sped away, arriving at the emergency department five minutes later. She was taken through immediately, and the doctors didn't wait for test results before starting treatment. As soon as they'd seen the rash and heard Mark relaying how quickly she'd gotten sick, they didn't waste any time. But their efforts were in vain, as two hours later she was dead.

Mark downed the rest of the beer, then thumped the empty bottle onto the coffee table. Although it didn't break, the loud sound shocked his eardrums, and he gasped for breath. He bit down on his lip, trying to stop the emotions of that day coming out, but they were too strong. Pain and grief spilled out of his eyes, though he tried to push them back with the heel of his hand. Sure, he'd cried when she died, and many times after, but then nothing for months. It was as though there'd been nothing left inside, like he'd dried out. But now, after opening that door to Sylvia, that door inside his heart that had been closed for so long, he'd remembered what it felt like to feel connected to someone. He'd felt the rush and the bliss, and then the ache, knowing that he'd never have that connection with his wife again. There was no guarantee that any woman could ever make him feel the way Cindy had made him feel. Being with Sylvia had given him a hint of hope, but also danger. There was no way he was prepared to fall for someone again and risk the pain of losing them. It was easier to keep that door to his heart closed.

Not at all hungry, Mark retreated to his bed, stripped off to his trunks and slid under the sheets. He looked at Cindy's photo on his bedside table, the one of her on their wedding day. He filled his eyes with her beauty, before turning out the lamp, filling his eyes with darkness.

CHAPTER TWENTY

'I could sit here all afternoon and listen to you, Grace.' William Randleman, the music teacher at Tarrin's Bay High School, leaned back in his chair and threaded his fingers together over the back of his head. 'Obviously, we'd be honoured to have you perform at the variety concert. You'll be the highlight of the show!' He removed his hands and wrote something on a piece of paper, shaking his head as though in disbelief.

'Where did you find this prodigy, Sylvia?'

'Oh, she just turned up on my doorstep one day,' Sylvia replied, smiling. Mr Randleman laughed. Little did he know how true that statement was.

Warmth gushed from Grace's face and permeated the air. She wasn't used to being treated like a star or called a prodigy, but after Mr Randleman's standing ovation on finishing her audition piece, well, she could get used to it! She just hoped she'd be able to conquer her nerves, performing in front of a few hundred people instead of only one.

'Well then, if you could let me know by the end of April the name of the piece you'll be performing on the night, that would be appreciated. And Sylvia, can I count on the clinic distributing some promotional flyers again this year?' Mr Randleman asked.

'Of course,' Sylvia replied.

Grace picked up her bag and thanked Mr Randleman, then walked out of the school hall with Sylvia, past a line-up of aspiring performers. A girl in a leotard had one leg stretched up the wall in front of her, making Grace wince. She wondered how anyone's body could physically do that. A teenage boy was practising a card trick, swearing when he dropped all the cards, revealing they were all the same. He quickly picked them up and shoved them into his pocket. And a woman who Grace thought she'd seen in the bookstore a couple of times stood by the wall, warming up her voice through a range of high and low notes. A variety concert indeed. Though she doubted the card trick boy would pass the audition. Poor bugger.

'Told you there wouldn't be a problem getting through,' Sylvia said as they walked outside. 'Looks like our shopping trip *is* on for tomorrow as planned.'

Grace smiled. 'What colour dress should I wear to the concert?'

Sylvia pursed her lips to one side. 'Definitely not black. You'd be camouflaged among the black of the piano and stage curtains.'

'True, I hadn't thought of that.'

'Red could be good, or blue perhaps?' Sylvia suggested.

'Do you think pink would be too... I dunno, little girly?' Grace asked.

Sylvia looked at her for a moment. 'I'm sure I've seen lots of girls your age wearing pink. If you're comfortable in pink, then pink it will be.'

'On second thoughts, maybe not,' Grace said, eyeing a

young, feminine-looking man bouncing up the steps wearing a hot-pink shirt and yellow bow tie, carrying an instrument case.

Sylvia raised her eyebrows. 'Looks like he didn't have anyone trustworthy to take him shopping.'

Grace laughed, all nerves from before dropping away. 'I hope you're trustworthy.' She looked cautiously at Sylvia.

'Of course, I'm very good at clothes shopping.'

'I hope so,' Grace said with a tinge of sarcasm.

Sylvia stopped dead in her tracks and gave an exaggerated gesture at her clothing. 'Would this SABA suit lie?'

They both laughed, and Grace knew she'd be in good hands with Sylvia. She always looked perfectly dressed and well-groomed. Not way out, but sensible and elegant. Although Grace hadn't heard of SABA suits before.

'Sorry I couldn't drive us to the shopping centre,' Sylvia said as they stepped off the bus the next morning.

'No problem. Doesn't worry me how I get somewhere, as long as I get there,' Grace replied. 'Oh, I forgot to thank you for leaving work early yesterday to take me to the audition.'

'My pleasure. Any excuse for an early mark on a Friday! And any excuse to hear you play,' Sylvia said. She seemed genuinely happy to be with Grace, but there was something in her eyes, something in her expression that Grace couldn't read. Like there was something on her mind that wouldn't budge. Probably nothing, she is a doctor after all, so maybe she just had a difficult week with patients.

'Well, thanks. So, which shops do you recommend in here?' Grace asked as they walked into the shopping centre, hit with a cool blast from the air conditioning. 'Do you think Target would have anything decent?'

Sylvia looked at Grace as though she'd asked if they should

eat their lunch off the footpath. 'We won't be going to Target, Grace. Come this way...'

She led Grace to a boutique hidden between a homewares shop and a mobile phone outlet. Not the sort of place Grace would think to look; it seemed a little old for her taste. Sylvia's eyes scanned the store, and within seconds she'd lifted three dresses from the rack.

'What do you think?' she asked.

She'd chosen well, but Grace wasn't sure about one of them. 'They're nice, I'll go try them on.' A sales assistant carried them into the fancy change room, and closed the curtain behind Grace. The first dress she tried was a bright blue halter neck. It was a little loose around the bust, but made Grace feel like she was twenty-five. The second was a rich red colour, with one shoulder strap that travelled diagonally across the front of the dress. And the third was pink, but Grace wasn't sure about the ruffles at the front. Too frilly.

'Wow.' Sylvia's mouth gaped open along with the curtain.

It actually looked fantastic. Somehow the ruffles spread out once the dress was on, and really flattered her petite figure. 'I like it,' Grace said, turning side to side in front of the mirror.

'It's made for you,' Sylvia said. 'But if you like, we'll look around at some other stores just in case.'

'I'm happy to go with this one.' Grace smiled, waiting for Sylvia's agreement as she had offered to pay for it, and closed the curtain to get back into her white cheesecloth skirt and lime green singlet.

When Sylvia got her purse out to pay at the counter, Grace saw it. Another dress. A *perfect* dress. Even better than the pink ruffle one. 'Um...' she started. 'Sylvia?'

'Yes?'

Grace pointed feebly in the direction of the other dress, an amazing satin creation with varying shades of purple and silver.

Strapless, the dress itself looked like an embrace, wrapping from the back around to the front and crossing over in the middle.

Thankfully, Sylvia didn't seem disappointed. In fact, she seemed in awe of it as well. 'How did I miss that?' she asked, moving towards the dress like a moth to a flame. 'This is exquisite,' she said, lifting the dress off the rack and turning it over in her hands.

Grace stepped closer, and her heart sank to her stomach. It was double the price of the pink dress.

Sylvia didn't seem to notice. 'Try it on, Grace. If you like it more than the pink dress, then we'll get it.'

'But...' Grace gestured surreptitiously towards the price tag.

'It's twice as much, so what?' Sylvia led Grace back to the change room, the sales assistant's face lighting up, probably in anticipation of her commission. 'Grace, I want you to wear the dress you like the best. If this is it, then this is it.'

This was it.

Grace didn't want to take it off. When she closed the curtain after showing it off to Sylvia and the sales assistant, she stood for a few moments, looking at herself in the mirror. Bloody awesome! She wished Jonah could see her now. Maybe he'd come to the concert, she could ask him tonight. After meeting his friends at Café Lagoon last Saturday night, Jonah had asked Grace if she would like to join them all at the annual Youth Festival in Miracle Park tonight. In Tarrin's Bay, there seemed to be a festival or some kind of event on almost every weekend. She couldn't wait to see him. Although it wasn't like a date; his friends would be there, but surely he wouldn't have asked her if he didn't like her in *some* way.

'Your daughter looks beautiful,' Grace heard the sales assistant say outside the change room. There was a brief pause and then a soft, 'Yes, she does,' from Sylvia. Grace wished she could have seen Sylvia's expression at Grace being called her daughter. It must be weird for her. Hell, it was weird for Grace too.

Grace took the dress off, changed quickly, and went straight to the counter before any rival teenager could grab it from her. There was only one in her size. She was so glad she'd noticed it before Sylvia paid for the pink dress, nice as it was.

'Half an hour and we're done, can you believe it?' Grace said as they walked from the shop, boutique bag in her hand.

'Told you I was a good shopper. Although it was you who found the dress. Maybe you didn't need me after all.' Sylvia chuckled.

'Are you kidding? I would never have gone into that shop if you hadn't brought me to it.' Oops, Grace hoped that didn't offend Sylvia. 'I mean, I usually go to the cheapest shops first,' she corrected.

'Then let's say it was a joint effort,' Sylvia said.

Grace nodded. 'So, where to now?'

'You'll need some jewellery to go with the dress, and a nice pair of heels.'

Wow. Grace hadn't thought beyond the dress. Shopping for fancy clothes without paying a cent, followed by a fun night ahead with a cute guy — this was every eighteen-year-old girl's idea of the perfect day!

CHAPTER TWENTY-ONE

G race was almost at the Wishing Fountain, the obviously popular meeting spot in Tarrin's Bay, when she received a text message.

> Soooo sorry Grace but I have 2 stay at work till about 9pm, 1 of the staff went home sick. U can still meet the others as planned. If u want to hang around, meet me at cafe at 9. Jonah.

Oh, crap. Should she go back to the caravan, or meet Jonah's friends? She barely knew them, and didn't want to tag along like the odd one out. But if she didn't meet them, they'd know she was only coming to see Jonah. How desperate would that look? She continued walking and came to the fountain.

They were already there. Everyone smiled to greet her.

'Hey, Grace,' Susie said, her arm around Josh. There was also another girl, Lauren, and two other guys, Chris, and, oh what was the other dude's name? Something difficult to pronounce. It was on the tip of her tongue.

'Did you get Jonah's message?' Josh asked, eyebrows raised.

'Yeah, just now,' Grace replied, holding up her phone.

'The bugger's always standing us up,' Josh said.

'I don't blame him wanting to rack up some extra bucks, he needs as much as he can get,' the nameless guy said.

'Jianyu,' Lauren whispered, nudging him discreetly in the ribs.

Jianyu! That was his name. She repeated it in her mind a few times to imprint the memory. Anyway, what was that nudging about? So what if Jonah needed money? Probably spends his income on the finer things in life. For a moment, Grace imagined Jonah taking her out to dinner at a fancy restaurant, candlelight warming his face, their hands entwined on the table...

'Let's grab some burgers,' Josh said, leading the group towards a stall set up in the park.

They all walked together, three girls and three guys, and strangely Grace was reminded of *The Brady Bunch*. When she was younger, she loved watching the reruns on TV, total comfort television.

Steam rose from the hamburger stall, and strong smells of onions, beef, and tomato sauce had Grace salivating. Mark Bastian wouldn't approve, but she wasn't about to tout her health plan in front of Jonah's friends. She held up her phone and took a photo of the festival while there was still some light.

They wandered around the park, hamburgers filling their mouths, live music filling their ears as it emanated from the stage. It was an alcohol-free event, and people wearing glow-bands around their wrists handed out brochures on the dangers of alcohol and drugs. Grace didn't need one, she wasn't stupid. Unlike some of the kids at school last year who drank themselves silly after the HSC, a couple of her friends included. All Grace wanted to do when it was over was go home, throw all her books out, and sleep for a week. All that effort, and she still didn't know what to do with her life. That was what this year was about — finding out where she came from and where to go from here. After yesterday's audition she had a twinge of hope that maybe she could pursue a music career; but, in reality, it would probably be really hard to make a living from playing the piano. If she could sing, well that would be another matter, but not that many people became famous pianists.

When they all finished eating, they tried out a few of the novelty games, like trying to throw a toy frog on a floating lily pad. Grace's frog kept landing on the edge, pushing the lily pad away and floating off with the other reject frogs. Three bucks down the drain. Lauren managed to get her last frog on a lily pad, winning a plastic toy bird who tweeted incessantly when you threw it up in the air.

'Here, you have it,' Lauren said, handing the creature to Grace.

Gee. Thanks. 'Aww, that's nice of you,' Grace replied, taking the bird. She bet if Jonah were here he would have got all three frogs to land on the lily pad, winning her one of the giant fluffy toys which would take up half her caravan.

As the late summer sun went down and was replaced by a moonlit sky, they lined up for the dodgem cars. They were clearly the most popular attraction, the crowd growing larger by the minute. Grace and Lauren took the last two dodgem cars, while the others had to wait for the next session. Grace enjoyed bumping and dodging the other cars, her head bobbing this way and that, despite the insistent ramming from behind by a creepy looking guy in a black singlet and beanie. Whenever she tried to go around him he'd cut her off, sniggering to himself. Idiot.

Soon the cars went limp and the girls clambered out, Lauren mouthing to the others, 'We'll meet you around back.'

'I haven't been in a dodgem car for ages!' Grace remarked.

'They're always fun,' Lauren replied. 'So tell me, what do you think of Jonah?'

Luckily it was dark behind the dodgem track so Lauren wouldn't be able to see her blushing. 'Um, he's nice I guess.' Grace shrugged.

'Just nice? C'mon, I saw the way your eyes sparkled when you watched him work at the café last Saturday night,' Lauren insisted.

Grace bowed her head, unable to withhold a grin. 'Is it that obvious?'

Lauren nodded. 'That's good, because I reckon he has the hots for you too. Big time.'

'What? Huh? Why? What did he say?' Grace's speech reverted to that of a five-year-old after a red cordial overload.

'Let's just say he's been talking about you. A LOT.'

Grace giggled like a child and covered her face with her hand. Just then an arm swung around her shoulders.

'Evening, darlin', lookin' good tonight.' It was the idiot from the dodgem cars, his beefy skin emitting a combination of alcohol and body odour. Grace shrugged his arm off and stepped back, but he swung his arm back around her, the other around Lauren, pulling them in close to his body.

'Hey, get lost, will ya?' Lauren had him off her in a second, holding an arm in front of Grace as if to shield her.

He didn't get the message. He leaned in towards Lauren, trying to put his arms around her. 'C'mon babe, show me some love,' he slurred.

Lauren pushed his arms down and away. 'Leave us alone. C'mon Grace.' They turned away and walked quickly in the direction of the crowd.

This only irritated the guy. He lurched forwards and grabbed Lauren's ponytail, pulling her head backwards. Grace's heart skipped a beat and she froze, not sure whether to run or help Lauren. She didn't have to do either. In an instant, Lauren had spun around, her forearm pushing his arm out of the way, before grabbing his shoulders and kneeing him in the groin. As he collapsed forwards, crying out in pain, Lauren grabbed Grace's hand. 'C'mon,' she said.

'You bitch, arghhh!' The guy tried to walk towards them again but couldn't, his hands cupped around his groin.

'Take that!' Grace yelled, throwing the plastic toy bird at him. It missed. But at least the sound of the bird's tweeting shocked him enough to wonder what the hell it was.

Lauren found one of the security guards who was covering the crowded area and pointed out the guy to him. Moments later he was escorted out of the park.

'You were amazing!' Grace told Lauren. 'I thought he was going to drag us off somewhere, but you... you kicked a grown man's arse!'

Lauren smiled. 'I didn't want to hurt him, he obviously just had a few too many, but when he grabbed my hair my instincts took hold.'

'Damn good instincts! I just froze. Great help I was,' Grace said.

'It was nothing. Just my training kicking in.'

'What sort of training?' Grace asked.

'Taekwondo. I got my black belt last year.'

'Awesome! I picked the right girl to hang with then,' Grace said.

'Actually, the others are black belts too.'

'All of you? Jonah too?'

Lauren nodded. 'That's how most of us became friends, we're in classes together. Susie and Josh also went to the same school as me, and I've known Jonah since I was a kid.'

'Wow. And I came here tonight feeling like the odd one out to start with, now I find out you're all ninjas!' Grace laughed.

'Actually, ninjas undergo different training. Anyway, no

need to feel like the odd one out, I'm glad you came tonight. You're a lot of fun.'

'I am?'

Lauren nodded and smiled.

It felt nice for Grace to have made a new friend. She missed her friends from Melbourne. 'So what do you do during the day, Lauren? Do you work, or study?'

'Study,' she replied, shaking her blonde hair loose from its ponytail. 'I'm in my final year of a dance degree at Welston Uni.' She scooped up her hair and retied her ponytail.

Grace's eyes widened. 'Wow, I didn't know you could do dance at uni. I'm starting dance classes in town soon, though I doubt I'll be any good. You must be awesome if you're in your final year!'

Lauren flicked her hand. 'Ah, it's what I love to do. I hope to start my own dance school one day.'

'So you're a *dancing* ninja,' Grace said.

Lauren chuckled. 'Yeah, maybe I should invent my own style of *entertaining self defence*.' She moved her arms in a beautiful flourish and followed up with a sharp punch in the air.

'Sounds like fun!'

'Who knows, it could be the next craze,' Lauren replied, then burst out laughing.

'What are you laughing at? Do I have food stuck in my teeth?' Grace slid her tongue across her teeth just in case.

'No, sorry,' Lauren said. 'I'm just remembering the way you threw that annoying bird at the guy. '"*Take that!*"' she mimicked Grace's earlier display of aggression, and they both folded forward in giggles.

'What's so funny?' Josh asked, the rest of Jonah's friends coming over from behind the dodgems.

'Oh, nothing,' Lauren said.

'Actually, Lauren just saved me from getting attacked by some creep. She was awesome!'

'Really? You okay?'

Grace nodded. 'I'm fine. He grabbed Lauren by the hair, but she got him where it hurts before he could do anything else.'

'Way to go girl. Is he gone now?' Josh asked.

'Yeah, he got escorted out of here.'

'You'll have to tell Master Jin at class next week,' Susie said, before turning to Grace. 'He's our taekwondo instructor,' she explained.

'I thought so, Lauren told me you guys all do classes together.'

'Hey, you should come along!' Lauren put her hand on Grace's arm.

'Yeah, beginners are always welcome,' Susie said.

Grace got a mental image of herself in a white suit, trying to high-kick but falling over. 'I dunno, I'm pretty uncoordinated.'

'It'll teach you coordination, Grace, and there are other beginners in the classes too.' Lauren hadn't let go of her arm yet.

'Um...'

'Master Jin gives newbies a free class to try it out, so why don't you come along next week? We've only just started back for the year,' Josh said.

'Well, okay. I'll give it a try, but promise not to laugh at me?'

'We promise,' they all said.

'Classes are on at seven from Monday to Thursday, you can come to any one,' Lauren said. 'At the high school hall.'

After finishing Year Twelve, Grace thought she'd seen the last of school halls, but it looked like she'd be paying the Tarrin's Bay High School Hall another visit.

At nine, Susie and Josh left, while Grace, Lauren, Chris and Jianyu headed over to Café Lagoon to meet Jonah. Grace's heart soared when she saw him. He smiled widely, and apologised again to Grace for not being there earlier. She so wanted to take a photo of him right now.

'It's okay, we had fun, didn't we?' Grace turned to Lauren.

'Sure did,' she replied. 'Even managed to convince Grace to join us at taekwondo next week.'

'Really?' Jonah's eyes widened.

Grace nodded feebly.

'Awesome,' Jonah said, pulling the apron off over his head. 'So, you know where to go?'

'Yeah, the school hall. I was there yesterday so I know where it is,' Grace replied.

'Oh yeah — your audition! How'd it go?' Jonah asked. Grace had told him about the upcoming audition last Saturday.

'I got in,' she said.

'Woohoo!' Jonah clapped. The others joined in, and she tried to flick their applause away.

'It's nothing. It's not like it's *The X Factor* or anything.' Grace tried to will her blushing away.

'Are you kidding?' Lauren asked. 'It's the biggest concert in town each year. They only let the *really* talented people perform, and they go way out with the sets and lighting. It's a great night.'

'So... you'll all be there, then?' Grace scanned everyone's eyes, lingering on Jonah's.

Everyone nodded. 'I'll *make sure* I don't have to work that night,' Jonah said with a definitive tone.

So not only would she have to work up the courage to perform in front of strangers, but new friends, and possibly her as-yet-unknown grandparents too. At least it was a few months away, time to get prepared and build up her confidence.

'I'm off now.' Jonah turned to a staff member, and came around the counter to the group. They walked across the road to Miracle Park, where some of the stalls were packing up, and hung out for a while by the stage where musicians were still playing. When things died down, Jonah looked at his watch. 'Only nine-thirty — anyone feel like catching a late movie?'

'Sure,' Grace said, nodding. Lauren nodded too.

'I've got an early morning mate, might give it a miss,' said Chris.

'Yeah, me too, I'm off to the city tomorrow,' said Jianyu.

So, it would just be Jonah, Grace, and Lauren.

Lauren looked awkwardly at Grace. 'Actually, I remembered I have to take my sister to... a, um... thing, early tomorrow before uni.'

Just Jonah and Grace. Alone. Together. *Would he still want to go, just with me?*

'Looks like it's just us,' Jonah said, raising his eyebrows at Grace. 'Shall we go?'

He held out his elbow and she took it. They said their goodbyes to the others, and Jonah led her in the direction of the car park around the back of the shops on Park Street. A tiny Italian restaurant Grace had never noticed before was lit by a frame of red and green lights, a sandwich board listing specials sat out front in the car park. It was so cute; Grace took a photo of it. Jonah smiled at her curiously.

'What?' she asked.

'You like restaurants I take it?'

'I like photography. I've been collecting photos since I came to Tarrin's Bay.'

'Cool. You'll have to show me what you've got so far, sometime.'

Grace nodded. 'Which movie should we see?' she asked, as they got into his car.

Jonah got out his phone and loaded up the session times for the local cinema. 'There's either *Time out*, or *Never Again* — both comedies.' He looked at Grace.

'Um… I like the sound of *Never Again*, wanna see that one?'

'Sounds good.' Jonah revved the engine and drove to the cinema in the next town.

Three hours later they were back in Jonah's car, driving home. Grace allowed a small yawn to escape her mouth. Although tired, she could easily stay up all night and hang out with Jonah if the opportunity presented itself. Unlike her friends from Melbourne, she hadn't had many boyfriends, nothing serious anyway. She'd never felt as strongly about anyone as she did about Jonah, and she couldn't get enough. Of his eyes, his smile, his laughter, and his gentle strength. Okay, so she didn't know him *that* well yet, but what did that have to do with anything?

At the cinema, their hands had brushed against each other when they both went to put their arms on the armrest between them. Jonah had moved his away, letting her arm take the spot. And then, amidst an episode of laughter from a funny scene in the movie, he'd put his arm back on the armrest, on top of her arm, entwining his fingers with hers. A tingle had rushed from her arm to the rest of her body, and she hoped he couldn't feel the goose bumps on her arm that felt as big as golf balls.

Grace hummed along to a song on the car radio, and Jonah joined in. He looked at her for a moment, a smile playing on his lips, then belted out the chorus of the song with one hand curled into a microphone-shaped fist in front of his mouth. He moved the 'microphone' to her mouth, and she did her best to outsing him. Soon, the car was filled with enthusiastic, out of tune singing, followed by laughing. After some unsuccessful channel switching to find another suitable sing-along-song worthy of their performance, they arrived at the caravan park.

'Thanks for the movie,' Grace said, walking as slowly as possible to her caravan, Jonah following.

'My pleasure. Sorry I wasn't there earlier for the festival.' Jonah slid his hands into his pockets.

'That's fine. It's more important all those thirsty people got their fix of gourmet coffee — Jonah style!'

Oh God. Did I really say that?

'True, and coffee is an in demand industry. People will *always* need their coffee.'

'Do you think you'll stay at the café long term, maybe take over the family business someday?' Grace asked.

'Who knows?' Jonah replied. 'Maybe. It does allow me to talk to people all day, I love doing that. And I get discounted food and coffee.' He removed his hands from his pockets and let them swing beside his body.

'That's a good enough reason.'

'What about you? Do you want to have your own bookshop one day?' Did Jonah step in closer to her just now?

'I don't think so. But I don't really know what I want to do yet. I'm just trying a few things out,' Grace said.

'What about music? That is, *if* you're any good,' he suggested, elbowing her cheekily in the ribs.

'You'll have to wait till the concert to find out.' Grace elbowed him back, a smile curving at the corners of her mouth. 'This is mine,' she said, coming to a stop in front of her temporary home.

'I like it, it's very... you.' Jonah glanced at the colourful garland of fake flowers she'd framed the caravan with.

'Do you mean to say that I'm *fake*?' she teased.

He tilted his head back with a chuckle. 'No. That it's pretty, like you.' He was looking straight at her now.

'Well, thanks.' Thank God it was too dark for him to see her blushing. 'And thanks again for tonight.'

Jonah simply nodded, and leaned in towards her. Grace felt her lips part ever so slightly, as she felt his warm breath on her face. Her dream guy was right here in front of her, coming in closer, getting ready to...

'See you again soon,' he whispered, pursing his lips and planting them on her cheek.

What happened to the perfect kiss she'd imagined? A combination of bliss from the sensation of his lips on her skin and disappointment from the anticlimax of the moment stirred around her heart, as he walked back to his car and waved before driving away.

CHAPTER TWENTY-TWO

I f she hadn't looked down to shy away from the glaring sunlight that welcomed her on opening the caravan door, Grace would have stepped on it. A rectangular package about the size of a book lay on the ground in front of her caravan. Gold wrapping paper reflected the sun's bright rays, and a red ribbon tied into a lopsided bow made her smile with curiosity.

She bent down to pick it up, and tugged at the ribbon to release the bow. Turning the package over to undo the sticky tape, she noticed a small card attached to the bottom.

HAPPY VALENTINE'S DAY was printed in a flourished font on the front of the card, and Grace brought a hand to her mouth in surprise. She didn't even realise it was the fourteenth of February today. She also wondered for a moment why Mrs May's Bookstore hadn't planned any sort of promotion for this global day of love; it would have been a perfect excuse to create a new, romantic window display.

Knowing who it must be from, she inched the card open and found obviously male handwriting that read:

*This is only half your gift, meet me at the café at
6pm and I'll give you the other half. Jonah.*

Quickly, Grace tore off the wrapping paper to reveal a
cardboard box. Inside the box was a beautiful silver photo
frame, covered with diamantes that glimmered in the sunlight.
She squinted as her eyes watered, both from the glare, and from
the fact that Jonah had remembered she liked photography. Like
a love-struck actress overacting her part, she held the gift to her
heart in a dramatic gesture, lifting her head to the sky, and
closing her eyes. Warmth permeated her eyelids and she felt like
the luckiest girl on the planet.

The day couldn't go fast enough. It was her day off, so Grace
kept as busy as possible, cycling, walking, reading, and catching
up with her friends on Facebook. Just after five she was
showered and dressed for her mystery evening with Jonah. She
wondered what the 'other half' of the gift would be.

As she had a half hour to spare, Grace plugged her phone
into her laptop computer to upload the latest photos from the
last few days. Then she opened her 'My Pictures' folder to have
a look at her growing collection. All of a sudden the screen
froze, and when she tried clicking nothing happened.

'C'mon, stupid computer!' she said, as though that would
make it behave. A pop-up window appeared and then disappeared
before she had a chance to read it, then her folder disappeared, and
the internet browsing windows she'd opened closed down. When
she tried opening up 'My Pictures' again, the folder was empty.

'What the...?' Grace's eyes furiously searched for a solution.
She tried opening the internet again, but it wouldn't load, and
all her pictures were gone.

Just like that.

'No!' she lifted her hands to her head and stared at the screen, as if the magic remedy would suddenly appear and fix the problem. It must be some kind of virus, she thought, as the computer began shutting down. Maybe she shouldn't have accepted that invitation from one of her friends to play 'Which movie star are you most like?' on Facebook. What if that somehow caused it? Then again, she'd also been Googling and reading blogs about 'How to tell if he's the one', and 'Ten things NOT to do on a date'.

Frustrated, she stormed out of the caravan, holding back tears. If she'd lost all her photos, she'd have to start her mother's memory album all over again. But it wouldn't be the same. She couldn't do anything about it now, she'd just have to find a computer expert tomorrow on one of her breaks from work. It was almost 6pm, and she had to go and meet Jonah.

Temporarily forgetting her problem when she saw Jonah coming out of Café Lagoon with a smile that could melt ice, she smiled back, and thanked him for the gift. Then she tensed up, a headache forming on her forehead.

'Is everything okay?' he asked.

'My laptop crashed, and I don't know how to fix it. I've lost all my photos!' Grace blurted out.

'Where's your laptop now?'

'At the caravan.'

'Let's go,' Jonah said, tugging on Grace's hand. 'I'll take a look at it.'

'You know much about computers?' she asked, a glint of hope in her voice.

Jonah leaned in to Grace's ear. 'Don't tell anyone, but I'm a bit of a geek-at-heart,' he whispered. 'Now I can't promise anything, but I'll do my best. Otherwise, there's a guy I know who's even more of a geek-at-heart than me.'

'Well, I hope you're enough of a geek to fix it, I really want my photos back,' Grace said.

'Maybe it'll help if I get into the zone,' he said, trying to pull his pants up high and walking in a daggy way.

Grace laughed and slapped him lightly on the arm. 'You really don't care what others think, do you?'

'Nah, I am who I am.' He readjusted his pants and resumed his normal walking style. 'Seriously though, you don't need to be a full on geek to fix a computer. You just need a little understanding of how things work.'

Grace flipped open her laptop when they arrived at the caravan. Strange green writing on a black screen appeared, like on a really old computer. Jonah clicked a couple of keys, waited a bit, clicked a few other keys, waited a bit more.

'You don't still have the photos stored on your iPhone?' he asked.

'Only the ones I took from Sunday till now, the rest I deleted because I uploaded them to the computer.'

'So you've still got the photos you took at taekwondo then?' He turned to face her.

She nodded. Grace went to her first class on Monday night. While the black belts practised their *poom sae*, or patterns of techniques, Grace snapped a few pictures of them in motion. When she was caught out, Jonah snatched the phone from her and took a few of his own while she was learning the basic stances with the other beginners. After the class, they hung around outside and took wacky photos of each other with Jonah's friends from the festival. She was like the black sheep in the group, the only one not in a white uniform. Master Jin would be bringing her a uniform and white belt next week.

Jonah tapped away at the keyboard, opening up windows she didn't know existed, until bam! — her photos reappeared in the 'My Pictures' folder. He sat back and circled his hands in the air. '*Voilà!*'

'You fixed it?' Grace shoved her face close to the computer screen.

'Uh-huh. Although if you created any documents in the last couple of days, they might have been lost, but everything up to last Sunday has been recovered.'

'Woohoo! Thank you so much!' Grace wrapped her arms around Jonah's neck, then pulled back, feeling slightly over-enthusiastic.

'Do you want to re-upload the new photos from your phone?'

'Yes, but I'm afraid to do it in case it crashes again.'

'Lucky I'm here then.' Jonah plugged Grace's phone into the laptop. 'All done,' he said after a few moments, handing the phone back to her.

Grace slipped the phone into the pocket of her capris, and scanned her eyes through the folder to make sure all the photos were there.

'Are there any you'd like to show me?' Jonah asked.

Grace was secretly pleased she hadn't taken any impromptu photos of Jonah while out and about. 'Sure.' She sat next to him, clicked on a photo to start the slideshow, and gave a running commentary on each photo.

'Why is there a photo of you and Dr Greene?' Jonah asked.

Oops, she'd forgotten about that one. 'Oh, you know Sylvia?' Grace twirled a tendril of hair around her finger.

'Everyone knows Dr Greene.'

'Um, we're kind of related,' she said.

'Oh yeah? In what way?' Jonah's curious eyes searched hers.

Should she tell him? Grace knew that Sylvia seemed keen on keeping this a secret, but she didn't want to lie to him. She took a deep breath and said, 'Let me start at the beginning.'

Grace's eyes became moist when she told Jonah about how her mother died last year, and how these photos were to be incorporated into a memory album to give to her father. She then explained how she'd been adopted, and came to Tarrin's Bay after finishing school to find her birth mother.

'Dr Greene? She's your real mother?' Jonah's jaw opened wide.

Grace nodded, and placed a hand on his arm. 'But don't tell anyone, okay? It was a bit of a shock, me turning up like this, and I don't think many people knew she had a baby when she was a teenager.'

Jonah slid his thumb and forefinger across his lips. 'I won't say a word,' he said.

'Thanks.'

'Wow, Grace. It sounds like you've been through a lot for someone your age,' Jonah said.

You don't know the half of it. 'Yeah, you could say that.' She ran a hand through her hair and looked away.

Jonah took hold of Grace's hand, concern on his face. 'How did you get through your HSC after dealing with what happened to your mum?'

'To be honest, I have no idea,' Grace began. 'I took a couple of weeks off school, then I just threw myself back into it. I think it helped distract me from the pain, and...' Grace felt her chin tremble a little. 'And... I wanted to do her proud.' She wiped at the corner of her eyes, swallowing hard and pushing back tears. 'So I stuck at it, and finished with a decent result.' Grace allowed herself a brief smile. Her hand became warm and she realised Jonah was rubbing it up and down.

'I have *no* doubt that she would be *very* proud of you,' he said, a genuine warmth in his eyes.

She mouthed a silent 'thank you', and stood. 'Anyway, enough reminiscing. What should we do now?' Grace stretched her arms above her head, as though preparing for a race. When she lowered them, Jonah took hold of them and stood to meet her gaze.

'I was thinking... this.' He leaned in close like he did last Saturday. Only this time his aim was better, his lips landing right on target.

Grace softened at Jonah's touch, and the butterflies that had become permanent residents in her stomach since meeting him collapsed in a love-induced haze. Heaven had definitely come down to earth for a visit. Maybe this was the other half of the gift he'd promised.

Jonah eased his lips off hers for a moment, smiling. 'I just remembered I haven't given you the rest of your gift yet,' he whispered.

Maybe not then.

'What is it?' Grace whispered, her face still within a few centimetres of his.

'Come with me,' he said, leading her outside.

They walked hand in hand to the beach, taking the steep concrete steps up to the top of the headland. From here, they could see forever. A man stood below, fishing rod extended far into the ocean, a couple walked barefoot along the shoreline, and in the distance, a flock of seagulls flew far away until Grace couldn't see them anymore. Warm blobs of orange and a tender glow of yellow swam around the sky as dusk fell.

Grace's pulse quickened as she felt Jonah's hand on her hip. He lifted the phone from her pocket. 'Hey! What's with the pickpocketing?' she teased.

He ignored Grace's question, simply turned her back to the horizon, stood next to her and held the phone out in front. 'Smile!' he said.

Click!

Jonah and Grace looked at the photo, a happy shot of them,

their skin glossy and glowing against a backdrop of sunset. 'Happy Valentine's Day,' Jonah said. 'This is the other half of your present — to put in the photo frame.'

A smile grew on Grace's lips, and she leaned in towards him, rising up on her tippy-toes. 'Thank you,' she whispered, kissing him gently on the lips. 'Only I didn't get *you* a gift.'

'Oh yes you did,' he replied, grasping the sides of her face with his hands and pulling her lips to his.

CHAPTER TWENTY-THREE

After moving through the resistance of the water in her swimming pool, Sylvia moved through the crowd of tourists walking the opposite direction to her. The footpath alongside the terrace shops was always packed on a Saturday. Resistance gave way as she came to Miracle Park and relished the open space. She took off her sandals to feel the lush grass beneath her feet as she walked diagonally across the park, before putting them back on to cross the road. While waiting for a break in the traffic going down Park Street, she glanced towards Café Lagoon to see if Larissa was there yet. They'd planned to meet for lunch at twelve-thirty, and it was now twelve-twenty-five. Nope. As usual, Sylvia was the first to arrive.

She saw Jonah standing outside the café, his back to her. A pair of young arms were draped around his neck, and he leaned forward, then back again. *Oh, he's found himself a girlfriend, how sweet!* Sylvia tilted her head to one side and smiled. Jonah was a great kid. No, a great *man*. He'd be about twenty years old by now, Sylvia thought. Very popular with the girls, but he never seemed to let it go to his head. As the young arms reluctantly dropped away from his neck, he turned back to the café, while a girl with red curls turned the other direction and bounced happily along. Grace. His girlfriend was Grace!

As Sylvia crossed the road she didn't know what to think. Of course Grace could have a boyfriend; she'd probably had a few by now, but this perpetual image of Grace as a child, a baby, kept surfacing in her mind. Part of her wanted to sit her down and talk, make sure she wasn't jumping into anything serious too soon. Maybe that was the maternal instinct that people talked about. She wasn't sure. The other part of her dismissed this and told her to stay out of it. Grace was old enough to make her own decisions, and her own... mistakes. Hell, Sylvia had been two years younger than Grace when she'd *had* her. Anyway, if she was going to hook up with anyone, she was glad it was Jonah. Sylvia knew his parents and was comforted by the fact he came from a good family.

Jonah stiffened slightly when he saw her. 'Oh, hi Dr Greene. Table for one?'

'Hi Jonah, two actually.' Sylvia sat as Jonah pulled out a chair at one of the outdoor tables. 'And, I think you know me well enough to call me Sylvia from now on, okay?' She smiled.

'Well okay then, *Sylvia*,' he emphasised. 'Although, it sounds a bit strange!' He blushed slightly and placed a 'reserved' sign on the table. She'd never seen Jonah blush before. His relaxed self-confidence was always palpable. 'I'll see you at the counter to take your order when your friend arrives.'

Sylvia nodded, and poured herself a glass of water from the carafe. Café Lagoon was one of the best café's in town. They had an efficient computerised ordering system that saved people waiting for a waiter to come and take their order. Their food was delicious, cooked on-site, and always quick to be served.

'Sylvia!' Larissa dumped an array of shopping bags on the

ground next to the table and flung her arms around her. 'It's so good to see you!'

'You too! How's married life treating you?'

'Extremely well, if you must know.' She winked. 'I'm so glad we were able to extend our honeymoon, didn't want to leave!' Larissa sat in the chair opposite Sylvia and poured herself a glass of water. 'Back to work on Monday, but this afternoon I'm doing a bit of decorating. Luke's place will never know what hit it!'

'Don't you mean *your* place?' Sylvia asked.

'Oh yeah, I keep forgetting it belongs to both of us now. Anyway, look what I got.' Larissa showcased her shopping spree piece by piece, and eventually they both got up to place their order at the counter.

Back at the table, Larissa suddenly leaned forward. 'Sorry, Hun, I'm still on the honeymoon high. You said in your text something about Mark?'

'The night of the rehearsal dinner, were you going to tell me about his wife?'

'That's right, we got interrupted. And then it completely slipped my mind. God! I've been so self absorbed lately! Anyway, I was going to tell you his wife died a while ago, so if you were keen on him to take it easy at first. Her death really shook him up. Luke had to go stay with him for a while after it happened.' Larissa took a sip of water. 'So he told you about her, is that how you found out?'

Sylvia shifted in her chair. 'Sort of. Well, no actually, he didn't tell me. Not until I confronted him about it after overhearing a patient's conversation. But I only heard he had a wife, I didn't know she'd died. And by then we'd already kissed, so I furiously told him off. I thought I was "the other woman", and needless to say it was extremely awkward when he told me the truth, and—'

'You kissed?' Larissa's eyes grew wide. 'And you told him off because you thought he still had a wife?'

Sylvia nodded.

'Oh no. What a mess!' Larissa brought her hands to her face.

'I know, I know. I should have gathered the evidence before coming to a conclusion. But when I heard he had a wife, and he was acting like he wanted to avoid me, it didn't even cross my mind that there could be an alternative to him being a lying, cheating, you-know-what.'

'So you let him have it, in your "I'm Dr Greene and no one messes with me" kind of way?'

'You could say that,' Sylvia said, hiding behind her glass of water.

Larissa's mouth tried to withhold a giggle. 'I shouldn't laugh, but I can just see you doing that,' she said. 'I can only imagine the shock on your face when he told you the truth.'

Sylvia ran a hand through her hair. 'I felt like such an idiot! I can't believe he's still speaking to me.'

'So things are... okay, between you?'

'Well, he pretty much said he's not ready to get involved, so I guess there isn't *anything* between us.' Sylvia straightened in her chair.

'But you'd like there to be?'

'He's not ready, that's obvious, and it's a bad idea to get involved with someone who's still grieving.'

'But, Sylvia, you'd *like* to be involved? If he was ready?' Larissa probed.

Sylvia thought back to the sadness on Mark's face when he told her of his wife's death, and how he'd removed his hand from hers. But then she thought back to the night of the wedding, when he'd launched himself at her with a passion she'd never felt before, and tingles ran up her spine.

'Yes,' she said. 'Yes, I would.'

Later that day, Sylvia sat staring at the blinking cursor on the computer screen. It shouldn't be this hard, should it? Sending an email to your parents to tell them the granddaughter they've never met is here, and wants them to come and watch her perform on stage?

Larissa had been brought to tears when Sylvia showed the photo of her and Grace at the beach. Grace had sent it to Sylvia's phone after their day out together.

'She looks just like you did at that age, minus the boofy teased fringe you had!' Larissa had said, before dabbing the corners of her eyes and saying how amazing it was that Sylvia's daughter had come all this way to find her. Sylvia told Larissa about Grace's musical talent, and the variety concert she'd be performing in, and Larissa had made her promise she'd contact her parents to tell them. 'They have a right to know,' she'd said.

Problem was, Sylvia didn't know if they *wanted* to know.

It would be so much easier to leave things as they were, without dredging up the past. The relief on her parents' faces when she'd agreed to the adoption was obvious, and they'd encouraged her to simply move on and forget about the baby. Besides, they were always travelling around Australia in their Winnebago, and who knew if they'd be able to stop by in June.

But, Larissa was right. They *did* have a right to know. And, she'd promised Grace she'd ask them.

Hi Mum & Dad,

No. Too Casual.

Dear Mum and Dad,

Just letting you know that...

No. That sounded like she was letting them know she'd left her scarf at their place and could they bring it round next time they visited. Oh man, how was she supposed to tell them? *Dear Mum and Dad, Guess what? Remember that baby I gave up when I was sixteen, well — she's back! Surprise!*

Maybe she should tell them over the phone.

No, email would be better. Then she could say what she wanted to say without getting into an awkward conversation. Sylvia drew a slow breath and typed.

Dear Mum and Dad,

I have some news I need to share with you. The baby I had eighteen years ago has found me. Her name's Grace, she's staying here in Tarrin's Bay for a while. She's even got a job at Mrs May's. Anyway, she's a great girl, and a very gifted pianist. She's performing at the variety concert on the first Saturday in June, and I was wondering if you would like to come and meet her then?

Sylvia.

There. All done. Sylvia clicked 'send' and turned off the computer.

CHAPTER TWENTY-FOUR

'I'll see you two lovebirds later,' Lauren said as she turned and wandered off. Grace had met up with Jonah and his friends at the Sunday markets in Miracle Park, and at just after two o'clock, some of the stalls were packing up for the day and the crowd had diluted somewhat. Grace finished off her chocolate ice-cream cone, while Jonah licked the remains of his from his fingers.

They slid their arms around each other, glancing at the stalls as they walked past. Grace stopped at a jewellery stall, admiring the unique ring designs.

'All Australian made, love,' the woman behind the stall said. 'And for the rest of the afternoon, fifty percent off.'

'They're beautiful,' Grace said, her eyes not moving from the glimmering display of rings.

'I'll buy one for you,' Jonah offered. 'Which one do you like?'

Grace touched them with her fingers as though doing so would help her see them better, then picked up a ring that caught her eye. She slid it onto her finger, the plastic backing board still attached. It resembled a sunflower, its stem wrapped in a diagonal circle around her finger, and the flower spreading out on top.

'This one,' she said, and then pulled at the ring. It wouldn't budge. 'Uh-oh, I think it's stuck.' Grace looked helplessly at Jonah and the saleswoman. Jonah tried to pull it off, but couldn't.

'Here, I'll have to cut off the plastic binding connecting it to the backing board,' the woman said. 'But I'm afraid you *will* have to buy it after that.'

Jonah grinned. 'It's okay, we'll take it.'

With a quick snap the binding was released, and the ring could now be easily slid on and off. Jonah paid, and they walked off, Grace tilting her hand side to side to admire the ring.

'I can't believe it got stuck!' she said.

'I can,' Jonah replied.

'What? Do you mean I've got fat fingers?' Grace joked.

'Of course not,' he replied, cuddling her. 'I just meant that it's stuck on you, like I am.'

Grace sunk into his grasp. 'Oh, you're so corny! But I love it,' she whispered.

***

Sylvia opened the door just as Grace was walking up the steps of the front porch. Well, floating up, more like it.

'Isn't it a beautiful afternoon?' Grace said.

Sylvia poked her head outside. 'Um, yes. It certainly is.' She welcomed Grace inside and led her towards the piano. Sylvia had told Grace she could come over and practise every Sunday until the concert. 'Can I get you anything? A drink?'

'No I'm fine, I just had an ice-cream,' Grace replied, twirling a curl in circular motions around her finger.

'Nice ring,' Sylvia said.

'Oh, thanks. I just got it from the markets. Actually,' she said, leaning closer to Sylvia, 'My *boyfriend* bought it for me.'

Jonah.

'Boyfriend?' Sylvia didn't want to embarrass Grace by saying she'd seen her kiss Jonah yesterday.

'Yep. Jonah DeRae. He works at Café Lagoon, you know him?'

'I know Jonah and his parents quite well, actually,' Sylvia replied with a smile, glad Grace had brought up the topic of boyfriends and not her.

'Wow, this *is* a small town,' Grace said. 'Everyone seems to know everyone.'

Sylvia nodded. 'So, let's get started. Would you like to perform an existing composition, or one of your own?'

'My own composition. That way if I stuff up people might not notice.'

'Grace, you won't stuff up, you're going to be great.' Sylvia pulled a dining chair over while Grace took her place at the piano. 'Show me what you've got in mind.'

For the next hour and a half, Grace showed Sylvia her ideas, stopping here and there for Sylvia's feedback, and to make adjustments to the composition. Sylvia agreed that an upbeat piece would be best, as Grace's fingers were so quick on the keys it brought the room to life. Plus it would suit her bubbly personality.

'Here.' Sylvia dropped a key into Grace's hand as she went to leave. 'Why don't you come by on Wednesdays to practise when you're not at work.'

'You sure? You don't mind me being here when you're not around?'

Sylvia shook her head. 'Of course not. It'll be good for you to get a chance to practise on your own without me hovering over your shoulder. Make yourself at home, and feel free to help yourself to any food.' *Just don't move the fridge magnets or rearrange the perfectly organised bookshelves.* 'Anyway, the house is closed up during the day so it would be a good chance to let some fresh air circulate.' *And remember to wipe the benches down after eating.*

'In that case, I'll be sure to open all the windows when I come by,' Grace said.

And be sure to close them before you leave. Sylvia bit her lip to avoid giving orders. It was strange to know that someone would be in her house while she wasn't home, but Grace was her daughter. She could trust her. Okay, she barely knew her, but they shared the same DNA. Surely somewhere in there was the sense of order and superb organisational ability that took up about eighty percent of Sylvia's DNA. Then again, Grace also had her father's DNA, eighty percent of which probably contained his childlike sense of fun and superb sporting ability.

Grace attached the key to her key ring, which only had two other keys on it, and dropped it into her bag. She turned towards the front door, then hesitated a moment before turning back around. 'Have you heard anything from your parents yet, about the concert?'

'Not yet, but they're on the road a lot, so they might not have had a chance to read their emails,' Sylvia replied. It wasn't the complete truth. She *had* received a 'read receipt', an automatic notification that they had opened her email, but no reply as yet. Disappointing. She'd told them the granddaughter they've never met was here, the least they could do was acknowledge that. As always, her parents would do what they wanted to do when they wanted to do it, and she would just have to wait until they were ready to talk. 'I'll let you know when I hear from them,' she added.

Grace nodded, and looked at her watch. 'Oh boy, I better go, I have to be ready in half an hour!'

'Where are you off to?' Sylvia asked, forcing a casual tone as she leaned on the doorframe.

Lately, she'd become increasingly concerned with Grace's whereabouts, wanting to know more about where she went and what she did. She would have been a basket case of a mother, always needing to know the exact movements, times, and locations of her child's social life. Had she reared Grace herself, she probably would have supplied her with a pre-programmed electronic organiser with curfew times and reminder beeps, emergency contact numbers, and a first aid instruction manual.

'Jonah's taking me to see a band in Welston tonight. It's gonna rock!'

Grace told her the name of the band, and Sylvia nodded as though she knew who they were. 'Well, enjoy!' *And don't stay out too late.* 'I guess you'll have a quiet night tomorrow after work then.'

Grace shook her head. 'Uh-uh. I now do taekwondo on Monday nights, and Tuesday is Pump class at the gym, Wednesday I've enrolled in a dance class, and Thursday is Pilates,' she explained. 'I'm on a bit of a fitness binge!'

Yep. Eighty percent sporty DNA. 'I do the occasional Pump class and Pilates too, but mostly I swim,' Sylvia said.

'Yeah, I noticed the pool out back.'

'Feel free to use it when you come on Wednesdays,' Sylvia said. *Just dry yourself off in the laundry before coming back inside.*

'Thanks! Anyway, better go, thanks again for letting me use the piano.' Grace trotted down the front steps.

'You're welcome, have a good night!' Sylvia threw her voice to catch Grace who was jogging off down the driveway, one hand in the air waving at Sylvia, not looking where she was going. Before closing the door Sylvia saw Grace give a wave to

Nancy Dillinger too. The comings and goings at Sylvia's house lately were probably better than daytime television for Nancy.

Back in the living room, Sylvia switched on her computer and logged into her email program. Fourteen new emails greeted her: a general practitioners newsletter, medical research subscription, a few from a Mr Gentleman trying to sell a bottle of Viagra for her dwindling manhood, and one from her parents. Although tempted to open the email from her parents right away, Sylvia followed her 'email-checking protocol' and deleted the spam first, filed the newsletters away to read later, and finally clicked open on the email with the subject: Re: I have some news.

CHAPTER TWENTY-FIVE

A month and a half since his run-in with Sylvia about his wife's death, Mark had only sorted through one box of Cindy's belongings. There were still eight more to go, and if the first was anything to go by, it wasn't going to be an easy task. Tentatively, he'd cut the tape that secured the box together and peered inside. It was filled with an assortment of mismatched items, probably from one of the drawers of her bedside table. Three or four paperbacks, notepads, pens, candles, hair bands, even tissues. When he was preparing to move house, Mark had told his brother to put everything belonging to Cindy in boxes, and not to throw anything out.

He could almost smell his wife's scent, feel the remnants of her touch as he ran his fingers over the items in the box. He took the cap off her favourite vanilla lip balm, and touched it to his lips for a moment, knowing it last touched hers. The welcoming scent and moist sensation sent shivers down the length of his spine, just like when he'd first kissed Cindy.

In the box he'd also found notes she'd written to herself: Don't forget to organise a quote for the new curtains; Remember to bring fitness gear to park tomorrow for outdoor session; Book appointment with hairdresser. Such trivial things, yet these were all aspects of her life. Cindy liked to make sure she kept on top of things. She'd often joked that if it wasn't written on a list somewhere it wouldn't get done, so Mark had started adding his own notes to her lists: Cook gourmet three-course dinner for darling husband; Give wonderful husband a luxurious massage; Breakfast in bed for Mark on Sunday. Now he wished he'd written: Go to doctor for a check-up; Tell husband you're really not well enough to be left at home.

Before a well of grief and regret threatened to drown his heart, he'd scrunched up the notes and tossed them in the bin. Waiting for his heart rate to normalise, he did the same with the lip balm, hair bands, and half burned candles. He tried scribbling with the pens. They still worked so he decided to keep them. The books he would take to the second hand store, along with some little trinkets.

He'd been about to toss what looked like an empty envelope into the bin, when he'd opened it just to make sure. Inside were two ticket stubs from the movie theatre when they'd had their first date. Mark couldn't believe she'd kept them. It brought a sliver of a tear to his eye, and he couldn't bring himself to throw them out. He retrieved a shoebox from his wardrobe and placed the ticket stubs inside. Anything else he came across that he couldn't bear to part with he could put in there and decide what to do with later.

Mark sat silently, heavily, the remaining boxes a weight in his mind. One was enough for now; he couldn't bear opening another. Afflicted with the sudden urge to move, he walked out of the tiny spare room, grabbed his house keys from the kitchen bench, went outside and flung the front door closed behind him.

Mark lifted his leg over his bike and cycled down the long hilly road towards town. Crisp autumn air nipped his cheeks and woke him from his reminiscing, and he felt strangely euphoric. The combination of the air on his face, the rapid intermittent pedalling pushing blood through his muscles, and the sensation of moving forward made him feel alive. He wasn't wearing a helmet, but didn't feel at all concerned with the speed he was travelling. In this moment, in his mind, he was invincible. Just like when he was a kid and he'd ride his bike down the steep hill around the corner from his house. Death Hill, the neighbourhood kids had called it. If you could descend it at full speed without stacking you were admitted into the Invincible Club. Since the inaugural 'death ride', only four kids had been inaugurated into the club by spitting onto the telegraph pole at the bottom of the hill and carving their name into it. Mark became the fifth. Two more followed, until someone stacked it badly and broke their leg and collarbone, and neighbours complained about the dangers to the local council. Eventually, a 'no cycling downhill' sign was erected, and the seven members of the Invincible Club became neighbourhood legends.

Mark had gone back to his hometown a few years ago and found his name still existed on the telegraph pole. He'd imagined taking his future son to Death Hill and showing him the carving, telling him stories about his own childhood adventures.

The son he was supposed to have with Cindy.

The son who would never exist.

He and Cindy had only just agreed to start trying for a baby a week before she died, but that dream died along with her. Pain ripped at Mark's chest at the injustice that Cindy never got to experience motherhood, something she'd always wanted, but 'only when the time was right'. How cruel that when the time finally *was* right, the opportunity was taken from her.

And him.

If she hadn't died, they might have been parents by now,

perhaps with a six-month-old baby. Mark would have been a father. Something he'd always wanted to be. Now, he was just a widower, who almost two years after his wife's death had only just started going through her things, and who still kept her photos in every room of the house. How was he supposed to move on when everything around him reminded him of her?

Forced to slow to a stop by the inconvenient stop sign at the next intersection, Mark shook the memories and unfulfilled dreams from his mind. Up ahead were two white figures, and for a moment he thought he was hallucinating, the bizarre thought that they were ghosts flashing briefly across his mind. He rode past them, and one waved. It was Grace Forrester. Trying to keep his balance he returned a quick wave to her, and continued pedalling. She was with a young man who was wearing a black belt, Grace herself in a white belt, and obviously wearing a martial arts uniform. *Ghosts!* Was he going mad?

Shaking that thought from his mind too, Mark remembered that Grace had cancelled her follow-up appointment last week. *Oh well, she must be doing alright then. Or maybe she was too busy.* He hoped she'd come back, though, there were other things he wanted to discuss with her. He decided if he hadn't heard from her within the next month he'd call to see how she was going and encourage another consultation. Mark didn't want another tragedy on his conscience.

'I've seen that guy around, who is he?' Jonah asked, after Grace waved to Mark as he cycled past.

'Mark Bastian. He's the naturopath who works with Sylvia.'

'Oh, right.'

'I should have asked him to give me something to settle my

nerves for today!' Grace fiddled with her uniform as they walked around the corner towards the high school hall.

'I can give you something,' Jonah said, drawing her in and kissing her lips. 'Anyway, you'll be fine. I don't know anyone who ever failed their first taekwondo grading. In another couple of hours you'll be an official yellow belt!'

Grace smiled. 'It would be good to bring some colour to this uniform, I feel like a ghost!'

Jonah wiggled his fingers in the air and sang, 'Doo-doo-doo-doo, Doo-doo-doo-doo,' in a spooky *Twilight Zone* voice, before wrapping an arm around her waist.

'You're crazy.' Grace laughed.

'That's what happens when people get haunted by ghosts, they go craazeee!'

Grace gave him a friendly slap across the chest, and within minutes the light-hearted mood Jonah had managed to create dissipated as they arrived at the check-in desk for the grading. Grace got her name ticked off, and Jonah led her to where she had to wait while he went to join the other black belts who were helping out for the day. She exchanged nervous glances with a few other white belts, and looked over at the blue and red belts, wondering if she'd ever get to their level, let alone black belt level.

Sitting around waiting was making her sleepy, so she wiggled her legs and took a few sips of water, and soon the official proceedings began. After a ten minute warm-up, the white belts were first to take their position and perform the stances, while a crowd of about thirty or forty people in the audience watched in silence — except for a few young children who chattered and giggled, parents shushing them.

Next, Grace performed the blocking techniques, followed by basic kicks and punches. Each movement had to be accompanied by an enthusiastic *gee yup*, or loud yell, a way of raising your energy and intimidating your opponent. At the first class she attended she'd felt awkward and embarrassed to yell, but once she saw other people doing it she got into it, proudly *gee yupping* with the best of them! Apparently, you lost points if you didn't *gee yup* with enough enthusiasm. So Grace thought she might as well perfect that aspect of the martial art in case she needed it to make up for lack of skill in any other area.

Before too long that portion of the grading was over, and Grace took her seat again, waiting and watching as each belt level performed their required techniques. It was great to watch some of the more advanced kick combinations from the red belts. Grace had tried a couple of them in the privacy of her caravan; but, the lack of room combined with lack of training resulted in her knocking over the plastic bowls and cutlery on her tiny kitchenette bench, and falling onto the bed causing it to fold backwards into its alter ego – the makeshift couch.

When all the techniques had been assessed, Grace and the other white belts rose from their seats for the sparring component of the grading. She was paired up with a girl a few years younger, but the same height as her. A female black belt in her twenties she'd seen at some of the classes stood near them, acting as a referee, and Jonah stood near one of the other pairs. Master Jin gave the instructions and they began sparring. Grace and her opponent kicked and punched while moving around, making sure not to contact each other. It looked more like playing than fighting and, with the girl's high-pitched *gee yupping* that sounded like a crow on helium, Grace tried hard not to laugh.

When all the belt levels had performed their spar, the students went through some cool-down exercises then sat on the floor while Master Jin talked about their results. He announced that everyone had passed, and even though Grace knew she had, she wondered what he would say if she hadn't. 'Everyone has passed, except for YOU, Grace Forrester!' and everyone would look at her and laugh until she ran from the room crying. Silly, but sometimes her mind thought up worst-case scenarios so that anything else would feel like a bonus.

They gathered everyone for a group photo and Grace managed to get a stranger from the audience to take a photo using her phone camera. If they ran off with her phone, she could always run up and attack them with a front kick, side kick, and double punch at yellow belt level. At least her *gee yup* might be black belt standard, and if anything, it might simply shock them into surrender. Unfortunately, her new skills weren't needed as she got her phone back safely.

'See, I told you you'd be a yellow belt by this afternoon,' Jonah said as he met her outside the school with a high five. 'Congratulations.'

'Thanks. Not as significant as a black belt though,' Grace replied.

'Hey, all black belts were yellow belts at one stage. It's all part of the journey.'

Jonah's other friends came over to chat to Grace for a while and when they finished, Grace swung around to see where Jonah was. He was deep in conversation with Lauren, and her hand was on his arm, leaning in close as though telling him something private. What was going on? An uncomfortable twinge pulled at Grace's stomach. Lauren was her friend, wasn't she? Did she have feelings for Jonah?

Lauren's hand dropped and she stepped back when she saw Grace glancing at her and Jonah, then she walked over to her. 'Well done Grace, you put up a good fight in the sparring.' Lauren held up her hand for a high five.

Grace awkwardly reciprocated. 'Thanks, Lauren.'

'I was just saying to Jonah we should all go get some food and hang out, you wanna come?'

She had to touch him *and* lean in close to suggest they all go and hang out? It looked more personal than that, and Jonah was now shifting awkwardly from one foot to the other.

'Um... to be honest, I'm totally wiped,' Grace explained. 'I think I'll go and crash for a while.' She'd rather be with Jonah, and rather Lauren wasn't with him alone, but a heavy fatigue was casting its shadow over her and she really needed to lie down. She'd been overdoing things lately — taekwondo, gym classes, cycling, swimming, work, and her busy new social life.

'You sure?' Jonah asked, and Grace nodded. 'How about we meet up for dinner then?'

'Sounds good. I'll call you later?' Grace asked.

Jonah nodded. 'I can walk you home if you like.' He gestured towards the road that led to the caravan park.

'No need, you guys go and hang out, I'll catch up with you later.' Grace kissed Jonah and he squeezed her tight. It felt good, but there was hesitancy in his touch, and she wondered what Lauren had said to him to shake his usual buoyancy.

As Grace walked up the road, she turned to look at the others who were walking in the opposite direction. Lauren was talking to Jonah again, and he was shaking his head. There must be something going on they weren't letting her in on. But how could she bring it up without sounding like she was being possessive? It could be nothing. After all, they had known each other since they were kids. Surely if they liked each other something would have happened by now.

By the time Grace got back to the caravan she didn't have the energy to think about it anymore. She took off her belt and pulled open the fold-out bed, flopping onto it without bothering to get out of her uniform. Minutes later she was fast asleep.

CHAPTER TWENTY-SIX

It had taken Sylvia's parents long enough to reply to her email about Grace, so it didn't surprise her that almost a month had passed before they called her on the phone. The email, written by her mum, said they were planning on being on the road around the time of the variety concert, but would give her a call down the track and let her know for sure. Then she'd written: *I thought this day might come. Your father and I agree that you should be careful not to get too close, we don't want to see you hurt or disappointed.*

So when Sylvia saw her mother's number on the caller ID, she took a breath and braced herself for 'the conversation' that had been eighteen years in the making.

'Hi, Mum,' Sylvia said light-heartedly.

'Hi, sweetheart, how are you?' her mother responded, and without waiting for a reply, she continued. 'Your father and I had a great time in Western Australia, such a big place so we'll probably go back for another trip again sometime.'

'That's good. Where are you off to in June?'

'June? Oh yes, South Australia. We're going on a winter getaway for seniors for two weeks, including a winery tour. We were planning on going during the first two weeks of June, but managed to adjust our booking for the second half of that month.'

Making them available for the variety concert. 'So, does that mean you'll...' Sylvia began.

'We'll be coming to watch the concert, and... meet Grace.'

Finally, a definite answer. 'Thanks, Mum, Grace will be happy to hear that,' Sylvia said. 'And wait till you hear her play, she's phenomenal.'

'Well, it does run in the family. Speaking of which, I'll have to give the old piano keys a workout when we visit.'

'Of course. Although they've been getting a workout with Grace's practising,' Sylvia replied.

'She's been practising on my old piano?'

'Yes, surely that's okay?'

'Yes, yes, that's fine. It's just strange, that's all. So, you've been spending a fair bit of time together?'

'A fair bit. Work takes up much of the weekdays, of course, but on weekends and some evenings we often get together.' Sylvia paused for a moment. 'She's a great girl, Mum.' Somehow a smidgen of moisture had worked its way out of Sylvia's eyes. Why was she feeling so emotional? She still hardly knew Grace, but couldn't help feeling a sense of pride at how she turned out. Obviously, Grace's adoptive parents had done all the work. But Sylvia wondered, hoped, that the little she contributed, if only genes and a healthy gestational environment, had some impact on the young woman Grace had become.

'Have you told anyone in town... about her?' Sylvia's mother asked tentatively.

'Only Larissa. People must have seen me with her, but no one's asked about the connection. Anyway, it was a long time ago; maybe it doesn't matter so much if people find out.'

Sylvia walked across the living room as she spoke, and waited for a response. 'Mum?'

'I'm here,' she replied. 'Your father and I think it's best if you keep it on a need-to-know basis. Yes, it was a long time ago, but many of your father's old colleagues still live in Tarrin's Bay and, as you know, we see them whenever we visit. The knowledge of an illegitimate granddaughter could still affect his reputation, not to mention yours. You're a pillar in the community to be looked up to, and—'

'Mum, many young unwed women have become pregnant,' Sylvia interjected. 'These things happen, and we shouldn't — *I shouldn't* — have to feel ashamed about it.'

'I'm not saying you should be ashamed, I'm just saying that some things are best left in the past. Why risk affecting your respectable status in the community by declaring you had a baby when you were only sixteen? You were so young, Sylvia, so young...'

Sylvia knew her mother would be shaking her head from side to side right now, remembering the disappointment of her daughter's youth and innocence being cut short. 'And yet despite my young age, I managed to get on with my life and build a successful career helping others. Surely that's something to be looked up to?' Sylvia was pacing up and down the room now.

'Of course it is, and we're very proud of you. We just... don't want you making a mistake by getting too close to this girl. She could up and leave at any time, probably will, and then how will you feel?'

'*This* girl? She's my daughter, Mum. And it just so happens that she lost her adoptive mother last year. I want to be there for her, to be a part of her life.' Sylvia thought back to the Wishing Festival, and smiled at the amazing events that had taken place since then. 'I wished I could meet Grace, and be given a second chance at being a mother. Now that I have the opportunity I'm not going to let it slide.' Warmth rushed to Sylvia's face and her bottom lip trembled. 'I won't let her go *again.*'

Although Sylvia knew she could never replace the mother who had raised Grace from birth, she wanted nothing more than to prove to Grace, and herself, that she was worthy of being a mother. That given the chance, she could rise up and take on the role with commitment and love, with the same passion she'd infused into her medical career. Her wish to be given a second chance was unfolding, and there was no turning back. Grace was in her life now. And not only did Sylvia want a second chance with Grace, but she also hoped for, *wished* for, another chance to become a mother. Properly this time. Meet the right man, have a baby, and this time, bring her baby home.

CHAPTER TWENTY-SEVEN

'Thirty-five today, huh? You've finally caught up with me,' Larissa said to Sylvia as they sat down to lunch at Café Lagoon.

'Yep, definitely getting old now!' Sylvia replied, smiling on the outside but shrieking on the inside, knowing all too well that once a woman gets to the age of thirty-five her fertility rapidly declines. She'd read the research and seen it all too often with patients. Plus the risk of miscarriage or conceiving a baby with genetic anomalies was higher after this age. That was the least of her worries right now though. How would she even be able to *have* another baby if she hadn't found the right man yet? She'd thought Richard might be it, but look how that turned out. Then Mark, but he was still grieving for his dead wife. Maybe she needed to get out of town, move to a place with a higher population of single men who were ready for commitment. If such a place existed. Nah, she was settled and happy in Tarrin's Bay, and she wouldn't dare leave her patients behind. 'Thanks for my present, Riss, I definitely need a "three-hour stress-busting forget-all-your-worries pamper treatment"!' Sylvia waved the voucher Larissa had given her in the air. This time she'd have to remember to keep visions of shaving cream far from her mind.

After eating lunch and splurging on her favourite hummingbird cake (it *was* her birthday), Sylvia slid her arms into her cashmere cardigan and secured the single button at the front, as a breeze left goose bumps on her arms. 'It's getting cooler, I might need to put the heater on at home in the mornings.'

'I already have. As soon as April arrives it goes on. Luke hates it; he sleeps in boxers all year long, never feels the cold,' Larissa said.

'So I'm guessing you hog all the blankets at night, yes?'

'Sure do. Luke just folds his half over onto me so I get double layers.' Larissa grinned. 'Although he takes up so much room in the bed I'm thinking we should switch to a king-size bed. Half the time I end up teetering on the edge of the mattress!'

The good thing about being single, Sylvia thought, was that you could sleep in the middle of the bed, have as many or as few blankets as you needed, and not get woken up by your partner moving, or worse, snoring. But, there was nothing like having someone to cuddle up with, and someone to talk to about your day.

Sylvia turned her wrist. 'Geez, that's gone fast. Time to get back to work.' Sylvia stood and leaned forward, wrapping her arms around Larissa. 'Thanks for my birthday lunch. And my voucher. *And* these,' Sylvia said, lifting the bunch of colourful gerberas.

'My pleasure, Hun. I hope you get an early mark from work,' Larissa said.

'Mark what?'

'An early mark, you know — go home early?' Larissa said slowly.

'Oh, yeah.' Sylvia's face flushed.

'Still got Mark on the mind, huh?'

'No, not really, I just didn't catch what you said at first.' Sylvia brushed a wisp of hair from her face. 'Anyway, things are okay. He's even coming out to dinner tonight with everyone else from work.'

'That's an improvement. Luke hasn't spoken to him in a while. Whenever he calls, Mark says he's on his way out, or just getting in the door, or something like that.'

'Yeah, he's been pretty quiet and distant, but seems better this past week. He even brought a fruit platter into work the other day to share. Although, he did say he simply needed to use up his supply of fruit at home before it went off.'

'Men. Always practical,' Larissa said.

'Not just men. I'm practical too,' Sylvia said.

'You're the Queen of Practical.'

'I know.' Sylvia smiled, and just then Grace walked slowly towards the café.

'Oh, hi, Sylvia,' Grace said.

'Hi, how are you? On your lunchbreak too?'

'Yeah, but I'm just grabbing some takeaway and going back to the caravan. Not feeling the best today, but I'll be right,' Grace replied.

She did look pale. 'You sure? I can take you to the clinic with me if you like and check you over.'

'No, no. I'll be fine. It's just... *women's* problems, if you know what I mean.' Grace made quotation marks with her fingers as she spoke.

'Oh, right then. Well, call me if you need anything, okay?'

'Okay.'

Sylvia rubbed a concerned hand up and down Grace's arm, then realised Larissa was frozen still, her mouth gaping. 'Oh, Larissa, this is Grace. Grace, this is my friend, Larissa.'

Larissa enveloped Grace's right hand with both of hers. 'It's so lovely to meet you. Wow, after all this time,' Larissa said, her eyes wandering over Grace's features, just as Sylvia's had when she first met Grace outside the clinic back in January.

'So... you know who I am?' Grace asked.

Larissa nodded. 'Sylvia and I have been friends since school, no secrets between us at all.'

'Well, it's nice to meet you too.' Grace smiled, then glanced at the flowers and greeting card Sylvia was holding. 'Is it your birthday, Sylvia?'

Sylvia nodded.

'I wish I'd known; I would have bought you a present!' Grace leaned in to smell the flowers.

Sylvia flicked her hand forward in the air. 'Don't worry about that, no need to celebrate my advancing age.'

'Why not? Every birthday you reach is a gift, you *should* celebrate.'

For someone with hardly any life experience she was right. How could her own daughter be smarter than her? 'That's true Grace. Well, I *am* celebrating tonight at Bayside with my work colleagues,' Sylvia reassured. 'You're welcome to come along, if you like?'

Grace shifted on her feet. 'Thanks, but I'll probably just take it easy and get an early night. Besides, I'd be out of place with your colleagues; you should just celebrate with them,' Grace replied.

'I guess you should rest, but the offer still stands if you change your mind, okay?'

'Okay, thanks.' Grace motioned towards the counter of the café. 'Well, I better go get some lunch and head back home.'

'Look after yourself, Grace, and don't hesitate to call me if you need anything,' Sylvia said.

Grace smiled and walked into the café, Jonah waving to her

from the kitchen, his hands busily picking up plates of food. He gave Grace a quick peck on the cheek as he walked past, and she whispered something in his ear. He gave her another brief kiss and pouted as he walked away to serve customers. Young love; so cute. Sylvia remembered her fleeting relationship with Grace's father. For a short amount of time, he was her world, but then everything changed.

Grace walked out of Café Lagoon with a chicken and salad wrap, munching on it as she walked. She couldn't help but rub her belly with her free hand, the cramps getting a bit worse. But walking seemed to ease them somewhat, even though she just wanted to lie down. She had some period pain tablets at the caravan, so she'd take them as soon as got back.

It was a shame she was feeling this way now, as she'd felt fairly good this morning, and was looking forward to the variety concert in a couple of months time. When Sylvia called last week to tell her that her grandparents were coming, excitement welled-up inside. And nerves. But as Sylvia had been telling her, she need only focus on the piano and remember to breathe, and she would be fine. Sylvia likened it to performing a medical procedure. If you worried about everything else going on around you, and what people were thinking, you'd mess up. But if you put all your attention calmly on the task at hand, and took it one step at a time, and in Grace's case, one key at a time, then you wouldn't fail. Grace wasn't feeling as worried about performing now.

And no longer was she worried about Lauren and Jonah either. When she'd woken from her nap after the grading last weekend and met up with Jonah for dinner, she'd asked him straight out whether there'd been any history between him and

Lauren, or whether he thought she had feelings for him. Jonah had seemed genuinely shocked, and reassured her that there wasn't any history between them, that Lauren was like a sister to him, and that she had in fact fallen head over heels for Jonah's cousin. It didn't completely explain their secretive exchange after the grading, but after Grace saw Lauren canoodling with an older guy in the park on the way to work this morning, she no longer felt concerned that Lauren was after her man. In fact, she felt kind of silly for thinking it, and bringing it up with Jonah. Thankfully, she hadn't scared him off, if anything, he was showering her with more attention than before. Which Grace didn't mind in the least.

When she arrived at the caravan, Grace swallowed the last two tablets from the packet of pain relievers with a gulp of water, and took to the bed like a lost bear cub reuniting with its mother. She woke a couple of hours later feeling much better, ducked out to the bathrooms, then went back to bed, deciding to read for a while and keep resting in order to be well for work tomorrow.

Hours passed, and darkness eased its way inside the caravan. Grace switched on the light above the bed, engrossed in a new release she'd picked up from work, although her eyes were straining a little. After a while she could no longer focus on reading, as a familiar ache resumed its hold on her stomach and lower back. Damn hormones! The tablets had given her relief, but they must be wearing off. She reached for the packet of pain relievers then remembered she'd used up the last of them. Crap, she'd have to walk to town and get more. Or maybe she could call Sylvia and ask her to bring some around? No, it was her birthday and she'd be enjoying dinner with her colleagues. She couldn't ask Jonah, that would be way too embarrassing. Lauren? Nah, she might as well go and get some now in case the pain got so bad that she couldn't.

Grace walked over to the bathrooms first, tidied up her hair a little, then walked in the direction of the town. Grumbles accompanied the growing cramps in her belly, and she realised she hadn't eaten since lunch. She'd have to pick something up in town, or eat the remaining half of the chicken wrap she'd failed to finish earlier. It was too late to join Sylvia, who'd probably be halfway through dinner by now, and Grace wasn't up for a social gathering anyway.

She walked discreetly past Bayside, peering in briefly through the gap between the top and bottom curtains to see Sylvia with a glass of wine in her hand, talking and laughing with five other people, including Mark Bastian. Hopefully they wouldn't notice her. It was now seven-thirty, and luckily the pharmacy stayed open till eight. Grace bought a packet of pain relievers and a bottle of juice, and took two tablets as soon as she walked back outside.

Her legs weak, it felt strangely like she was trying to walk through water. And a wave was coming in from the side, causing her to wobble a little. The footpath appeared distorted in shape, and she couldn't quite sense her feet on the ground. Grace grasped hold of a telegraph pole as an uncomfortable flutter inside her chest took her breath away. And then another. She'd had a few of these heart palpitations recently, but they were over before they began really, so she'd dismissed them. But now, they kept coming. It felt like her heart was made of bubbles, and at any moment they'd all burst, releasing blood throughout her chest and paralysing her with weakness inside a pit of darkness.

Okay, breathe Grace. Breathe. In and out. She looked for a bench to sit on but the nearest was several metres away. She wanted to sink to the ground but kept hold of the pole, urging her heart to beat normally. Maybe it was low blood sugar. She wolfed down some juice, but didn't feel any better. Tears of fear formed in her eyes, and Grace's first thought was that she wanted her mum, but she was gone. And her dad was far away. Then in her mind she saw Sylvia, felt her gentle hand on her arm, and without thinking she mustered all her energy and hauled herself over to Bayside and leaned heavily against the window, her chest rising sharply with shallow breaths. Grace grasped hold of the door, but couldn't find the strength to open it, nor could she bang on the window. Her eyes strained to see as her surroundings became darker, and they urged Sylvia's eyes to look this way. Why had no one noticed her yet? *Please see me, Sylvia, I need help!*

CHAPTER TWENTY-EIGHT

'I don't think I can fit in dessert now,' Sylvia said, as she leaned back in the chair at the dinner table and lifted her glass to her lips. She had no problem fitting in more wine.

'You have to, it's your birthday!' Joyce said. 'And the waiter needs something to put a birthday candle on,' she added.

Mark nodded in agreement. 'You know you're getting old when you only get one birthday candle. It's too much hassle to count out the correct amount,' he said with a charming smirk. 'Either that or there's not enough room to fit them all on,' he added. Everyone erupted in laughter and Sylvia kicked him under the table. He simply grinned, then winked at her. 'Just teasing,' he said. 'You look great for someone your age, Sylvia.' She kicked him again.

They say that one of the best signs that someone is recovering well from illness is the return of their sense of humour. Sylvia wondered if the same could be said for grief. When she'd first met Mark, his humorous charm had attracted her, but after their discussion about his wife's death, he'd lost that charm. He'd become quiet and serious. Lately though, she'd begun to see a subtle re-emergence of his sense of humour. Tonight, it was obviously back in full force.

'Look, Sylvia, there's lemon meringue pie.' Joyce held the menu in front of Sylvia. 'And coconut panna cotta with raspberry coulis and almond biscotti. Or what about Death by Chocolate?'

Maybe she *could* fit in some chocolate. 'That sounds like a good way to go,' Sylvia replied. 'I mean, in terms of dessert choice, not death,' she added with a chuckle, and hoped the mention of death wouldn't upset Mark. She'd tried to keep their few discussions at work light-hearted, but that was difficult considering her profession. The subject of death was bound to come up occasionally. Thankfully, Mark didn't seem rattled in the slightest, and in fact continued to mock her 'old age' by suggesting she tuck her napkin into her shirt collar and ask for her dessert to be pureed for ease of consuming.

'Is the naturopath allowed any dessert?' Sylvia asked Mark.

'Of course. All things in moderation,' he replied. 'Tell you what, I'll splurge on Death by Chocolate too.' Mark placed his menu down on the table and signalled a waiter.

As the waiter made his way towards the table, Sylvia noticed Grace outside the restaurant. Strange, she thought. It's a bit late to change her mind about joining them for dinner. Well, she could always just have dessert; there was room to pull up another chair. Sylvia was about to wave at Grace to come inside when a sense of dread filled her stomach. Grace looked different. Ghostly, in fact. And she was clinging to the window. A strange facial expression crossed Grace's face as their eyes connected. Fear mixed with relief, Sylvia recognised. And within moments of their gaze locking on each other, Grace's eyes rolled back and she slid down the window like a raindrop losing its grip on the glass.

The lower curtain on the restaurant's front window

obscured Sylvia's view. Her chair skidded loudly as she pushed it back and ran outside.

'Grace!' She knelt down and patted her cheek, not unlike the first time they'd met when Grace had fainted. Back then, she'd come around quickly. This time, Sylvia could tell there was something wrong. She'd had a feeling earlier today when she'd seen Grace at lunch; now she wished she'd insisted on checking her out. 'Grace, can you hear me?' Sylvia urged. She went to put two fingers on the side of Grace's neck when she found that Mark had beaten her to it. He was on the other side of Grace, and kept still as he felt for her pulse.

'Pulse is weak and thready, but fast,' he said calmly.

Just then Grace's lips moved, and she opened her eyes and tried to get up. After feeling like her heart was frozen in time, Sylvia's heart resumed beating as relief flooded her chest. 'It's okay, Grace, I'm here. Stay put for a moment and tell me what happened.' She noticed a slight tremor in Grace's hands as she nestled Grace's head in her lap.

'I'm sorry, I... felt so weak, and...' Grace mumbled. 'Your birthday... sorry, it's just...'

'It's okay, take a deep breath, Grace. Just tell me how you feel.' Sylvia tucked Grace's hair behind her ears, and caressed her cheek. Mark was holding Grace's hand, and was now checking the pulse on her wrist.

'I was feeling really weak, and... and... then my heart kept going funny, like it was missing beats,' Grace explained breathlessly, while tears glossed her eyes. 'I felt like, like I was going to die.' Grace inhaled short sharp breaths, and sobbed.

Sylvia kissed her on the forehead. 'It's going to be okay.' Then she looked at Mark who said what she was thinking.

'Let's get her to hospital, I'll drive. It'll be quicker than waiting for an ambulance.'

Sylvia nodded.

'No, no hospital. I'm... okay,' Grace protested, clambering to get up, before clasping her chest and looking like she was struggling to get air into her lungs.

'No you're not,' Mark said, tossing his car keys into Sylvia's hands and sliding his arms underneath Grace to lift her up. 'Let's get you some help hey, so you'll feel better.'

Sylvia mouthed 'sorry' to Joyce and the others who were standing next to several shocked onlookers from the restaurant.

'It's okay, go,' Joyce mouthed back, tossing Sylvia's handbag towards her.

Mark walked quickly over to his car parked on the side of the street, and Sylvia clicked the unlock button on the key ring and opened the back door. 'Sylvia, in the boot there's a BP monitor in the first aid kit, can you grab it?' Mark said as he helped Grace into the car.

Sylvia lifted the huge bag from the boot. Man, this guy was prepared for anything. It contained even more emergency supplies than *her* kit. She closed the boot, and tossed the keys over the top of the car to Mark as he opened the driver's side door. Sylvia slid into the back of the car next to Grace, and rested Grace's head on her lap as she unzipped the blood pressure monitor.

Grace startled every few seconds, mumbling, 'My heart, my heart... keeps palpitating,' while Sylvia inflated the cuff.

'What's her BP?' Mark asked, as he drove.

'Ninety over sixty, pulse one-twenty-five.'

'What's happening?' Grace looked upwards at Sylvia.

For a moment Grace appeared to be like a small child, and an ache stabbed at Sylvia's heart, as though sympathetically feeling her daughter's distress. 'It's okay, it isn't too bad. I'll check it again in a few minutes, and the doctors at the hospital will find out what's going on. You just focus on breathing deeply and staying calm, okay?' Sylvia caressed Grace's cheek.

Hopefully the emergency department wasn't too busy tonight. But Grace would get seen to right away, as any heart complaints were considered a high priority. Unless, of course, an ambulance wheeled in an unconscious patient bleeding to death from stab wounds. Grace would need to have blood taken and an ECG. Sylvia found her mind going through the tests she'd order if she was the doctor on duty.

As hoped, Grace was taken right through, but after the nurse got the details on what happened, she asked if Sylvia and Mark could wait outside the curtain while they got her hooked up to electrodes and performed tests. After a while, Sylvia could hear the doctor asking Grace some questions, but couldn't make out what they were saying. Should she go in? No, surely Grace would ask the nurse to get her if she wanted Sylvia there. Mark kept looking like he was about to say something, but didn't. He simply held onto the small of Sylvia's back in a gesture of support. He still didn't know Grace was her daughter. Or did he? Anyway, it didn't matter. Sylvia just wanted to know what was wrong with Grace and that she'd be okay. Grace had mentioned her mother's death; maybe there was a genetic heart complaint? But then she remembered that *she* was Grace's biological mother, and Grace's father was fit as a fiddle, so that possibility was impossible.

The doctor came out and said the ECG was normal, and that it was likely she was experiencing ectopic beats. He went on to explain what that meant until Sylvia interrupted and told him she was a doctor too. His choice of words immediately changed from layman's terms to medical terminology, then with his work completed for now, he walked away and disappeared inside another curtain.

Every now and again the nurse would emerge from the curtain, walk away for a while, and come back again. 'She's stable, just resting now. I'll let you know when we know what's going on,' the nurse said.

Sylvia wanted to go in, but she didn't want to disturb Grace if she was resting. Mark had suggested he grab them a coffee, but Sylvia couldn't drink or eat anything right now. Not until the blood results came back. So they simply sat in the small corner where a few chairs were placed, and waited in silence. Three other people soon joined them, looking similarly anxious.

After more waiting, the doctor from before slipped back inside Grace's curtain, along with the nurse. Sylvia perched on the edge of the chair. He emerged soon after and went straight over to another patient who was thrashing about in distress on the bed. Moments later, the nurse came out and Sylvia walked over to meet her.

'You're Grace's mother, right?' the nurse asked.

Sylvia glanced for a moment at Mark who was standing back a little, but still close enough to hear. 'Yes, I am,' she replied.

'Grace will be okay, but we'll keep her in overnight for monitoring, and I've put her on a drip. She's anaemic, so she'll need iron replacement for a while, and her calcium and potassium levels are a little low. With all of that combined it may have affected her blood flow, and the way her heart was beating. Panic could have contributed somewhat too, probably worried that the cancer had come back, poor girl. But don't worry, there's no sign of that in the blood. Her white cells and platelets are normal.'

A jolt of shock rooted Sylvia's feet to the floor. 'Cancer?'

'The leukaemia. But as I said, no evidence that it's returned, which is good news,' the nurse explained.

'She had *leukaemia*?' Sylvia asked, her forehead aching from the furrowing of her brows.

The nurse looked confused. 'Surely you knew?'

Sylvia shook her head. 'I *am* her mother, but we only met three months ago. I gave her up for adoption after she was born.' As the words stung her throat with guilt, she barely registered Mark's touch as his hand returned to the small of her back.

The nurse brought a hand to her mouth. 'Oh no, I'm so sorry. I just assumed... oh, I'd better contact her adoptive parents, do you have their details?'

Sylvia didn't answer. She went straight towards Grace's bed and pulled the curtain aside.

CHAPTER TWENTY-NINE

'Why didn't you tell me?' Sylvia rushed to Grace's side and sat on the bed, grasping her daughter's hand gently, careful not to disrupt the sticky piece of tape securing the IV line.

'The nurse told you? About the cancer?'

Sylvia nodded.

'I didn't want you to find out.' Grace tilted her head away from Sylvia, the tears from earlier resurfacing. Sylvia wiped them away with her thumb. 'I didn't want you to think...'

'Think what?'

'That I only wanted to find you in case... in case I needed a bone marrow transplant.' Grace's voice shook.

'Oh, Grace, I wouldn't have thought that! And even if you *were* looking for me for that purpose, I wouldn't have hesitated to be tested. *Or* go through the procedure if I was found to be a match.' Sylvia tucked some wayward curls behind Grace's ear.

'I wouldn't expect you to though, I mean it's such a big ask.'

'Not as big as what you went through.'

'Anyway, they said it's just anaemia, and apart from a couple of other things everything else is normal. So it doesn't look like I'll be needing bone marrow anytime soon,' Grace said, attempting a smile.

'How long have you been in remission?' Sylvia asked.

'Two years.'

'What type of leukaemia was it?'

'AML. Acute myeloid leukaemia,' Grace replied.

A thousand thoughts ran through Sylvia's mind, and she wanted to know all the details. How old Grace was when it appeared, what subtype it was, the treatment protocol used, the prognosis and chance of recurrence, how she coped with the chemotherapy. But she was here as Grace's mother, not her doctor.

As if hearing her thoughts, Grace added, 'I was diagnosed when I was thirteen. My teenage years were just beginning when the cancer appeared. It all happened so quickly. I started feeling tired all the time, I'd bruise at the slightest bump, and I could never seem to shake off a minor cold.'

Sylvia nodded as she listened to Grace relay how she was diagnosed and began treatment right away. It broke Sylvia's heart to imagine her baby girl going through the debilitating treatment, and she had to bite back a sense of guilt at not being there for her. Not that she was to know but, nonetheless, regret seeped through her heart. While she'd been helping save the lives of strangers, her own flesh and blood had been suffering from a deadly disease.

'The doctors and nurses said I was a fighter, that I never complained and just *got on with it*. But to be honest, it was easier to not talk about it. So I kept distracting myself as much as possible, with reading mostly.'

'That's how you became so knowledgeable about books,' Sylvia said.

'I guess so. While my friends were reading magazines and hanging out with boys after school, I was in bed dreaming of a fantasy world. It passed the time, and stopped me feeling too overwhelmed.' Grace's eyes stared straight ahead but appeared distant, as though looking into the past. 'But there were many times I didn't even feel well enough to read. Sometimes all I could do was just lie there and be with the illness. I kept wishing I'd wake up one morning in my own bed and the cancer would be gone, and I'd dress up and go out with my friends, and do all the normal things a teenager would be doing. But when I'd wake, everything would be the same. And funnily enough, even when the tests gave me the 'all clear' just before my sixteenth birthday, all I wanted to do then was study and finish school, get my HSC.'

'Which you did.'

'Yes. I told my mind that the more I focused on my studies the less room the cancer would have to take up residence in my body again.'

And the less room there'd be for guilt to take up residence, Sylvia thought as she remembered her gruelling final two years of school, just after having Grace. Study saved her from seeing Grace's baby face in her mind, feeling the silky touch of her tiny hand. By the time she was at university she had no time to think of the past.

'My follow-up tests kept coming back normal,' Grace said. 'And with each passing month I grew more hopeful. By Year Twelve at school I finally felt like I'd turned a corner and the cancer was lost somewhere in the past. But only a few months before the HSC exams, everything changed again.' Grace wiped a new tear from the corner of her eye.

'Your mum.' Sylvia shook her head gently from side to side at the unfairness of it all, at the incomprehensible trauma of going through cancer, then recovering, only to lose the mother who's cared for you your whole life.

Grace nodded, wiping away another tear. 'I thought I'd

done something wrong to deserve such pain. Dad and I were inconsolable for a while. But then I remembered Mum's face as she'd told me how proud she was of me, getting stuck into my studies again and working hard for my future. I knew I couldn't give up, so I decided I'd get through the HSC successfully no matter what.' A triumphant smile grew on Grace's face, and she readjusted her position on the bed, seeming stronger already.

'She'd be even more proud of you now, I'm sure of it,' Sylvia said.

When she'd handed Grace over after she was born, she never imagined her baby would end up going through all of this. Sylvia spent time with teenagers and young children suffering from cancer during her oncology placements as a trainee doctor, and the thing that struck her most was their sense of being older and wiser than others their age. Their experience etched onto their faces, hiding the innocence and invincibility that once lay beneath.

'I'm proud of you too, Grace,' Sylvia whispered as she exhaled slowly, her tense concern from earlier softening into acceptance and admiration.

'Thanks, that means a lot,' Grace replied. 'And from now on, I promise to be more consistent with my medical check-ups. I can't believe I ended up in here — it was exactly what I was trying to avoid!'

'Well now that I know your secret, don't expect me to forget it. If you miss any appointments or tests you'll have me to answer to, young lady,' Sylvia said, waving her finger at Grace.

'Oooh, I'm scared.' Grace pretended to hide under her blanket, and Sylvia laughed. 'I'm sorry I ruined your birthday. Of all the days for this to happen.' Grace sat up.

'Don't worry about that, your health is much more important. Besides, you saved me from overindulging in a fat, sugar, and cholesterol-laden dessert. You may have saved *my* life, you know!' Sylvia said, glad to see a smile on Grace's face.

'I don't know about that, you've got to enjoy life while you've got it. Eat the dessert, I say!'

'I won't tell Mark you said that.'

'Good,' Grace replied. 'I'm glad Mark was there tonight, he was like a knight in shining armour, rescuing me from my moment of distress.' She giggled.

Mark. He was still out there waiting. Sylvia felt incredibly grateful he'd been there tonight; he seemed more in control than she was, and that was saying something. For a moment, she felt she should check on him, wondering if being here was triggering memories he'd rather forget.

'I feel bad though, I didn't follow through with the tests he told me to get,' Grace continued. 'When he did the live blood analysis he said my red blood cells weren't of "optimal shape and size" and that I should get a full blood count, and iron studies done, along with some other things, but I can't remember. Maybe if I'd listened to him this wouldn't have happened.'

'Mark suggested that?'

'Uh-huh. But I became so sick and tired of having tests. I dreaded the thought of seeing the look on the doctor's face again, knowing without him telling me that the cancer had recurred. This year was supposed to be about feeling free, finding out where I came from, and experiencing some of the things I missed out on as a teenager. I didn't want blood tests and hospitals to be part of it.'

'I can understand.'

'So when I began feeling more tired than usual, I refused to believe anything could be wrong. Rather than taking it easy and doing less, I started doing more — more exercise, more social stuff, keeping busy with work. Then I would have something to blame the fatigue on,' Grace said. 'Until it got too bad and my heart started doing funny things. That was enough to wake me up and realise I couldn't avoid getting checked out.'

'Luckily anaemia is something easily fixed,' Sylvia stated.

'Yeah, I have to take tablets and eat more steak apparently. I was supposed to do that back when I was sick too, but I couldn't stomach much meat,' Grace said. 'And just now, when they told me I was anaemic, I still felt worried because I thought they were just starting with the "good" news, and getting ready to tell me the "bad" news. I had anaemia along with the cancer too, you see, so I thought that had returned along with *it*.'

'But there was no bad news.' Sylvia smiled.

'No, and I asked about three times, "So that's it? Nothing else?" and the nurse put her hand on mine and said, "You're going to be fine, Grace".'

They sat silently for a moment, Sylvia taking in everything she'd just learned, and working out what to do next. 'I'll pick you up tomorrow and you can stay at my place for a few days, or as long as you need,' Sylvia said, lifting a hand to thwart Grace's beginning attempts to protest. 'And how about I book you in to see my colleague, Dr Bronovski? He can monitor you from here on, and refer you to any specialists if necessary.'

Grace nodded. 'Okay, if you think he'd be the best person to see.'

'Yes,' Sylvia replied, then added, 'And maybe you should book another appointment with Mark, I'm sure he can help you take good care of your health.' Whoa, that would have to make it into the *Guinness Book of Sylvia's Records* for the most out of character thing she'd done all year. She'd never referred anyone to a naturopath before, not seeing the need to. But perhaps he *could* be helpful to have around. Not that she was a convert to natural medicine now or anything; Sylvia still believed her way was best, but when it came to her daughter... the more help available to her the better. She wouldn't take any chances of losing her again.

'I think that's a good idea,' Grace agreed.

'Well, I think that drip's doing the trick, you're looking much better now,' Sylvia commented. She had an urge to check her chart hanging on the end of the bed but resisted. She didn't need to know *everything*, only what mattered. Of course, there was always a risk of the cancer recurring, especially within the first five years of remission, but right now, at this moment in time, Grace was going to be alright.

Mark had suspected that Sylvia was Grace's mother. They looked alike, of course, but he'd also noticed they shared a sense of 'I know what's best and I'll do it my way', which was both frustrating and charming. Grace hadn't seemed keen to talk about her family medical history, so he didn't probe for the full information at her first consultation. When he'd first met Grace at his market stall and she'd called Sylvia by her first name, he'd thought perhaps she was her aunt, but when he found out Sylvia was an only child he'd thought perhaps they were cousins. When he'd seen them together around town, they looked just like mother and daughter, although he knew Sylvia would have had Grace at a young age if that was the case. And it was.

Mark sat on the cold hard chair at the hospital, bouncing his foot up and down while he waited. He went over the night's events in his mind: seeing Grace collapsing, rushing to her side to check her pulse, hearing Sylvia's calm words to Grace yet seeing the panic in her eyes. His instinct told him to get her to hospital without delay, and for a moment he'd imagined she was Cindy, and he'd been given a second chance to save her life. But she wasn't Cindy, and there would be no second chances.

He also wondered if it would have been easier had Cindy been sick for a long time, so they both had time to prepare. But maybe that would have been worse, living with the fear of the inevitable and not knowing when she'd go. If only he'd had just one more day with her. One more day to talk to her, tell her how much he loved her, and say... goodbye.

'Mark, thanks so much for waiting,' Sylvia said as she appeared from behind the curtain and approached him.

'No worries, how is she?' Mark stopped bouncing his foot and stood, his head only a couple of inches higher than hers.

'She's okay, resting now. I'm coming back first thing in the morning to pick her up.' Sylvia fiddled with the handbag strap on her shoulder. 'You knew, didn't you, about the leukaemia?'

Mark pressed his lips together and nodded. 'Grace cancelled her follow-up appointment, and I was going to call her in another week or so to see how she was doing. Should have called earlier by the looks of it,' he said, wishing he'd been more insistent.

'Don't worry, she confessed she was in denial, didn't want to admit she was feeling unwell. Grace has learned her lesson now though,' Sylvia said. 'And it's only anaemia, plus low calcium and potassium, so nothing sinister.'

'That's good news,' he replied, slipping his hands into his pockets.

'Did you know about me, too?' Sylvia asked.

'That you're Grace's mother? No. I wondered, considering the resemblance, but I wasn't sure.'

'Well, you're one of only a few people that know, so...'

'I'll keep it to myself.'

'Thanks.'

'So, how are you?' Mark asked, noticing the weariness in Sylvia's eyes.

'How am I?'

'Tonight would have been a bit... traumatic for you.'

Sylvia's eyebrows rose briefly, as though she wasn't used to anyone asking how *she* was.

'I'm okay, thanks. It was a shock to see Grace like that, but I know she'll be alright, so it's all good.' Sylvia smiled.

'You never got to eat any Death by Chocolate,' Mark said, a smile sneaking from the corner of his mouth. 'There's still an hour and a half left of your birthday, how about we try and catch Café Lagoon before they close and grab something to take away?'

Sylvia's smile grew wider. 'As Grace told me today: "every birthday is a gift worth celebrating", so I think it's my duty to make the most of it.'

'Especially at *your* age,' Mark said, spicing his words with sarcasm.

Sylvia twisted her lips to one side and gave him an evil glare. 'Watch what you say mister, or—'

'Or what?'

'Or... I'll thump you with my walking stick.'

Mark snorted. 'In that case, I'd better think before I speak.' It felt good to muck around with Sylvia, especially after the stress of tonight. 'Anyway, in all seriousness, I think your Grace is one wise girl.'

'She sure is,' Sylvia replied, accepting Mark's offer of his outstretched hand.

At ten minutes to eleven they pulled up outside Café Lagoon, and Mark jumped out, before ducking his head back in the car. 'What can I get the birthday girl?'

'I'll have a hot chocolate,' Sylvia replied.

'And to eat?'

'Um... surprise me.'

Mark smiled and rushed inside. A staff member was wiping down tables and the last of the customers were filtering out. He paid for his order then got back in the car, placing the cardboard tray containing the hot drinks on Sylvia's lap, and the paper bag containing her 'surprise' between the two front seats.

'Let me guess... a dandelion chai for you?' Sylvia asked.

'Of course.'

She tried to peer into the paper bag but he stopped her. 'Uh-uh, wait till we get to the lookout. It's a surprise, remember?'

A minute later they were parked at the top of Lookout Point. Sylvia got out of the car and walked towards the edge of the lookout, leaning on the railing. Mark opened the boot and withdrew a picnic rug and blanket, laying them out on a spot of grass overlooking the leathery black ocean. Only a small amount of light shone from the moon and a distant streetlamp down the hill. Sylvia walked over and sat on the rug, lifting the blanket around her shoulders and taking the hot chocolate from Mark's hands. He went back to close the car, then returned with two blueberry friands on a plastic plate, along with two plastic forks from his picnic set.

'Is there anything you don't have in your car? I thought I was the only person who planned for every imaginable contingency,' Sylvia said.

'I like to be prepared,' Mark replied.

'Me too. But I bet you don't have an inventory in your car.'

Was she serious? 'You have an inventory in your car?'

'You already know one of my deep, dark secrets. You might as well know another.' She took a sip of hot chocolate and ran her tongue over her top lip.

'So, the purpose of the inventory is to...?'

'To make sure I keep the car fully stocked with all the essentials, and remember what needs replacing. Nothing worse than being stuck in traffic without a book to read, or getting caught in the rain without an umbrella, or—'

'Having a late night impromptu birthday celebration without a plastic plate and a couple of forks,' Mark added.

'Exactly.'

'Luckily, I also brought these.' Mark took a birthday candle and a box of matches from his pocket. Striking one against the box, a burst of light from the flame illuminated Sylvia's face, and a surprised smile emerged as he lit the candle and pressed it into the centre of Sylvia's friand. 'I'd sing *Happy Birthday* but I'm a terrible singer and it'd ruin the moment.'

'I'll take your word for it.'

'And I would have put thirty-five candles on it, but as I said before, it's too hard to fit that many on,' Mark said.

'Hey! Remember what I said about the walking stick.'

'I do, but I don't see any walking stick nearby, so I think I'm safe,' he replied with a grin.

'Actually, you're right. There's only room for about five candles max on this little thing.'

'The café only gave me one candle anyway,' Mark said.

'Oh, so you *don't* have everything in your car.'

Mark shook his head. 'They gave me the matches too. I must remember to add birthday candles and matches to my inventory. But first I must remember to *make* an inventory, or find someone passionate enough about them to make one for me. Know anyone?'

Sylvia laughed and pushed her hand playfully against his arm, then looked right into his eyes. 'Thanks for this, Mark.'

'My pleasure. Oh, before you blow out the candle, don't forget to make a wish,' Mark said, just as Sylvia opened her mouth into an 'O' shape. She stopped and looked at him funnily. 'What? Oh, you probably don't believe in wishes, do you?'

She didn't answer his question, but gave a sharp blow of air in the direction of the candle, eliminating the flame and leaving a sinuous wave of smoke in its wake. A waxy scent wafted through Mark's nostrils, reminding him of Cindy's thirtieth birthday. Her last birthday. He didn't know if she'd made a wish that night, but *he* wished she'd made one to be alive to see her next birthday. If Mark could make a wish, he used to think he'd wish for her not to have died and, of course, he still wished her life hadn't been cut short. But tonight, for the first time, he realised that if he could make a wish, it would be to be able to move on and start a new life. Whether Sylvia was destined to be a part of that life he wasn't completely sure, but all he knew was that each moment he spent with her felt one step closer to that goal. And that was both scary and liberating.

Sylvia dug the plastic fork into the friand and lifted a chunk of it to her mouth, her eyes closing momentarily. 'Mmm...' she said. 'Delicious.'

'Happy birthday, Sylvia,' Mark said, digging into his friand. 'And many more to come.'

CHAPTER THIRTY

Grace stepped out of the shower and dried off her skin with one of Sylvia's fluffy white towels. It was like she was in a hotel. How Sylvia had time to keep this place spotless she had no idea. The caravan park facilities were sufficient, but it was nice to shower in luxury for a change, not to mention sleeping in a proper bed. Sylvia had picked her up from the hospital and brought her back here yesterday, and had prepared the guest room for her arrival with books on the bedside table, fresh flowers, and even a chocolate on the pillow.

Grace rubbed some moisturiser onto her face, and moistened her lips with lip balm. On the way back from hospital, they'd called by the caravan to pick up a few items of clothing, her toiletry bag, and her laptop. Just the essentials. She'd probably only be here a few days at the most, although Sylvia insisted she not go back for at least another week.

Grace squeezed a tube of body lotion above her leg which was propped against the bathtub, but only a miniscule blob emerged. 'Damn, its run out,' she said to herself. Hoping it was okay to look in Sylvia's bathroom cabinet and borrow some of hers, Grace opened the cabinet gingerly and peered at the perfectly arranged items. Cleanser, toner, moisturiser, eye cream, and some sort of serum were placed equal distance from each other on the middle shelf, all the same brand; Christian Dior. Glass jars containing cotton buds and make-up remover pads were on the bottom shelf, along with an array of expensive-looking cosmetic items stored in a purpose-made stand. The contents of this cabinet were probably worth about a thousand dollars, more even. All Grace had was a pink cosmetic bag that had come free with a magazine, which she'd filled with a collection of different branded cosmetic items she'd bought from the 'two-dollar bin' at Priceline.

On the top shelf, a large tube of 'body-firming cream' with a gold lid stood elegantly. This seemed to be the only body lotion Sylvia owned, so it would have to do, although Grace felt guilty as she lathered it on her skin. It felt amazing; like silk. She'd have to buy more lotion of her own, or ask Sylvia if she wouldn't mind picking some up from the supermarket next time she did her groceries, which according to the schedule stuck to the fridge, would be tomorrow morning.

As Grace placed the lotion back onto the shelf, a perfume bottle caught her eye. A small amount of golden coloured liquid remained in the bottle of Trésor, hidden behind a full bottle of J'Adore. Grace carefully withdrew the bottle of Trésor from the shelf and took the cap off, lifting the bottle to her nose. Suddenly she felt as though her mother, Maria, was with her, could visualise her head peering around the side of the bathroom door, asking, 'Are you almost finished in there, sweetie?'

Trésor had been her mother's signature fragrance, and after she'd died Grace would often spray it around the house, just to make it feel like she was still there. Eventually it ran out. She'd considered buying more, but her dad said it was time to let it go. To let *her* go. Interesting, that both her adoptive mother and her biological mother shared the same taste in perfume.

Holding back tears, she quickly replaced the bottle, careful to put it back exactly as she'd found it. She shouldn't be going through Sylvia's things like this. Grace stepped into her jeans and pulled a long-sleeved top over her head before walking out of the bathroom and into the kitchen and dining area, where Sylvia was busily flitting about.

'Good morning, I was hoping to get back before you woke. I left a note just in case. Just popped into town to pick up some fresh breakfast and the Saturday newspaper,' Sylvia said.

A plate of croissants was on the table next to some sliced ham and cheese, along with a platter of fruit. Two glasses filled to the brim with orange juice glowed in the morning sunlight.

Then the tears came.

In the centre of the dining table was a single sunflower, extending out of a slim vase.

'Grace, what is it? What's wrong?' Sylvia rushed over and put an arm around her shoulder.

'I'm sorry, nothing's wrong. This is all, so... perfect, thank you,' she replied. 'It's just... my mum used to bring me sunflowers when I was in hospital.'

'Oh, Grace. I'm sorry, I didn't mean to upset you. I remembered you telling me they were your favourite,' Sylvia said.

'They are. Mum would give me one on the first day of each month, as a way of reminding me that I was still here, and how far I'd come. To encourage me not to give up.' Grace dabbed at her eyes, and took a deep breath. 'I began looking forward to receiving them. It kept me going, knowing I just had to hold out for the next sunflower, and then the next. On my sixteenth birthday, when I achieved full remission, she gave me a whole bunch of them. Twelve to be exact. She said it was in advance for the next twelve months of good health I was bound to have.' Grace smiled at the memory. 'She gave me another bunch on my seventeenth birthday. On my eighteenth, she wasn't there to give me any, so I bought some and put them on her grave.' Her chin quivering, Grace touched the stem of the sunflower, running her finger up towards its large bright yellow petals.

Sylvia dabbed at her own eyes. 'That's beautiful. Your mum sounds like the loveliest person on the planet. I wish I could have met her.'

'I think you would have got along well with her,' Grace said, regaining her composure with a smile.

'Do you want me to take the flower away?' Sylvia asked feebly.

'No, leave it. It's nice to see one again.'

'Well,' Sylvia began, sniffing and wiping at the corner of her eye. 'We'd better eat this breakfast while it's hot.'

Starved, Grace sat down and devoured three croissants, two glasses of juice, and a plate of fruit, stopping halfway through to take a multivitamin and iron tablet. It was time to take responsibility for her health, build herself back up again, and keep 'the sunflower promise' to her mother. There was no way she'd give up. Ever.

After finally getting up from the table, Sylvia lifted the lid on the piano and Grace took a seat.

'You sure you're up to practising? If you'd rather rest, then don't hesitate to make yourself at home,' Sylvia said.

'Nope, I'm alright. I'll have a little lie down later, after lunch. My fingers are itching to play.' Grace twiddled her fingers then rubbed her hands together, before warming them up on the keys. 'Oh, and I've come up with a name for my composition for the concert,' Grace said. '*Reunion.*'

A smile slowly grew on Sylvia's lips.

'Inspired by you and me, meeting again after all these years,' Grace added.

'Grace, I... I don't know what to say. What a lovely gesture.'

'You don't have to say anything, just listen. This new melody came to me last night before I fell asleep.' Grace's fingers gently pressed on the keys, and Sylvia closed her eyes as though to prevent other sensory stimulation from interfering with the melody. The notes were like warm liquid, flowing easily from one to the other in rapid succession.

'What do you think?' Grace asked as she placed her hands on her lap and leaned back a little.

'I can see why you haven't bothered with more lessons. You're a natural.'

Grace's cheeks showed a hint of rose as she smiled.

'You should seriously consider trying to make a career out of it. Give it a go while you're young,' Sylvia suggested.

Grace shrugged. 'Ah, I dunno. The industry is hard to get into, and I think I should get some professional training first anyway.'

'So do it then. There are plenty of courses you could enrol in, and you could even audition for a music degree. I think you'd get in no problem.'

Grace sat silently for a while, staring at the piano keys. 'It's just... If I commit to something like that I know I'm going to be totally in my element. But... I'm scared the cancer might come back and I'd have to give it up again.'

Sylvia perched on the edge of the piano seat next to Grace. 'Like last time?'

'Yeah. Although I didn't completely give it up as such, but not long after I started lessons, the cancer was diagnosed, so I didn't play for a long time. I just don't want to get my hopes up for a career that may never happen.' Grace's chest rose with a tense breath.

Sylvia didn't want to push the issue. Although Grace had a unique talent that could bring her success, she still needed time to heal, physically and emotionally; and time to build up her self-confidence again. 'Well for now, let's just get you better and prepare for this concert, shall we?'

Grace nodded. 'That's about all I can handle right now.' Her fingers returned to the keys as she played around with a few notes, stopping suddenly when there was a knock at the door.

Sylvia stood and welcomed Jonah inside, who was carrying a bunch of flowers.

'Where's the patient?' he asked.

Sylvia led him to where Grace sat at the piano.

'I thought you'd be resting. Can't stop a musician from getting their fix, hey?' he said, leaning in to give her a kiss on the cheek.

'It'll take more than a night in hospital to knock me down,' Grace replied, standing to accept the flowers.

'I'll just be, ah... in the bathroom,' Sylvia said, leaving the lovebirds alone. As she washed her hands at the bathroom sink, she could hear them talking.

'Why didn't you tell me you'd been sick?' Jonah pleaded, concern in his deep voice.

'I'm sorry, I didn't want to upset you. I just wanted to feel like a normal person and not a cancer sufferer.'

'Survivor, you mean,' Jonah insisted. 'You've still got the all clear, right?'

'Yep.'

There was silence for a moment, and Sylvia suspected they were embracing or kissing, or something. Or perhaps he was tucking coils of hair behind her ears, running his fingers across her cheek. She waited for them to resume talking before she returned to the kitchen and made herself look busy.

'Anyway, my shift starts soon so I better go. You — rest, okay?' Jonah pecked Grace on the forehead then turned to Sylvia. 'See you soon Dr —, I mean, *Sylvia*.' He smiled awkwardly and gave a subtle wave of his hand as he walked out the door.

Jonah had obviously been upset when he'd heard about Grace, but lately he'd seemed anxious anyway. Not his usual boisterous, jolly self. Probably just working himself to the grindstone at the café. Not to mention the fact that he was always working out in the park or at the beach whenever Sylvia went for a walk. The boy never sat down.

'He's a nice guy, that Jonah of yours,' Sylvia commented.

Grace's eyes glossed over. 'He sure is.' She turned to Sylvia and opened her mouth but then closed it.

Sylvia held her gaze. 'You were going to say something?'

Grace flushed. 'It doesn't matter.'

'No, tell me, what is it?'

Grace leaned on the kitchen bench. 'Was my father a nice guy?' She looked away from Sylvia and fiddled with a notepad and pen beside the telephone.

Sylvia took a deep breath. It was time. Time to tell her how she came to be in this world. Well, not exactly *how*, but it was time to talk about her father. 'Yes, he was a nice guy,' she said. Probably still was, although she hadn't crossed paths with him since it all happened. Sylvia gestured for Grace to sit on the couch, and pulled a newspaper from the categorised magazine rack against the wall. She only ever kept four newspapers at a time, and when she bought a fifth, one from the rack was recycled. That way she could refer to recent news or articles if she needed information on something, plus she had spare newspaper to lay down in case of painting, or craft, or things like that which she never did. But you never knew when they might come in handy. The other three sections on the rack contained medical journals which she sometimes flipped through on a Sunday afternoon just for fun, cooking magazines, and shopping catalogues. That was the extent of her publication collection, she wasn't interested in fashion magazines; she'd rather just go to a store and buy something well-made and stylish, with classic appeal. Nor was she interested in celebrity gossip magazines. After talking with patients all day about their lives, the last thing she wanted was to read about whose love child some famous actress was having and how skinny a popular catwalk model was becoming. If a magazine didn't have some useful purpose to it she wouldn't give it a second look.

She sat next to Grace and opened the newspaper to the sports section. 'Home Grown Olympian Makes Comeback', the headline said in bold black type. Sylvia tilted the article towards Grace and she peered at it closely. Then realisation dawned on her daughter's face as she turned her head slowly towards Sylvia. 'You mean...' Grace looked at the picture accompanying the article. A tall muscular man with a slight dimple in his chin stood proudly holding a basketball. Grace looked at Sylvia. 'Max Reeves is my father?'

Sylvia nodded, and relief seemed to fall from the top of her head like a loosely placed cap. 'Yes.'

'I can't believe it. All along I've actually known him. I mean, known *of* him.' Grace studied the picture closely. 'Now that I know, I can kind of see myself in him.' She traced a finger around his chin in the picture, then looked at Sylvia. 'But I'm glad I inherited your hair and not his!'

Sylvia agreed on that one. When Max was a teenager he had a full head of ruffled brown hair, but now he had a short cut and receding hairline. Still had that spark in his eyes though, an alluring stare that, like a charm, drew the attention of any female in close proximity, and his sporting prowess was a bonus attraction. He was still a good catch (no pun intended), but it wouldn't have worked out. They were too different. Sure, opposites attract, they say, and they did in this case, but Sylvia and Max were only meant to be a short-lived couple. If you could have called them that. Their relationship was over before it really began.

Sylvia waited while Grace read the article. It talked about his return to professional basketball after a long absence due to injury, and his plans to compete in the next Olympics — perhaps his last chance to win a medal. It also mentioned his recent marriage to a woman named Tina, and how they were expecting their first child. *Tina's* first child anyway.

Sylvia wondered if Max's wife knew he'd become a father as a teenager. She didn't even know if Max had told his own parents. When Sylvia called to tell Max the news over the phone, he'd already moved away from Tarrin's Bay with his family, and she'd had to find out his new phone number from a friend of a friend of a friend of his. She used the excuse of Max having left something of his with her. Which wasn't a total lie.

Before giving him a chance to react, Sylvia told Max she planned on giving the baby up for adoption, so he didn't have to worry about anything. Terminating the pregnancy was never an option for Sylvia; she preferred the idea of giving the child to parents who desperately wanted one. So what if she had to grow a large belly for nine months and endure the pain of childbirth? She knew she'd recover and be able to resume following her dreams, and Max could continue training to reach his goal of playing basketball for Australia. Max had seemed taken aback that she wasn't asking him for anything, and kept asking, 'So, you're sure about this?' and, 'You'll be okay then?' and told her to call him after it was all over. Which she did, as soon as she returned home from hospital. She told him that although it hurt like hell, everything went smoothly and the result was a healthy baby girl, given to a couple in their thirties who weren't able to have a baby naturally. It seemed ironic and unfair at the time that so many people who wanted children couldn't have them, and so many who didn't plan on having them, at least not right away, became pregnant easily. But Sylvia consoled her guilt with the thought that maybe it was the job of people like her to bring a baby into the world to help infertile couples. That made her feel better, for a while at least.

'That means I'll have a half-brother or -sister in a few months time,' Grace remarked.

Sylvia nodded. 'It's good that you know the truth. If you feel you want to get in contact with him, I'm sure we can arrange something.' Sylvia wondered if Grace would want her to come along if she ever met Max. The thought made her heart race and her muscles tense. She hadn't seen him since the night of his farewell party. The night when they both knew it was now or never. It was unlikely they'd see each other again, so there were no expectations, but the attraction that had been growing between them since the start of the school year was too strong to stay locked inside.

'Um... maybe someday. I just need to let it all sink in for a while,' Grace replied, then shook her head in what seemed to be amazement and disbelief. 'Max Reeves! Who would have thought?'

Sylvia was glad he wasn't a celebrity of unfavourable character. Although trying to keep the past behind her, she'd followed Max's career, watched him in the Olympics, seen him being interviewed on numerous occasions, and even voted for him when he competed on *Dancing with the Stars*. But when he'd made a brief visit back to Tarrin's Bay to give a talk at the high school, she wasn't in town at the time and didn't have to deal with the idea of seeing him in person again.

'Did he always want to play basketball for a living?' Grace asked.

'Yes. He told me it was the only thing he was good at. The one thing he was passionate about, and that life wouldn't be the same without it.'

Grace nodded. 'That's how I feel about my music.'

'I understand,' Sylvia replied.

'Yeah, that's how you must feel about medicine, isn't it?' Grace folded the newspaper and placed it on the coffee table.

'Oh, of course,' Sylvia replied. And it was true, although she was thinking of something else. Something else she was passionate about that hadn't been part of her life for a long time. Sylvia quickly pushed an old memory back to its allocated place in her mind, and folded her hands in her lap.

Grace appeared to think for a few moments, then brought up another memory for Sylvia. 'Did I cause you much trouble, you know, when you were pregnant with me?'

'Well, apart from turning my flat stomach into a bulge the size of a large watermelon... nah, no trouble!' Sylvia tried to make light of it, preferring not to remember how special she'd felt, carrying a growing being inside her. Because then she'd feel sad, having missed out on the bit that comes afterwards, the bit that most parents can't wait for, the bit that she willingly handed over to someone else. Not that she necessarily regretted giving Grace up, she'd made the decision she and her parents thought right. But that maternal part of her, however immature it was at age sixteen, somehow longed to take her baby home and care for her. 'I had a bit of morning sickness, but not as bad as some women get, so I was lucky,' Sylvia said. 'Apparently, my experience with pregnancy and childbirth was a "text book" case. Although at the time I didn't appreciate being likened to a text book, especially considering I was studying and my days were spent reading them!'

Grace laughed. 'So you'd rather be likened to a large watermelon then.'

'Of course!' Sylvia laughed too. 'Then I've got one over Baby who only carried a watermelon for a few minutes. I carried one for nine months!'

Grace looked at Sylvia with a face of confusion.

'You know, *Baby*, from *Dirty Dancing*... the famous line, "I carried a watermelon"?'

Grace shook her head. 'Sorry, nope!'

How can she not have seen *Dirty Dancing*? It was a classic. 'Never mind then. But you should watch it sometime, it's a trademark movie from my youth!'

Grace smiled a cheeky grin. 'So I guess it's in black and white then?'

Sylvia picked up the newspaper and whacked her playfully on the arm. It sounded like something Mark Bastian would say. Although, he was only a couple of years younger than her degenerative age so it wouldn't be as ingenious a joke. 'Don't feel too pleased with yourself, you'll be as old as me one day.'

'I hope so,' Grace said quietly.

Oops. Sylvia made a mental note to be more careful with things she said. Grace was obviously still unsure of her future and whether she'd stay free of the cancer. Sylvia placed a comforting hand on Grace's. 'Of course you will. I'll tell you what, when you turn thirty-five, I'll even throw you a huge party, how about that? I'm sure I would have been "event-planner of the year" in a past life, if I had one.'

'Sounds good. I'll hold you to that,' Grace replied. 'Although, by then you'll be fifty-one, so do you think someone of that age could handle the responsibility?' Grace shuffled away from Sylvia on the couch to avoid the inevitable newspaper whack, but it came too quickly, then she snatched it off Sylvia and whacked her with it, until Sylvia picked up a cushion and used it as a shield to defend herself.

They collapsed on the couch in laughter, and for the first time since they met, Sylvia actually felt like Grace's mother. But then she felt guilty that Maria Forrester was missing out on this, and that somehow Sylvia had taken Grace from her, perhaps subconsciously willing Maria out of this life so she could get the chance she didn't take eighteen years ago. Why did she always experience these conflicting emotions? Sylvia had grown so used to the guilt that as soon as she felt anything other than that around Grace, she'd feel guilty for not feeling guilty anymore, and then everything would go back to the way it was before; feeling as though she'd had her chance to be a mother and blew it, and didn't deserve another one. Silly, she knew, but the subconscious mind was a complex thing. Grace seemed genuinely okay with having been given up for adoption, but Sylvia's scientific mind needed proof; she needed to hear her say it.

CHAPTER THIRTY-ONE

Despite it being the first day of winter, Sylvia took off her jacket and rolled up her sleeves in anticipation of her six-monthly cleaning ritual at the clinic. They had a professional cleaner, of course; it was necessary in an environment frequented by tons of sick people, not to mention children with perpetually runny noses and the odd insect stuck in a bodily orifice. But this was a different cleaning job. This was the biannual complete rejuvenation of her consulting room, and she thoroughly enjoyed it. No cleaner, professional or otherwise, could do as good a job as she.

She'd remove everything from the desk, shelves, storage cabinets, and even removed the pictures from the wall, in order to clean every corner and crevice of the room. Then she'd discard old items, and reorganise the others, putting them away in the most appropriate place to allow for a clutter-free look and efficient withdrawal when the item was needed. It was a shame Dr Bronovski didn't aspire to such heights. Once, when Sylvia went to his room to borrow a book on spinal injuries, she'd opened the book only to have a spider crawl out and onto her hand; her reflex response causing the spider and the book to be flung against the wall behind her. Probably giving the spider a spinal injury of its own, the poor thing.

'Hi, Dr Greene,' a woman said as Sylvia exited the storeroom carrying a stepladder, an array of cloths, and a bottle of Spray & Wipe.

The woman was a heavily pregnant Samantha Roseford. 'Samantha, how are you?'

'Pretty good. Could pop any day now,' she said, rubbing her belly. 'All's looking good for a natural birth at this stage, which is good, but scary at the same time!'

'Natural is better whenever possible. Have you just had an appointment with someone?' Sylvia asked.

Samantha nodded. 'The physio. My back's been killing me. Feels much better now, but there's only so much you can do when there are two human beings pressing on my nerves. Not to mention my bladder.'

Sylvia nodded in sympathy. 'Well, take it easy. And remember, early labour can sometimes feel like a backache, so if it persists or gets worse, make sure you contact Dr Engelstein or the hospital, okay?'

Sylvia remembered the sensation. A dull, crawling ache spreading throughout her lower back, like a grey storm cloud looming on the horizon. Then the tight pain, extending around to her front, sharp like one gigantic hailstone trying to erupt. And just when you think you can't take any more, the relief comes like a breath of fresh air. But only for a moment. Soon, the stormy pain becomes a tornado within, increasing in intensity with each heartbeat. Sylvia winced at the memory. It was like nothing she'd ever experienced before. She thought she'd been prepared, but nothing could have prepared her for the enormity of the pain, or how feverish and out of control she'd felt during each contraction.

'Yep, don't worry, I'm going straight home to put my feet up.

Mike's on cooking duty till these munchkins are born, and probably for a while after, I'd say.' Samantha hobbled past Sylvia then stopped, curiously eyeing the cleaning equipment. 'I didn't know you were a cleaner as well as a doctor.'

Sylvia laughed. 'No, I'm just giving my room a bit of a spring clean — in winter.'

'Feel free to come by my house anytime, Dr Greene,' Samantha said, winking.

Sylvia farewelled Samantha and made her way into her consulting room. She opened up the folded stepladder and placed it below the wall shelves, before placing her hands on her hips and surveying the scene, mentally planning her mission.

An hour and a half later the mission was nearly complete. Sylvia stood on top of the ladder putting folders and archive boxes away on the top shelf, when a knock sounded on the door. Mark Bastian popped his head around the door.

'I'm off, you right to lock up?'

'Of course,' she replied.

'Good.' Mark disappeared for a moment before popping his head back in. 'How's Grace? She must be feeling a lot better by now?'

Grace had been taking the required tablets religiously, so she said, since her hospital visit almost two months ago. Sylvia had managed to get her to stay a whole week at her place before Grace said she didn't want to impose any further, and that she'd be fine back at the caravan. She'd cut back on her sporting endeavours, but returned to taekwondo, and kept up a consistent practise schedule on Sylvia's piano.

'She is, thanks for asking. Levels aren't completely back to normal, but they're well on their way.'

'That's good. She came in a few weeks ago and was much better then, so I was hoping things were still improving,' Mark said.

'Yes, she mentioned how she quite enjoys her acupuncture sessions now. Says they're relaxing. But how anyone could enjoy having tiny needles stuck into their skin is beyond me!' Sylvia managed a friendly laugh.

'You should try it sometime, you might be pleasantly surprised.' Mark's lips formed that incredibly charming smile, and Sylvia looked away.

'Hmmm... we'll see.' She placed the last folder on the top shelf and stepped onto the rung of the ladder below her feet. Her right toe didn't quite grab though, and it slipped downwards. A sting burned her ankle and a jolt jumped up through her body as her bottom landed with a thud on the floor.

'Are you alright?' Mark asked, kneeling on the floor next to her.

All she could do was scrunch up her face as though she was in labour. 'Ow!' A red swelling grew on her ankle, and she clutched at it in effort to stop it.

'Here, let me get you up on the bed.' Mark gathered her in his arms, just as he'd done with Grace the night she'd collapsed. Mark didn't make a sound as he lifted her, but Sylvia knew he held back a grunt. She wasn't that heavy, but lifting another adult usually required at least *some* verbal strain. He paused in front of the examination bed, Sylvia still in his arms. 'On second thoughts, let's get you onto *my* bed. I mean, the bed... table thingy in my room... the one I use for acupuncture.' Mark's face was almost as red as her ankle, but she wasn't up to making a joke about it. Mark, along with his cumbersome load, swivelled around quickly towards the direction of the door, but Sylvia's ankle collided with the bed.

'Owwww!'

'Sorry.'

'Christ! Why did you have to go and do that?' Sylvia yelled. 'Holy Mother of God this hurts.'

Sylvia bit her lip to stifle the pain, and Mark swivelled this way and that, seemingly unsure of whether to put her down or continue with his decision of transferring her to his table. As Sylvia continued her blasphemous expletives, Mark scurried into his room and placed her onto his acupuncture table, elevating Sylvia's leg on a pillow.

'Ice. You need ice. Hold on.' Mark disappeared then returned with an ice pack covered in a flannel pouch. He placed it on her ankle and wrapped a bandage firmly around it.

'Arghh! Too cold!'

'Tough. You need it. You know — RICE?'

'What are you talking about? I don't need rice. Arghh!'

'Not rice, R-I-C-E. Rest, Ice, Compression, and Elevation. Basic first aid?' Mark teased like she'd forgotten the sum of two plus two. 'The ice will numb it a little soon, then I'll see what magic I can summon from my bag of tricks.' He smiled at her, clearly amused by her low pain threshold.

'Magic my arse, get me some painkillers now!'

'Sylvia, don't be so quick to resort to drugs. I can help you, just trust me.'

Trust me? Whenever anyone uttered those words the situation never ended well. *Dear God, help me!* Although, he probably wasn't listening to her now after all her cursing.

Mark left the room and returned with a glass of water. He took a container of something off a shelf, and paused before opening it. 'You're not on any blood-thinning medications or immune suppressants by any chance are you?'

'No. Why?'

'Take these, it'll help.' Mark held three capsules and the glass of water in front of Sylvia, and she scrunched up her face even more.

'What are they?'

'Anti-inflammatory and pain-relieving herbs, plus some nutrients.'

'Forget that, get me some Nurofen, please!'

'Sylvia, just give these a go. It's the same formula I took to heal my old soccer injury. They're perfectly safe, and very effective,' Mark urged.

'Oh yeah? Show me the clinical trial results.'

'They've had some basic studies done on them, but unfortunately there's no funding for the incredibly expensive process of a clinical trial,' Mark said. 'That doesn't mean they don't work though. I can trawl through the research on the ingredients now if you like, might take me an hour or so. Or...' Mark held the capsules close to Sylvia's mouth. 'You can open your mouth and swallow the bloody tablets.'

'Okay, okay.' Sylvia put one capsule on her tongue and took a swig of water, before swallowing the remaining two. 'There. Happy now?'

'Not yet. A combination of therapies works best.' Mark ripped open an alcohol swab.

'What are you doing?' Sylvia inched her head back, cowering in her vulnerability.

Mark smiled. 'Looks like you'll be trying acupuncture sooner than you thought.' He peeled back the hem on her trousers, rolling it up to the knee.

Despite being still in pain, Sylvia quickly leaned forward, trying to remember if she'd shaved her legs. Some days in winter she'd give it a miss, but she couldn't stand the stubbly feeling and was usually a regular shaver. Relieved to find no stubble in sight, it finally registered what Mark was about to do.

'You're not going to stick needles into my sore ankle, are you?'

Mark repositioned the ice pack to the underside of Sylvia's ankle and wiped the alcohol swab on a few areas of her foot and leg. He then picked up something small and held it just under her kneecap, and tapped at it. When he removed his hand a tiny hair-like needle protruded from her skin.

'That's it?' she asked.

Mark simply smiled and nodded, before doing the same thing twice more, to a spot at the base of her toe, and then, right on the ankle. She didn't even feel them go in.

'Dr Greene, you are now experiencing the benefits of acupuncture,' he said smugly.

'I don't know about benefits, the pain's still there,' Sylvia assured.

'Give it time. I'll also do some other points to help with your anxiety.' Mark opened another alcohol swab.

'Anxiety? I'm not anxious, I'm in pain.'

Mark swabbed a spot on her wrist, and another on her ear.

'My ear? Don't you dare stick a needle in my ear!'

He tapped a needle into her wrist, then brought his hands to her ear. 'I see you've got your ears pierced. This'll be nothing to you.'

Sylvia braced herself, but a quick tap later it was done. Nothing. It didn't hurt. But she probably looked like a pincushion.

'I'll leave those in for about fifteen minutes. Just close your eyes and try to relax, while I make a herbal compress for your ankle.' Sylvia watched as Mark put his iPhone into a dock on his desk, then went to the bench on the side wall to make whatever he was going to make.

Relaxation music softly permeated the room, and she finally did as she was told and closed her eyes, trying to relax despite the rhythmic throbbing in her ankle. After a while, Mark came over to her and began removing the needles, pushing down on her skin with a cotton ball after he removed each one.

'It's not so bad now, is it?' he asked.

The pain had certainly reduced, it was no longer a 'Holy Mother of God!' type of pain, but more of an 'Oh, Geez!' type of pain. 'I think the ice has numbed the pain a bit,' was all she was prepared to say.

'Now I'll remove the ice, you still need some blood flow to the area.' Mark gently pressed a herb-soaked cloth into her skin, and wrapped it around her ankle. 'Leave this compress on for a while, then alternate between that and the ice every twenty minutes.'

'Okay, but... I do have to get home you know; I can't stay here all night.'

'It's alright, I'll drive you home. But I think you should give work a miss tomorrow so you can keep the ankle elevated, and use the ice and compress every two hours.'

'I can't miss work. My hands and brain still work, I can just stay seated and elevate my foot at lunchtime,' Sylvia demanded.

'Well, it's up to you, but my advice would be to rest. Otherwise you could have a sore ankle for a few weeks, but if you follow my advice it may only be a few days of discomfort,' Mark said. 'Look, while we wait for the compress to do its magic, why don't I call Joyce to let her know what's happened, and I'll call the patients booked in tomorrow to reschedule them?'

He was right. And Sylvia decided she'd much prefer to recover from this injury sooner rather than later. 'Okay then, *Dr Bastian*,' Sylvia said. 'As long as you don't mind?'

'No problem,' he replied, and turned the music up a little before walking from the room.

Wow. He was prepared to play receptionist for her? That would be a lot of phone calls he'd have to make. Plus, Mr Benson was due in tomorrow. He'd probably keep Mark on the phone for hours. Sylvia took a deep breath, deciding to make the most of the time by mentally planning her day tomorrow. If she was going to stay home she didn't want it to be a waste. First, she'd catch up on reading the medical journals she'd stored away. Then, she'd call her parents to double-check they were all set to come to the charity concert this weekend. Then, she'd indulge and spend time reading a novel, which she normally only did in the evening before bed. She could keep some food on her bedside table, and order a pizza delivery for dinner. Hmm, apart from the sore ankle, this might actually be *fun*. In a way, it was nice to be a patient for a day instead of a doctor.

'How you manage that much of a patient load I have no idea,' Mark said as he came back in the room over an hour later. 'And Mr Benson likes to talk, doesn't he? How's the ankle?'

'Resting is helping,' Sylvia replied. She wasn't yet prepared to say his treatment was helping.

'I'm sure it is.' Mark grinned. 'I've put the herbal capsules and a bottle of liquid herbs to use for the compress in this bag.' He held up a paper bag. 'You'll need to take three capsules every two or three hours, but don't exceed eighteen capsules in the one day, got it?'

'Got it.'

'And every two hours, put ice on the ankle for twenty minutes, then the compress for another twenty minutes, okay?'

'Okay.'

'Good. I've brought the car round front, so let's get you home.' Mark slid his arms underneath her, ready to lift.

'Wait. I need my handbag, it's in my room,' Sylvia said.

Mark walked out and soon came back, the bag strap across his shoulder.

'Nice look, Marky,' Sylvia teased.

'Yeah, yeah.' He went to lift her again, but Sylvia stopped him.

'I think I can walk out, if you grab me some crutches from the store room?'

'Alright then. You'll be needing them at home anyway.' Again, Mark left the room and returned, this time with crutches under his arms, one foot off the ground, pretending to be Sylvia. 'Holy Mother of God,' he exclaimed in a high-pitched voice.

'Ha ha, very funny. I'd like to see you deal with a sprained ankle that's been whacked against a hard surface by an indecisive man.'

'I'd like to see you try to lift a grown adult from the floor onto a bed,' Mark rebutted.

'I reckon I could,' Sylvia replied.

Mark grinned as he helped Sylvia off the bed, wedging the crutches into her armpits.

Twenty minutes later they were sitting in Sylvia's living room, Sylvia's foot propped up on the coffee table, eating Thai food and discussing their past injuries and illnesses.

'When I was about seven, I was standing next to a see-saw in the park when my friend jumped on the other end of it, the wooden seat flying up and hitting me in the chin. Eight stitches, I needed,' Sylvia said proudly.

'Beat this: my brother and I were skateboarding one day when I was about eight, and we sat on them to roll down a steep hill. I careened into some shrubbery and a branch scraped into my leg as I rolled past. Fourteen stitches,' Mark said even more proudly than Sylvia.

'Well, when I was sixteen I spent thirteen hours in excruciating pain that no acupuncture needle could ever fix. As for stitches, I won't even go there!'

'Okay you win,' Mark said, smiling.

Childbirth. Barring large kidney stones, it always won out for the most painful experience. Although during her hospital training in the emergency department, Sylvia had seen things that seemed contradictory to that. She'd enjoyed the excitement of the emergency rotation, but couldn't do it all the time — too unpredictable. Chronic care in a relaxed clinical setting was more her thing.

'I better get going and leave you to get some sleep,' Mark said, getting up from the couch. 'I'll send you an itemised bill for tonight's treatment, shall I?' He raised his eyebrows.

Was he serious? Sylvia searched his face, his expression straightlaced, before it softened into a wide grin. *The bugger.*

'Got you there, didn't I? Don't worry, I'll put this one down as a free trial,' he said. 'Now let me help you get organised for the night before I go.' He switched off the lights, leaving the hall light on, and put the empty food containers in the bin. 'I'll put these in your room,' he said, lifting up a bottle of water, the herbal capsules, and her handbag. Then he came over to Sylvia and despite her protest, lifted her up and carried her into the bedroom, placing her gently on the bed. He brought the crutches in and laid them against the wall, and wrapped a newly soaked herbal compress around her ankle. 'Do you have an old stretchy sock you can wear over the compress to hold it in place and prevent staining your sheets?'

'Top drawer, the one on the right.' Sylvia gestured to her dresser. Thankfully her socks were kept neatly bundled in there along with only stockings and scarves. Her underwear was in the drawer on the left.

'I guess you never have the problem of odd socks,' Mark said as he opened the drawer. Her drawers had little narrow trays inside that housed everything neatly, in groups of like-colours.

'I don't understand how people say their socks go missing. You wash them, hang them to dry, roll the pair up and put them away. How hard is it?' Sylvia said.

Mark simply smiled his recurring smile and held up a pair of thick woolly bed socks. 'These do?'

Sylvia nodded.

He slid them onto her feet, careful not to irritate her ankle, then pulled the blanket and quilt over her body. 'If you're right for work on Wednesday I'll pick you up on the way,' he offered.

Sylvia yawned and nodded at the same time. All this excitement had worn her out and she was desperate for sleep. Mark just sat there, on the side of her bed, looking at her with an expression that seemed familiar. When had he worn that face before? Of course. It was the night they'd played candlelit scrabble. The night before they almost…

Just as Sylvia recognised the expression, Mark's face came closer and his breath warmed her face as his lips gently met hers. Tentatively at first, he cushioned her mouth with his, then pressed more firmly, gathering her bottom lip between his hungry lips. All the pain melted away. Forget acupuncture and pain killers, kissing won out big time. 'Is that part of your treatment protocol for my ankle?' Sylvia whispered when they pulled away from each other.

'I'll add it to the bill,' he said, kissing her one last time before closing the door behind him as he walked out.

CHAPTER THIRTY-TWO

When Mark arrived at work on Friday morning Sylvia was in the kitchen, washing out her coffee mug. He'd driven her to and from work the last two days, but today she assured him she could make her own way, as she was meeting Larissa for an early breakfast in town. He'd had dinner with her every night this week too, and spent each evening talking, laughing, and cuddling with her on the couch; except last night as Grace was there practising piano. Things were looking up, and the stab of guilt he'd usually feel around Sylvia wasn't as strong anymore, more like a subtle tap on the shoulder. He didn't feel completely ready for a relationship, but this was a start. They could just take things slow.

'Good morning. I see you're walking around quite normally now,' Mark said as Sylvia put her mug away and walked up to greet him.

'Yeah, it's not too bad now,' she said casually.

'Not too bad?'

'Okay, it's much better than I'd imagined it would be at this stage.'

'So you're a total convert to natural medicine now?' Mark asked expectantly.

'Not quite. Let's just say I'm... pleasantly surprised.'

'That's good enough for me, doctor,' Mark said, giving her a peck on the lips. 'How's Grace? Is she excited about the concert tomorrow?'

'She seems fine. But I think she just wants to get it over and done with. I'm going to join her at the dress rehearsal tonight.'

'Well, I can't wait to see her performance. And the others, I hear there's quite a line-up.'

Sylvia nodded. 'Should be a good night.'

'Hey, I forgot to ask, where did you have to rush off to yesterday?'

'Oh. One of my elderly patients died. I had to examine the body and sign the death certificate,' Sylvia said.

'Sorry to hear that, are you okay?' Mark rubbed Sylvia's arm.

'Yeah, I've done quite a few, I'm used to it. She was a sweetie though, Mrs Johnson. Her husband died right before Christmas last year, and her sister told me she'd never stopped setting the table for him every breakfast, lunch, and dinner. When I went into the bedroom to examine her body, I noticed a photograph of her husband on the pillow on his side of the bed. The sister told me she always kept it there, couldn't bear the thought of sleeping without him by her side. Poor thing.'

Sylvia was silent for a moment, and Mark realised something. He knew exactly how Mrs Johnson had felt. He understood completely why she did those things. He never set a place at the table for Cindy, but he still had her picture on his bedside table, and on the wall in the entry foyer of his house. Cindy was everywhere. And there was still that mountain of boxes to sort through.

A yell from the waiting room broke the silence. 'Sylvia, come quick!'

Mark and Sylvia rushed from the kitchen to see Joyce fussing over a patient in the waiting room. The overweight man was clutching his chest and had half collapsed onto the chair next to him. Another patient sat nearby, clenching the armrests of her chair, her face lined with concern.

'Mr Benson,' Sylvia said as she approached the patient. 'It's Dr Greene, are you having pain in your chest?'

So that was the talkative bugger he'd spoken to on the phone on Monday evening. Mark felt a twinge of guilt for feeling annoyed with him, and hoped he'd be okay.

Fear darkening his eyes, Mr Benson nodded. 'And my shoulder. So tight!' Tiny buds of sweat grew on his forehead. 'Dizzy too,' he panted.

Sylvia calmly turned to Joyce and asked her to call an ambulance, then took a few pillows from the Kids Corner of the waiting room and placed them under Mr Benson's head, lifting his feet onto the row of chairs so he was semi-reclined. 'How bad is the pain on a scale of one to ten?'

'Nine,' Mr Benson strained.

'Do you have your nitroglycerine pills with you?' Sylvia asked.

He nodded and pointed to a leather zip-up folder under the chair. Sylvia unzipped it, allowing it to lie open on the floor. Inside were what appeared to be copies of blood test results, prescription forms, handwritten notes, and a compartment holding a pill dispenser which Sylvia immediately opened, taking a pill and placing it inside Mr Benson's mouth. 'Let it dissolve under your tongue, okay? It'll take the load off your heart and help it get more oxygen. Now concentrate on taking slow deep breaths — in and out,' Sylvia breathed the words as Mr Benson tried to slow his breathing.

Mark shifted back and forth from one foot to the other, adrenaline bubbling up inside. He went to ask if there was anything he could do, but refrained, as Sylvia looked like she had everything under control. And no doubt she'd yell orders if help was needed. He *could* help reduce the anxiety by applying some acupressure, a simple way of assisting the body without any acupuncture needles, but he'd never seen Mr Benson as a patient before, and he might become more anxious if Mark began pressing on his skin without understanding what he was doing.

Sylvia placed two fingers on Mr Benson's wrist and looked at her watch for a few seconds. Within a minute or two, his breathing slowed and his chest relaxed a little, however the deep furrows on his face still conveyed pain.

Dr Bronovski came out of his room to see if his assistance was needed, but Sylvia shook her head, so he motioned to his terrified-looking patient sitting awkwardly in a chair to come through for her consultation, although her head remained turned in the direction of Mr Benson. Like a car crash you couldn't help but look at.

Sylvia checked her watch again. 'Okay, how bad is the pain now on a scale of one to ten?'

'About seven,' Mr Benson replied.

Concern creased Sylvia's forehead, and she turned her face towards Mark. 'Mark, could you get the portable BP monitor from my room?'

Mark nodded and dashed through the hallway. He grabbed the one from his own room instead which was closer to the waiting room, and gave it to Sylvia who wrapped the cuff around Mr Benson's arm and pressed the inflation button. Mark leaned discreetly over to see the blood pressure reading. It was actually quite low. Uncommon for a man of his size, unless he'd overdosed on anti-hypertensive medication, but when associated with chest pain it could indicate a heart attack.

Sylvia took another pill from the container. 'Take another

pill now, hold it under the tongue.' She put it in Mr Benson's mouth and reminded him to breathe slowly.

Five minutes later, Mr Benson was still reporting his pain as a seven. Mark hoped like hell he'd make it to the hospital in time without going into cardiac arrest. They had an emergency defibrillator in the storeroom, but Sylvia had mentioned that in the time she'd worked at the clinic they'd never needed it. Yet.

Through the clinic windows Mark saw the ambulance at the bottom of the hill, so he went outside to wave it over. A middle-aged female paramedic and what looked like a young recruit followed Mark inside as he explained the situation. Sylvia told them what medication she'd given and when, and Joyce brought over a print-out of Mr Benson's patient file. *Good thinking, Joyce,* Mark thought. Although it looked like Mr Benson's whole medical history was inside his leather folder. Mark picked it up and carried it outside as they wheeled the patient into the ambulance, and handed it to the older paramedic as she got into the back with Mr Benson.

'They'll take good care of you, Mr Benson, hang in there,' Sylvia said before they closed the ambulance doors.

Sylvia had been amazing. So calm, efficient, and caring. No wonder she was popular. She may believe that her way was the only way, but she did her job well. Although maybe now she'd refer patients for acupuncture and herbal treatment after having experienced the benefits herself.

As Mark watched the ambulance disappear down the hill, its siren waking up the neighbourhood, he realised that if Mr Benson survived, then Sylvia had quite probably saved his life by acting so quickly. He also realised something else. Without Sylvia in his life he wouldn't have made any headway in moving forward through his grief over Cindy's death. Sylvia's presence, although triggering his guilt at first, also motivated him to move on. If they were going to make a go of things, he needed to step up and take responsibility for himself.

It was time to save his own life.

The rest of the day couldn't go fast enough, and by the time Mark arrived home that evening his blood was filled with adrenalin for what needed to be done. He chucked his wallet and keys on the kitchen bench and charged straight into the spare room.

He lifted the largest box first, and ripped off the masking tape holding it closed. He tipped the box upside down and piles of clothes fell out into a heap on the floor. Various fitness outfits, jeans, tops, and... Cindy's wedding dress covered in a protective slip. A sudden sense of her presence made his knees buckle and head dizzy, but through gritted teeth he picked up another box, ripping it open and tipping it over like a wild animal on a rampage for food. Books, CDs, and magazines spilled out on top of the clothes. The next box was heavy, so he pulled out the items one by one — various trinkets, candle holders and framed prints. Things that made a house a home. He opened another box, tipping its contents on the floor, and then another, until all the boxes were empty and the floor was littered with the rubble of his grief, his own kind of Ground Zero.

Splinters of pain wedged themselves in his heart as he sorted through the piles, bit by bit. It could take him hours, all night even, but Mark didn't plan on stopping till it was done.

CHAPTER THIRTY-THREE

Sylvia was finishing off her ham, cheese and tomato sandwich out on her back deck when a knock sounded at the front door. Curious furrows creased her brow. Grace wasn't due for another few hours. The weather was uncharacteristically warm for this time of year, and Sylvia reluctantly stood from her sun-drenched chair and walked through the kitchen to the front door.

'Mark, hi,' Sylvia said. 'Come in.' She thought he might give her a 'hello' kiss or even a hug, but he didn't.

'Thanks,' he said, giving his shoes a quick wipe on the doormat before walking inside. 'Have you heard anything about Mr Benson?'

'Yes, I called the hospital this morning. It *was* a heart attack, but he's stable now,' Sylvia replied.

'Good to hear. It's lucky you were there to help him.'

'It's lucky you rescheduled him to Friday for me, otherwise he may have had the heart attack at home with no one there to help him.'

'Team effort, then.' Mark smiled.

'Yes, a team effort.' Sylvia smiled back, then noticed Mark's smile disappeared as quickly as it had arrived.

'I won't stay, I know you'll be helping Grace get organised for tonight.' Mark scratched the back of his head. 'I just wanted to tell you that I'm going away for a little while.'

'You are? When? Where?' A wave of discomfort rolled through her body. Mark still wasn't ready. She knew it'd been a bad idea to let him kiss her again.

'I'll still be at the concert tonight, but I'm leaving tomorrow morning. Going to see Cindy's parents to give them some of her belongings I've been holding onto. Then I'll take a drive up north, go camping and spend some time in nature.' Mark stood there with his hands wedged in his pockets. 'I've spoken to Joyce, she'll let my patients know. I've already called those booked in for Monday. I feel bad, but this is something I need to do,' he said. 'I'm no good to my patients if I can't be one hundred percent focused on them.'

Sylvia's head nodded up and down, while her heart shook side to side in protest. But she had to let him go so he could figure out what he wanted. If he wanted *her*.

'When will you be back?'

'Not sure. Shouldn't be too long. I'll reassess after a couple of days and let Joyce know. I just need to go with the flow for a while and have time to think.'

Sylvia nodded again, while mismatched words moved around her mind, trying to sort themselves into a coherent sentence. She'd never go away somewhere without knowing when she'd be back. Heck, she'd never go away without having a detailed itinerary broken into hourly increments. Something inside told her she should try it sometime. Head off into the sunset and see where the road led. Be spontaneous. Maybe Mark had come into her life to teach her that.

'Well, I guess I'll be going. I'll see you tonight anyway,'

Mark said, leaning forward and giving her a light kiss on the cheek.

Again, it seemed all Sylvia was capable of was nodding.

'Take it easy on that ankle for a while.' Mark pointed to her foot. 'No climbing ladders or running around the block, okay?'

'Okay.'

'And tell Grace I said good luck for tonight.' Mark walked down the steps and got on his bicycle, and Sylvia's eyes followed him as he rode off down the hill.

Later that afternoon, Sylvia woke from a brief nap and went to the kitchen to boil the kettle. While she waited for the rewarding click of the switch as the water boiled, she unloaded the dishwasher. Glancing out the kitchen window, she saw Nancy Dillinger sitting as still as a statue on a wrought-iron bench in her garden. Her eyes were closed, and for a moment Sylvia thought she might be dead, what with Mr Benson's close call and Mark's dead wife playing on her mind. She went out on the back deck to get a closer look, and saw Nancy's chest rising slowly up and down. Phew. Sylvia realised she must simply be taking advantage of the warm sun. It was good to see her outside, getting some vitamin D.

At the exact same moment, Nancy opened her eyes and looked right at Sylvia, and a sudden pop burst from the kettle. Sylvia jumped backwards a little, her hand flying to her heart. It was like in a horror movie when you think the bad guy's dead and then he opens his eyes.

Sylvia gave a feeble wave and called out. 'Hi, Nancy. I was just, er...' She looked at her watch. Grace would be there in just under an hour. '...Wondering if you'd like to come over for a cup of tea?' After years of neighbourly waves and nothing more than a simple 'hello', Sylvia had finally broken the ice.

Nancy's eyebrows rose. 'Oh, um... I don't want to put you to any trouble.'

'No trouble. I've just boiled the kettle.'

'Um,' Nancy said, looking at her watch. 'Reruns of *The Golden Girls* will be on soon, so um—'

'I have scones,' Sylvia interjected. 'With jam and cream.'

Nancy pushed herself up from the garden bench. 'Well, in that case. I'm sure you don't want them to go to waste.' She walked to the front of her garden with quite efficient speed for someone in their late seventies. Although the promise of a Devonshire tea could get many a tired body moving, Sylvia was surprised she hadn't done a hop, skip, and a jump over the side fence to arrive sooner.

Sylvia went through the kitchen and opened the front door just as Nancy was walking up the steps, and she led her out to the back deck to take advantage of the low sun before it faded away. Sylvia set down a plate of scones, still steaming after she'd heated them in the microwave, and went back in to get the tea, milk, and sugar.

'These are delicious,' Nancy said with a piece of scone in her mouth. 'Did you make them?'

'I'd like to say yes, but no. Picked these up from the bakery this morning.' Sylvia lathered a scoop of cream onto a scone and lifted it to her mouth.

'So, you don't bake?' Nancy glared at her like she'd sinned.

'Sometimes. But I prefer to cook meals rather than cakes and things.'

'Do you cook butter chicken?' she asked with a fierce curiosity.

Just how much could Nancy see through that window of hers? Sylvia had cooked that only a week ago. 'Yes, I cook a mean butter chicken, actually.'

'A what?'

'Many. I've cooked it many times.' No point trying to explain that *mean* means *really bloody good*.

'Oh. Good. That's my favourite meal, you know.'

It looked like Sylvia now had Nancy's stamp of approval. 'Well in that case, I'll be sure to drop some over to you, next time I cook it.'

A sudden glow lit up Nancy's face. 'Please do. That would be delightful.'

'How long have you lived next door, Nancy?' Sylvia asked, after she'd swallowed the last mouthful of her scone.

'Thirty-six years and four months.'

Sylvia smiled. It seemed she wasn't the only one who liked to be specific with things. 'If you don't mind my asking, was there a *Mr Dillinger*?' Sylvia covered her chin with her teacup, blowing the surface of the liquid into tiny ripples as gentle steam circled above the cup.

'Oh yes. But I divorced him,' Nancy stated.

'Sorry about that. So, how long have you lived alone here?'

'Thirty-six years and four months.'

'Oh.' Sylvia realised that amount of time was more than the whole time she'd been alive. Such a long time to be alone.

'I'm not lonely you know,' Nancy piped up, seemingly reading Sylvia's thoughts. 'I like living alone. I get to watch the shows I want to watch. Don't have any dirty towels or smelly socks to pick up from the floor. And besides, I have eight hundred and fifty-seven Facebook friends to keep me company.'

Sylvia almost inhaled the mouthful of tea she'd just sipped. Nancy Dillinger was on Facebook?

'Don't look so shocked. I did a seniors computer course at the community college a while back, so I'm pretty nifty with the internet. Although I don't use that tweeter garbage or whatever it's called now. How anyone can have anything useful to say in one hundred and forty characters or less, I have no idea.' Nancy sculled the last of her tea and placed the cup back on the saucer.

Sylvia held in a snort of laughter. Nancy was probably more technologically savvy than many teenagers. Certainly more than her. Sylvia had a Facebook account but never checked it. 'And did you and Mr Dillinger have any children?'

Nancy softened a little and nodded her head. 'One daughter,' she said, staring into her empty teacup. 'But she died when she was twelve.'

'Oh, Nancy. I'm so sorry, I shouldn't have asked.'

Nancy flicked her leathery hand towards Sylvia. 'Don't apologise. It was a lifetime ago. All water under the bridge now.' Nancy lifted the teapot and poured the black liquid into her cup, adding a splash of milk and two heaped teaspoons of sugar. 'What will be, will be,' she added.

As a doctor, Sylvia's curiosity couldn't be detained. 'Had she been sick, your daughter?'

'No. Fit as a fiddle. It was a wretched accident that took her life. Bert... *Mr Dillinger*, was adamant that our young Rose attend boarding school, as he and I did when we were young. And despite my reluctance — I wanted to have her near, you see — he talked me round. So she packed her bags, and caught a bus with a couple of girls from town who were going to the same school. An hour later two police officers came to the door. The bus Rose was on had been in an accident, thanks to some hooligan who'd been speeding around a corner. They said the bus had swerved to miss the car but toppled sideways. The other people on the bus were only injured, but my Rose wasn't so lucky.' Nancy seemed composed in her recall, although her teacup was shaking a little.

'Oh, Nancy. I... I don't know what to say. I can't imagine how difficult that must have been for you.' Sylvia placed a hand on Nancy's forearm, if only to steady her shaky teacup.

'It was a very difficult time, to say the least,' Nancy said. 'And Bert and I, well, we just couldn't get past it. I couldn't help but blame him. If he hadn't demanded Rose attend boarding school it wouldn't have happened. I couldn't look him in the eyes anymore, hence our divorce four years later.' Nancy's voice cracked a little and she took a sip of tea. 'But after I moved here, I realised that maybe it had just been her time. If Rose hadn't caught that bus, perhaps she would have gone some other way. Maybe she would have ended up dating a hooligan herself and getting into another accident. Who knows? But I thank my lucky stars I at least had twelve good years with her. Bert and I weren't able to have any more children you see, Rose was my one and only.'

Sylvia was no stranger to the subject of death, but found herself blinking away tears. For years she'd seen Nancy as a quiet but nosy old lady, and now in a matter of minutes she was seeing Nancy for who she was. A grieving mother who'd toughened up over the years to cope with a tragedy, a woman who'd experienced something so awful and unexpected that she'd shoved it aside and replaced it with a life of predictability and routine. Nancy drew comfort from her controlled life. She knew what was going to happen and when. She knew that if she kept things the same something bad was less likely to happen, and by distracting herself with the lives of others, and keeping focus on what was 'next' in her day, she never allowed herself time to think. Or feel. Sylvia wondered if Nancy knew how alike they both were.

'I've been wondering,' Nancy said, a curious glint in her eye. 'Who's that pretty girl that's been visiting a lot lately?'

'Grace? She's ah... actually, she's my daughter.' She might as well bare her soul too. No point being vague with the usual 'we're related' speech.

'Oh, really?' Nancy asked, but Sylvia knew that Nancy already guessed that.

'Yes. I had her when I was young, so she was adopted out.'

Nancy swivelled in the chair to face Sylvia, her eyes widening. 'And you've recently been reunited?'

Sylvia nodded.

'Tell me all about it, love,' Nancy said, settling comfortably in the chair with a scone in one hand and teacup in the other.

'Good luck tonight, Grace!' Olivia called out as Grace walked out of Mrs May's Bookstore, having finished her Saturday shift.

They'd offered to give her the day off in preparation for the concert, but Grace said she'd rather keep busy to settle her nerves. She'd practised and practised already and could probably do the composition in her sleep by now, and she was more nervous about meeting her grandparents tonight than anything else. She'd thought long and hard about whether to try getting in contact with Max Reeves, her father, but decided to wait a while. She didn't want to interrupt this special time in his life, preparing for a baby, by turning up and announcing, 'Hey, I'm your illegitimate daughter!' After the baby was due to be born she'd reconsider, but for now, Grace was happy having met Sylvia, and now, about to meet her grandparents. What should she call them, Grandma and Grandpa? That would seem weird. First names might be best, or maybe Mr and Mrs Greene.

Grace ached to see Jonah, and hopefully score a quick 'good luck kiss', so she walked in the direction of Café Lagoon where he was working till six, having promised to be at the concert in time. She'd pick up a quick hot chocolate and drink it on the walk to Sylvia's house, as she was due there soon to get ready for tonight. Her dress was packed in the bag she had hanging from her shoulder, along with shoes, hair clips, jewellery, and make-up.

The café was packed when she arrived, and she waited in line behind a middle-aged couple at the counter. Jonah was serving them, but hadn't seen her yet.

'Thanks, Jonah,' the man said, taking one large cardboard cup and handing it to the woman, before picking up his own. 'I saw your mum the other day, said she was very proud of you, working extra hard to save money for the big trip,' the man said. 'When do you leave, next month isn't it?'

'Yeah, sixth of July,' Jonah replied.

The man nodded. 'She said you might be gone a whole year. Do you think you'll stay in the UK for most of it, or spend more time backpacking around Europe?'

'Not totally sure yet, I'm just going to see...' Jonah began his reply but trailed off when he saw Grace, staring at him in disbelief. 'Grace, hi, I didn't see you there, I was just—'

'Europe? The UK? You're going away for a year and didn't think to tell me?' Her blood boiling, she stormed out of the café.

'Grace, wait!' Jonah rushed out after her. 'Let me explain, please!'

She turned around momentarily, wanting to ask 'why?' but she couldn't face him. The truth was clear. He'd deceived her, led her on. And next month he'd be gone.

Jonah, looking torn between having to man the café and wanting to catch up to Grace and explain his deception, hung awkwardly at the perimeter of the café, several patrons watching and probably wondering what the fuss was about.

'Let's talk about this, don't run off,' he pleaded.

But Grace turned and walked further away, her footsteps almost burning holes in the footpath. *How dare he? I knew he was too good to be true!* Just when things were going right for her, Grace was dealt a hard hit. Right in the heart. It hurt like hell and she wanted to curl up and cry, but anger kept her walking towards Sylvia's house. She wondered if Sylvia knew about this. Surely she would have told her if she did.

A few minutes later she arrived, out of breath, at Sylvia's front yard. She went to walk up the steps but heard voices around the back, so she went around to the side gate. Sylvia was probably on the deck enjoying the final moments of sunshine. Grace heard an elderly woman's voice, but couldn't make out what she was saying. *It must be Nancy from next door*, Grace thought. Sylvia had finally become neighbourly and invited her over. As she unlatched the hook on the side gate and pushed it open, she heard Sylvia's voice. Could only hear fragments of what she was saying, but enough to have the words send shockwaves through her heart, still raw from Jonah's revelation.

'...Too young to be a mother... a mistake to have her... if I could turn back time...'

A mistake? Yes, that's what she was. She wasn't supposed to have been born. That's probably why she got cancer — a cruel trick by the universe trying to send her back to where she came from. These thoughts rushed through Grace's mind as tears rushed to her eyes. She took her hand away from the gate and turned away, the gate falling closed behind her with a loud clang.

She was at the end of the driveway when Sylvia called out. 'Grace, where are you going?'

Grace turned around. 'I shouldn't have come.'

'Grace, if you're nervous about the concert you needn't be, everything's going to be fine.' Sylvia rushed to meet her, but Grace took a few steps backwards.

'I mean, I shouldn't have come *here*. To Tarrin's Bay. It was a mistake, just like me — a mistake!' Grace stormed off.

'Oh, Grace, wait. Come back.'

'Leave me alone!' Grace yelled, before turning back briefly. 'That's what you always wanted, isn't it?'

She trudged down the hill quickly, then sped up to a run, knowing Sylvia wouldn't be able to chase her with a bad ankle. And it was for the best. She didn't want to talk to anyone right now, just wanted to get out of there.

Sylvia's chest rose and fell rapidly in short sharp bursts. Grace had run off too fast for her to catch. She wouldn't have cared if her ankle hurt, but if she tripped and fell she'd be no good to anyone tonight. The car. She'd get in the car and drive after her. Sylvia went to rush inside to get her keys, when Nancy stopped her.

'Let her be for a while,' she said.

'I have to talk to her. She must have overheard us talking and took things thing the wrong way. I have to make it right,' Sylvia said, walking up the steps.

'Sylvia. Give her some time to calm down, you don't want to talk to her while she's so upset.'

Hesitating, Sylvia looked at her watch, and not having registered the time, looked at it again. 'She's performing tonight. We don't *have* a lot of time.'

Nancy placed her hand on Sylvia's arm. 'She'll come round, love. Why don't you wait a half hour and then call her. If she doesn't answer, then drive over to her. Whenever my daughter was upset with me, she'd run into her bedroom and lie on her stomach on the bed until the tears dried up. Then we'd talk and everything would go back to normal.'

Sylvia allowed Nancy to lead her inside. She sat at the kitchen table, and Nancy brought in the tea and scones from outside. 'Maybe I'm just not cut out to be a mother,' Sylvia said.

'Now, don't go talking like that, love. You can't give up at the first argument. Motherhood is a rollercoaster ride; you have to take the ups with the downs.'

'But did you see the way she looked at me? She didn't want to be anywhere near me.'

'Look, love, as many mothers will tell you, that's normal. And she's at a vulnerable age, finding her independence in the world. It can be scary. Somehow, she only heard what she was fearing, and assumed the worst.'

Sylvia had never experienced anything like this before. An unfamiliar and very uncomfortable sensation sat in her stomach. To see Grace hurting hurt her too. She sat there listening to Nancy's advice, and after a while she tried calling Grace. No answer. 'I'm going now. I can't sit here and do nothing.' Sylvia thanked Nancy and told her she could let herself out when she was ready, and grabbed her car keys and handbag. A few minutes later she pulled up at the caravan park to find Grace carrying a couple of large bags and about to get into a taxi. Leaving the engine running, Sylvia lurched from the car. 'Grace!' She rushed up alongside her. 'Don't go. What about the concert?'

'Tell Mr Randleman I'm very sorry,' Grace said, opening the taxi door.

Sylvia pushed the door closed. 'Wait. I don't know what you overheard back there, but you must have misunderstood what I was saying. I said it would have been a mistake *not* having you. Please just—'

'You said "a mistake having her". Sounds pretty clear-cut to me.' Grace opened the door again. 'I know I'm not wanted here. And Jonah's going overseas so he obviously doesn't care about me anymore, so I'm going back to Melbourne, where I belong. Dad will be glad to see me.'

'Jonah's going away? And Melbourne? No Grace, please. I

do want you here, and...' Sylvia looked at her watch. '...We have to get ready for the concert, you've spent so much time preparing, don't let it go to waste. And, and, my parents are coming! This is your chance to meet them,' Sylvia urged, her hands waving about relentlessly.

Grace looked Sylvia directly in the eye. 'If they wanted to meet me, they would have by now.' She got into the taxi and closed the door, and Sylvia was forced to step away when the taxi reversed, its tyres crunching on the gravel driveway as though poking tiny holes in her heart.

Sylvia stood in the driveway, hands on her head in disbelief, as she watched her daughter being driven off into the distance, not knowing if she would ever see her again.

CHAPTER THIRTY-FOUR

When disbelief and worry had given way to helplessness, Sylvia returned home. She sat slumped in the chair on the back deck, the metallic tingling of the wind chimes hypnotising her. Their sweet sound conjured an image of the ocean on a summer morning, sparkling under the sunshine as though stars were scattered across the rippling surface. For a moment she felt nature's peace, its reassuring embrace. Amazing how something as simple as a sound could evoke such clear images and feelings. As though different sounds were keys that could unlock every possible emotion in the heart.

Suddenly, she knew what she had to do.

With resolve, Sylvia picked up the phone. 'Hi, William, it's Sylvia Greene. I'm sorry to tell you this, but Grace Forrester won't be performing tonight after all. I'm afraid something important came up.'

She listened for a moment to his cries of, 'No! She was going to be the highlight of the show!' and 'Everyone's going to be so disappointed!' before putting him out of his misery.

'William, it's okay, I know someone who can fill in for her.'

'You'd be hard pressed to find anyone as talented as her, who could possibly take her place?' William asked.

'Me,' Sylvia replied.

She didn't have long to prepare, and didn't even know if she could pull it off, but Sylvia knew she had to do it. People were expecting a piano performance tonight and that's exactly what they would get. It was time to put the past behind her, stop hiding, and show the world the real Sylvia Greene.

She lifted the lid on the piano. The smell of old timber and varnish wafting up to her nose transported her back to a time when she was younger, more carefree. She could feel her mother's breath above her as she sang and played with Sylvia's hair. Her father, sitting in his armchair tapping his feet, sipping whisky.

Sylvia's fingers touched the smooth white keys, and she pressed lightly, tentatively, getting a feel for it. Then, as though she'd turned on a switch, it all came rushing back, and a flood of emotion poured from her heart to her hands. Her fingers danced across the keys in a foxtrot of high and low notes; quick steps from one key to the next, rhythmic and fluid, yet each tap definite and strong. It was as though they had a mind of their own.

She swayed forwards and backwards, putting her whole body into it. A smile found its way to her lips as she lost herself in the music. Or more so, *found* herself in the music, remembering who she was. It had been over eighteen years since she'd played, but it was as though she'd never stopped. All that skill, stored away, waiting to be used again, had resurfaced.

Surprisingly, Sylvia didn't feel guilty like she thought she would. Somehow, the thought of playing again after giving up her child had seemed selfish. She'd failed to accept the responsibility presented to her back then, and denying Grace her real mother made her think it only right to deny herself of something too. Concentrating on her studies after Grace was born made it somewhat easier, and soon playing piano was as distant to Sylvia as the memory of her daughter's eyes.

But now, she'd feel guilty if she *didn't* play. How could she encourage Grace to play piano if she wasn't prepared to make use of her own talent? Apart from being a good doctor, this was her gift. This was her passion. And it was time to share it.

When it came time for Grace's scheduled performance at the end of the concert that night, Sylvia walked out from behind the curtain on to the stage, her heels on the wooden stage floor piercing the silence. She went up to the microphone at the front corner of the stage, and adjusted its height. 'Good evening, everyone. There's been a slight change to this evening's program. Unfortunately our pianist had to cancel at the last minute due to unforeseen circumstances, so... I'll be performing instead.' Taking a deep breath, she glanced around the auditorium, knowing her secret was about to be revealed. One of them anyway. 'I hope you'll enjoy my composition, which I've called *The January Wish*.'

Despite her nerves quivering when she sat at the piano, Sylvia soon found her groove as she began playing. The slow rhythm of the song was calming, and although she was too focused to see the audience, she could feel their eyes on her. It felt good. Real good.

Finally, her music was out of her mind and spreading throughout the auditorium. It was a huge release. The emotion from everything that had happened: the day she gave Grace up; the day she wished to meet her again and be given a second chance; their reunion and relationship over the past few months; and now her hope that they'd be able to reconnect, found its way into her composition.

When the last note faded to silence, Sylvia left her hands hovering over the keys momentarily, energy still pulsating through them. Then she placed them on her lap and looked sideways at the audience to see everyone on their feet, clapping. Her heart rose with them, and a wide smile grew on her lips.

She stood and gave a subtle bow of her head. Just as she was about to walk off the stage, a figure came into view in the middle aisle of the auditorium, light bouncing off her red curls as she neared the stage.

Her breath caught in her throat, Sylvia stared as Grace walked up the steps to the stage, wearing the dress they'd bought that day they went shopping together, and smiling her infectious smile.

'I'm so sorry I ran off. Am I too late?' Grace gestured towards the piano, the audience silent as they watched with intrigue on their faces.

'It's never too late to do what you need to do.' Sylvia placed a hand on Grace's cheek, warmth spreading through her fingertips, before walking up to the microphone.

'Thank you all, for your kind applause, I'm so glad you enjoyed the performance. And now, it looks like our star pianist *will* be playing after all.' Sylvia turned towards Grace and smiled, watching as her eyes sparkled and her soul glowed, overwhelmed by a sense of maternal love. Then Sylvia revealed her other secret to the audience. 'I'd like to introduce the amazingly talented Grace Forrester. My daughter.'

Sylvia stood behind the curtain as her daughter commanded the stage, bringing the room to life with an upbeat composition resembling a garden full of bright, colourful butterflies. Grace had transformed from a regular teenage girl into an accomplished and mature woman and performer, and Sylvia's heart overflowed with pride.

The energy in the room soared as the audience rose to their

feet again. Grace humbly accepted their applause, her hand over her heart as she mouthed 'thank you' in all directions.

William gave Sylvia a happy little squeeze of her shoulders from behind, before giving a 'thumbs-up' signal with his hands as he walked past, up to the microphone to conclude the concert.

Grace scurried over to Sylvia backstage. 'I'm so sorry, I shouldn't have left like that, it was selfish of me, and—'

'It doesn't matter, you were upset,' Sylvia interjected, placing her hands on Grace's arms. 'I'm sorry you overheard some of my conversation with Nancy Dillinger, I just wish you'd heard all of what I'd said. I was talking about how people always call teenage pregnancies a mistake, and I said, "But it wasn't a mistake to have her... it would have been a mistake *not* to have her".'

Grace's head dropped. 'It looks like I made a fuss over nothing, didn't I? I should have let you explain, instead of rushing off in that taxi, only to ask the driver to turn around when we were almost at the airport! He wasn't happy, and I lost a bit of money, but I don't care. When I'd had time to think, I realised I must have misunderstood something, you seemed so genuinely shocked that I was angry. And apart from that, I knew I couldn't let Mr Randleman and the children's oncology department down, I mean — I used to *be* one of those kids. How could I not support them now that I'm okay?'

'It's all water under the bridge now. You're here, I'm here, that's all that matters.' Nancy's words of wisdom hung in Sylvia's mind. Nancy wouldn't get a second chance with her daughter Rose, but Sylvia would, and she wasn't going to waste it.

'What else did you say to Nancy, something about "turning back time"?' Grace asked.

'Oh yes. I said, "Sometimes I think if I could turn back time, just maybe, I'd take my baby home with me."'

Grace sniffed, and wiped at the corner of her eyes.

'And before all of that, I told her how glad I was that you'd come back into my life, how I'd wished more than anything to meet you again, to be a part of your life. And most importantly how proud I am of what you've accomplished, and how you've handled the difficulties in your life with such, well... grace!' Sylvia wiped a tear from Grace's face with her thumb, and kissed her forehead.

'Now I can see where I got my talent from. You were amazing!' Grace's chin quivered. 'I love you,' she said as she fell into Sylvia's body and held on tightly, as Sylvia wrapped her arms around her.

Their first embrace all those years ago was brief, and surreal. Over before it had really happened. Now here Sylvia stood, eighteen years later, holding her baby properly for the first time. But this time she wasn't going to let her go.

She'd done it. She'd finally performed in public. Grace was buzzing, on a high, made higher by the fact that the misunderstanding between her and Sylvia had been sorted out. So the perfect boyfriend had not turned out to be so perfect after all, but there were more important things in life than guys. Now that she'd had a taste for performing, she wanted to keep doing it. And to think that Sylvia had been hiding her own talent all this time! It felt special to Grace to know that she could attribute something to a parent. While other kids she'd known at school had their father's eyes, or mother's smile, she didn't know who she took after. It'd been like she was an alien, and landed here on earth by herself, with no family background.

Now, she felt like she belonged. She knew where she got her red curls from, she knew where she got her chin dimple from, and she was extremely grateful to have been given the gift of musical ability.

As she and Sylvia walked through the backstage door into the foyer, they were bombarded by people coming at them from all angles, saying how much they enjoyed their performances. Then a woman with short grey hair came up to Sylvia. 'Sylvia, it was so good to hear you play again!' The woman hugged Sylvia, then turned to Grace. 'And you were absolutely brilliant.' She stared at Grace in a look of amazement, and held out her hand. 'I'm Lillian Greene, Sylvia's mother.'

Her grandmother. Her *real* grandmother. Grace took her soft hand and shook it gently. 'It's so nice to meet you.'

'And I'm Robert Greene,' said a tall man with a grey beard and moustache, holding out his hand too.

Her grandfather. She shook his hand, and smiled. The moment was surreal, and Grace felt she was in a dream. But this was real.

'Rob, great to see you back in town! You have a very talented daughter and granddaughter there,' a man said as he came up and shook her grandfather's hand.

'Indeed I do,' Robert replied, looking proud.

'Well, I'll leave you all to it and catch up with you later. Nice seeing you, you too Lillian,' the man said.

Lillian nodded happily at the man, then turned to Sylvia. 'If the weather's anything like today, why don't we all meet in Miracle Park for a picnic lunch tomorrow?'

Sylvia glanced at Grace and raised her eyebrows. Grace nodded. 'Sounds nice!'

'Lovely, say about twelve?' Lillian asked.

Everyone agreed, and Sylvia excused herself as a couple of people approached her. Grace recognised one of them as the lady from the clinic. Then she saw Lauren in the crowd trying to get Grace's attention, and Grace waved.

'There are probably a lot of people wanting to congratulate you. You go and talk to them, Grace, and we'll get a chance to talk tomorrow,' Lillian said.

'Thanks so much for coming tonight, it's really great to meet you,' Grace said, shaking Lillian's and Robert's hands once more, and walking over to Lauren.

'Good stuff, girlfriend, that was awesome!' Lauren high fived her. 'I am so jealous of your talent; I can't even play *Twinkle Twinkle Little Star* on the piano!'

'Thanks, but I'm jealous of you, your reverse turning kicks are the best in the class!'

Lauren shushed her. 'Stop it, tonight's about you.'

Grace sidled up closer to Lauren. 'You knew, didn't you, about Jonah going overseas?'

Lauren nodded and bowed her head. 'I'm sorry, I wanted to tell you, tried to get *him* to tell you, but he made me promise to keep it secret. Said he planned on telling you after the concert, and didn't want to upset you after you'd been sick and all.'

So that's what that exchange between Lauren and Jonah had been about. She was trying to get him to tell her the truth. 'He still should have told me, it really hurt, knowing he'd kept it from me,' Grace said.

'Maybe you should tell him that,' Lauren said, pointing to the doorway that led outside.

Jonah stood leaning against the doorframe, his hair covering one side of his face, and he signalled for her to come over. Grace didn't want to argue, she just wanted to enjoy this night, but somehow she found herself walking towards him.

'You didn't tell me there was a song named after you,' he said.

'What do you mean?' she asked, confused.

'*Amazing Grace.*' Jonah smiled.

There he goes again, Grace thought. *Putting on the charm.* She turned her head away from him. 'You really hurt me, you know. I don't know why you didn't just tell me.'

'I was going to, not long after we met, but then things started getting serious, and it got harder and harder to tell you. I didn't want to risk losing you. I thought you'd break up with me if you knew I wasn't going to be around much longer.'

'But you should have left that up to me to decide. Who's to say I wouldn't have stayed with you — to make the most of the time we had?' Grace said, finally looking him in the eyes.

'Yes, I should have. I'm so sorry, Grace. We were having so much fun together, and I didn't want anything to muck it up. Then you went to hospital and I found out about the cancer, and there was no way I wanted to tell you then, so I thought after the concert would be best. Guess things didn't quite work out as planned,' he said, bowing his head. 'If I'd known you were going to come into my life I don't know if I would have even booked the trip. I even thought of cancelling, but I'd already paid a deposit, and I've spent years saving money.'

'I wouldn't want you to cancel your trip, it'll be an amazing experience.' Grace smiled, the hurt from before dissolving away as she realised, he'd only kept it secret from her because he really liked her. Maybe even loved her.

'I know. It's going to be the trip of a lifetime.' Jonah held onto her shoulders. 'And I want to share it with you.' His eyes looked straight into hers. 'Will you come with me, Grace?'

CHAPTER THIRTY-FIVE

The next day, Robert Greene and Grace were tossing bread crumbs towards a growing army of birds, all lined up in readiness to charge forward at the flying crumbs, when Sylvia noticed a tear falling gently down her mother's cheek.

'Mum?'

'I'm sorry,' Lillian replied, wiping the tear away quickly as though she'd walked into a spider's web. 'I don't know what's come over me. It's just... she's beautiful, Sylvia.'

'She sure is,' Sylvia replied, glancing towards Grace, now competing for the birds' attention with a child nearby, who was enthusiastically throwing large chunks of bread. The sun had carried over its warm reign from yesterday into today, and as tomorrow's forecast was for cold winds and rain, many people were in Miracle Park enjoying the favourable weather.

'I'm so glad you finally took up piano again, Sylvia. It's been far too long.'

Sylvia nodded, her fingers still tingling from the euphoria of performing last night. 'I know. If it wasn't for Grace, I wouldn't have.'

'I hope you'll keep it up,' Lillian said.

'I don't think I'll be able to stop now. I have eighteen years of unsung music waiting to be born.' Sylvia smiled. 'When I got home last night I thought about how powerful music can be, and I want to do something with it to help people who are sick. Maybe visit the nursing home and play for the residents, and I could go to the children's oncology ward at the hospital too.'

Lillian's face lit up. 'And you could even teach the children some basic tunes on a keyboard,' she said.

'Good idea. And you know, I might talk to Joyce and my colleagues about having relaxing music playing at the clinic, instead of that daytime TV rubbish,' Sylvia said.

Lillian sat there with Sylvia at the picnic table, looking into her eyes. 'It's good to see your spark back.'

'My spark?'

'The spark you had when you were younger, before you had Grace. The spark you had when you'd show us the new compositions you'd created. You were meant to be a doctor, Sylvia, but you were also meant to play the piano. It's part of you, just like it was for me.'

Sylvia looked at her mother's arthritic hands. 'Are you sure you can't fit the piano at your place, Mum? I'm sure we could squeeze it in somewhere.'

'No, it should stay at your place, you'll get more use out of it now than me. I'd rather only play if I can play *well*. But I'm afraid my time has been and gone,' Lillian said, rubbing her knobbly fingers.

Sylvia pursed her lips to one side. 'Actually, I know something that might be able to help with your arthritis.'

'But I'm already doing everything you've suggested.'

'Yes, but I haven't suggested acupuncture or herbal medicine yet,' Sylvia replied.

Lillian eyed Sylvia curiously. 'Who are you and what have you done with my daughter?'

Sylvia laughed. 'Let's just say, I've had a few eye-opening experiences this year.'

'Well, it's getting worse, so I'll do anything.'

Sylvia opened up her purse and took out a business card, handing it to her mother. 'He's away at the moment, but give him a call in a couple of weeks and see what he says. I don't know if you'll be able to come back to Tarrin's Bay often enough, but if anything, he might be able to point you in the direction of someone closer who could help.'

'I'll do that, thank you.' Lillian winked at Sylvia. 'I just won't tell your father.'

Sylvia smiled, and looked at her father, tossing a crumb to the birds, talking and laughing with Grace. He looked different somehow, less rigid. More... at ease.

'Your father would never tell you this, Sylvia, but last night he asked me if I thought he'd been right in encouraging you to give up Grace for adoption.'

'He did?'

Lillian nodded, then looked down. 'And I have to wonder the same thing myself.'

'Mum, what's done is done. And she's here now.'

'Yes, but if we hadn't been so... insistent about it, *would* you have made the same decision?'

Sylvia thought back to the shock of her positive pregnancy test; those two pink lines that silently told her she was expecting a baby. Two potential realities awaited her: life as a single teenage mother, frowned upon by others, her dreams of being a doctor shattered. Or, life as she had always planned it — top of the class in medical school and a rewarding, important career, her daughter being raised by two parents who wanted her desperately. 'Yes, I would have made the same decision,' Sylvia said. Although whether Grace would have chosen it, she wasn't sure. It can't have been easy, being different to the other kids, not knowing where she came from.

Lillian placed her hand gently on Sylvia's and nodded, relief on her face. 'I'm sorry we've become so distant. We'll make the effort to visit more often.'

'It's okay, I've been distant too. And I'll make the effort to visit *you* more often.' Sylvia removed her hand from under her mother's and curved it around her mother's back, Lillian leaning in and resting her head on Sylvia's shoulder.

After saying goodbye to her grandparents, and eagerly accepting their offer of free accommodation whenever she visited Sydney, Grace began walking up the hill to Lookout Point where she was to meet up with Jonah. A cool breeze resisting her forward movement, she wrapped her scarf in an extra circle around her neck.

At a park bench under a naked skeletal tree, she saw him. Elbows resting on his knees, and hands clasped together, looking out at the wide expanse of ocean. So still, which was unlike Jonah. Grace veered off the footpath and onto the grass, and when her footsteps neared him, he turned around and stood, his smile warming her deep inside. She smiled too, and in that moment wanting nothing more than to wrap herself around him and stay close to him forever.

'So, you've forgiven me?' he asked.

Grace nodded. 'I understand why you kept it from me, and I'm flattered actually.'

'And have you had time to make a decision, about coming overseas with me?' Jonah held on to her hands and swung them gently from side to side.

Grace tightened her grip on his hands, stilling the movement. 'Jonah, I'd love to...'

The downward tone in her voice communicated her conflicting emotions, and though defeated, he smiled. 'But?'

'But... I can't.' Grace looked away, then back at him. 'It's *so* tempting, believe me. I thought about it last night, about running off overseas with you, seeing the world. And I almost called you then and there to say yes, but it just isn't right for me, not now. And then I thought maybe I could go for a month or two and fly back on my own, but I knew if I went, I wouldn't want to leave, and that would be even harder.'

Jonah stood silently, nodding, his lips clamped together in reluctant acceptance.

'After performing last night, I realised that's what I want. I want to live and breathe music. I've been holding back so long, scared of getting sick again, and I can't do it anymore. I have to pursue my dreams, and make the most of being well. Who knows what'll happen down the track, but I can't live in fear anymore.' Grace fought back tears, but a rogue one escaped.

'I wanted so much for you to come with me, but you're right, you have a gift and you need to make a go of it.' Jonah wiped the tear from Grace's cheek with his thumb.

'I've decided to audition for the Sydney Conservatorium of Music,' Grace said. 'In November.'

Jonah's eyes widened. 'Wow. You'll get in for sure, I know it.'

Grace shrugged. 'We'll see, but I hope so. I've been looking at the website and I'm really excited.'

'If you perform anything like you did last night you'll blow them away,' Jonah said. 'And you've got the complete package — the skill, *and* the looks.'

Grace smiled, and ran her finger around his jawline, taking in a deep breath. 'I'm going back to Melbourne next week to stay with Dad until my audition. I want to spend as much time as I can with him before I move to Sydney, that is, *if* I get in.'

'You'll get in.'

'Sylvia's coming with me, just for a few days. She wants to meet my dad,' Grace continued. 'So, it looks like I won't be back this way until November, and by then... you'll be gone.' Another tear escaped Grace's eye and, as she looked down, it dropped to the ground before Jonah could wipe it away. When she looked up, Grace saw that Jonah's eyes were red and glossy, and his lips were clamped tighter together than before.

'I'll miss you, Grace Forrester.' He pulled her close and kissed her with such emotion that Grace felt she would have collapsed had it not been for his arms wrapped tightly around her. She didn't want it to stop, knowing it would be their last kiss, her mind trying hard to store the memory of the moment.

'I won't forget you,' Grace said as they reluctantly pulled away, arms still entwined around each other.

'I won't forget you either,' Jonah replied. 'How could I? You'll be a household name before too long, and I'll be in the audience of one of your sell-out shows, that's for sure.'

'I might even write a piece of music about you.'

'You would?'

'Yeah, I reckon I will. But I won't let you hear it until one of my 'sell-out-shows', so you'll have to try and guess which one it is,' Grace said.

'So you won't be calling it something obvious like *The Most Amazing Guy In The World*?' Jonah grinned.

'Ha ha, no. Sorry. It'll be something cryptic. Although *Geek at Heart* might be a good title.' Grace giggled.

Jonah tickled her under the arms. 'Don't you dare expose my secret!'

Laughing and wriggling, Grace urged him to stop. 'I promise, I won't. I promise!'

'You sure?' Jonah intensified his tickling attack, until he succumbed to her protests and enveloped her in his arms again. His warm breath on her neck masked the cool breeze as it leapt up from the ocean.

'So I guess this is goodbye,' Grace said.

'For now. I'm sure you won't be able to stay away from Tarrin's Bay forever.'

'I'll visit often, I'm sure.'

'Well, when I get back from overseas and go back to work, I'll be sure to keep a *morange and ango juice* chilled for you.' Jonah winked.

Grace laughed at the memory. 'Will it be *squeshly freezed?*' she asked.

'Nothing but the real deal for you, Grace.' He kissed her one last time, briefly, as though to not dilute the passionate one from before.

Grace wanted to tell Jonah how much he'd meant to her, how much more magical this year had been because of him, and how he was her first real love. But now seemed the most appropriate time to leave. She wanted to remember him as he was now, smiling and joking around. Sure, they might see each other again someday, but as Grace knew all too well, life could change in an instant, and nothing was guaranteed. So she took a step backwards, and then another, her hands still holding his, until they dropped away gently and the only thing connecting them to each other was the gaze of their unblinking eyes. She didn't look away until the hard surface of the footpath met her feet. And as Jonah waved and flashed his delicious smile, Grace turned and walked down the hill, engraving the memory of his eyes in her mind alongside the memory of his kiss, the warm tingle of it still lingering on her lips.

CHAPTER THIRTY-SIX

'Olivia was sad to see you leave Mrs May's, Grace. She said you were the best sales assistant they'd had.' Sylvia walked with Grace down the pebbled path leading into the cemetery, an icy Melbourne wind throwing their hair all about.

'I'll miss it, and them. I feel bad leaving on such short notice, but with it being the anniversary of Mum's death, I thought now would be the best time to come back here,' Grace said. 'And anyway, my friend Lauren is looking for casual work, so I got her an interview at the bookstore.'

Although she was coping well, Sylvia had noticed the deep sadness in Grace's eyes this morning as they'd eaten breakfast at the hotel. They'd been to the theatre the night before, and were going to be spending a few days together in the city. Then she'd leave Grace with her dad, and fly back to Sydney. Back to Tarrin's Bay. Back to the life she wasn't sure if Mark was still to be a part of. But work would keep her busy as usual, especially now that Mr Benson was out of hospital, he'd need more regular care. She'd felt bad leaving town for a few days, knowing Mr Benson would want to see her, but Dr Bronovski assured her he'd take care of him.

'There he is,' Grace said, pointing to a thin man with silvery hair, standing with his hands in his pockets in front of a grave. Grace ran towards him, her shoulder bag bouncing up and down, and he met her halfway with an enthusiastic embrace.

'Sylvia, this is my dad, David. Dad, this is Sylvia,' Grace said when Sylvia caught up with them.

What do you say to the man who raised your daughter? The man who'd fed and provided for her since birth, taught her how to ride a bike, consoled her when she was sick? Weariness surrounded his pale eyes, but an expression of kindness overshadowed it. You could tell by looking at him he was a decent man. A man who stood by his family and loved them unconditionally.

'It's so nice to meet you, David.' Sylvia held out her hand, but he didn't take it. He stretched out both his arms and welcomed her with a hug. At first, Sylvia's shoulders stiffened, then softened as he whispered, 'thank you', in her ear. They might not have met before, but they were inextricably connected, and their combined love for Grace was powerful beyond measure.

Words seemed unnecessary as they walked over to the grave of Maria Forrester and laid down a bunch of flowers, staring at the headstone, as though waiting for some kind of response. Some sign that she knew they were there. Grace stood in between Sylvia and her father, and as she sobbed softly, Sylvia put a hand on her pulsing back. David did the same, though he was surely hurting too. Fallen leaves wafted around the headstone, gently lifted up and down by the wind, and the noise of the nearby city seemed to fade away. Although standing in front of the grave of a woman she'd never met, Sylvia felt she'd come to know Maria through Grace, and found herself becoming teary-eyed as well.

After a while, Grace straightened up and turned towards

her father. 'Dad, there's something I want to give you. I was going to give it to you for Christmas, but I can't wait till then.' She led him to the comforting shelter of a nearby tree and as they sat on the small bench, Grace withdrew the memory album from her bag, handing it to her father. She'd shown Sylvia the album at the hotel. It was a beautiful monument in remembrance of Maria, and a promising reminder of the woman Grace had become. Sylvia had smiled at the photo of the sunflower Grace had drawn in the sand, that day they'd walked along the beach together.

David turned the pages of the album carefully, and Grace sat there smiling. Then she turned a few of the pages over and pointed to a picture, obviously eager to show her father. Sylvia didn't know which picture they were looking at, but it made the corners of David's mouth turn up. He spoke to her softly, before putting the album aside to embrace his daughter.

Sylvia turned away to give them privacy, and leaned over Maria's grave to place down the single sunflower she'd brought with her. Silently, she thanked Maria. Thanked her for taking care of Grace, for loving her, for being the mother Sylvia wasn't able to be back then. She wished she could hug her the way she'd hugged David, but she couldn't. She simply placed a hand on the cold, rough headstone, and somehow hoped to communicate just how thankful she was that her daughter had been well cared for. Maria's life may not have been long, but Sylvia knew it would have been fulfilling, having Grace in it. And suddenly Sylvia felt a strong sense of responsibility, that although she wasn't taking Maria's place, she *was* taking on a new role in Grace's life. At sixteen, it wasn't her time. But now, at thirty-five, it was.

'It's not goodbye, it's just see you later,' Grace said as she stood next to Sylvia and her suitcase, waiting for the taxi to take Sylvia to the airport.

They'd both stayed at Grace's family home last night, and Sylvia had tried to keep her composure while being given the tour, but Grace could tell she'd felt quite emotional. Grace had lived in this house since she was a young child, and knowing this was where her daughter had lived all this time must have been a strange sensation for Sylvia. Grace's dad showed Sylvia their photo albums, with pictures of Grace as a baby, a toddler, and on her first day of school. There was even a lock of her red curls taped to a page in the album. He'd shown her all of Grace's school photos, although some years were missing; the years she'd been sick. Within only an hour or so, Sylvia had seen a compressed version of Grace's life up till now. What pictures would take up residence in the photo albums of years to come she didn't know, but she knew there'd be plenty of her at the piano. And maybe she'd meet some nice like-minded people if she got accepted into the conservatorium, and they'd become lifelong friends. Who knows, maybe she'd even meet a nice new guy, although she couldn't bear the thought of that just yet. Her heart still ached for Jonah, but she'd try her best to move on. Empty albums awaited, and Grace was eager to fill them with new experiences.

'Of course, it's only a few months till your audition. I bet the time flies by,' Sylvia said.

'Make sure you keep in touch, okay?'

Sylvia picked up Grace's hand. 'I was going to ask you the same thing.'

Grace smiled. 'I'll be busy preparing for my audition, but I'm sure I can find *some* time to talk to you occasionally.'

Sylvia nudged her daughter's ribs. 'You better. And make

sure you look after yourself. Get enough sleep, eat well, and take your tablets.'

'Yes, Mum.' Oops. She'd meant it as a figure of speech, but an awkward moment hung between them. Grace preferred to call her Sylvia, as 'mum' was... *had* been, reserved for Maria. The only mother she'd known until this year.

'You know what, Grace?' Sylvia said after a few moments. 'I know I was young when I had you — too young to give you the life you deserved — but I'm so glad you were born. You're the best thing that's ever happened to me.'

Something tugged at Grace's heart. 'I am?'

Sylvia cupped Grace's face in her hands, and kissed her forehead. 'You bet.'

Grace wrapped her arms around her mother and held on until the taxi pulled up in the driveway. The past few days had gone so fast, she didn't want them to end. But Sylvia needed to get back to work, back to her life. And for Grace, *her* life was just starting. Her dreams were within reach and she was going to stand on her tippy-toes and grasp them with all her strength.

As she finally let Sylvia get into the taxi, Grace bit her lower lip to stop it from trembling, and as she waved goodbye while the taxi drove off, she could have sworn she could smell her mother's perfume. Maria's perfume. Her signature fragrance, Trésor. Maybe Sylvia had been wearing it? But she hadn't seen it in her cosmetic bag in the hotel bathroom, and she hadn't noticed the scent until now. Now that Sylvia was gone. The sweet fruity scent danced around her and accompanied her back inside the house, where her father was waiting with open arms.

CHAPTER THIRTY-SEVEN

Mark had been away eight days when he knew it was time to go back. He packed up his tent and set off early Monday morning, arriving home by 11am. The sun was intermittently making an appearance through the clouds, the sky mostly overcast. In contrast to the fine weather he'd had up north, Tarrin's Bay was at its coldest. Although not known as a particularly cold area, it still had those days in winter where you were better off indoors with a hot drink and a heater.

Anxious to make the most of the day, Mark quickly packed away his belongings so he could get started. There were three things he needed to do. First, he went to his bedroom and picked up the photo of Cindy from his bedside table. Saying a silent 'thank you' for the memories they'd shared and the part she'd played in his life, he turned the photo frame over and removed the picture, placing it inside a photo album that contained pictures of his previous life at Welston. He put the empty photo frame back on his bedside table. When the time was right, he'd fill it with a new photo.

Then, he lifted the framed portrait of Cindy from the wall in the entry foyer and removed the picture, placing it inside the photo album too. In its place in the frame, he put a print he'd bought at a local art and craft market last week. It was a picture of a silhouetted person sitting on a lush green hill at sunrise, with a quotation that grabbed Mark as soon as he'd seen it: *'You are the writer of your own life story. So get a pen, turn the page, and start writing!'*

The quotation had a double meaning for Mark. Not only was he moving forward towards the life he wanted for himself, he had a forgotten dream he needed to pursue. He fired up his computer, opened up his documents, and clicked on the folder titled 'Books'. In there was a file called 'BoostingAthleticPerformanceNaturally.doc' and he double-clicked on it. The last sentence he'd written was, 'taking this supplement twenty minutes before exercise has been shown to...' and then he'd stopped. Cindy had screamed when she found a spider in the bathroom, and Mark had left his computer suddenly to see what was wrong. Then the phone had rung, and one interruption after another had prevented Mark from finishing that sentence. Then life took over and the manuscript went into extended hibernation, until now.

Mark still remembered what he'd been about to write, so without pausing to acknowledge this significant moment in his efforts to move on, he typed and completed the sentence... 'improve oxygen uptake by fifteen percent, making it an excellent option for enhancing performance, endurance, and recovery'. He added a reference number in superscript, and updated his 'references' file that was to be included at the back of the book.

Mark tapped furiously at the keys, and by two o'clock found himself irritated by an inconvenient grumbling in his stomach. He defrosted and reheated a mug of vegetable soup he'd stored in the freezer, and sipped it while writing. The wind whipped at the branches of the tree outside, slapping the leaves at his window, as years of research and knowledge poured onto the screen, and he typed at a speed he couldn't quite believe. It was as though he was racing down Death Hill again, but with his mind not his body.

At dinnertime, he ordered a Thai home delivery and sat briefly at the dining table to refuel; rushing back to his desk before he'd finished swallowing his last mouthful. Just like when he'd sorted through Cindy's boxes, he seemed to work best in sudden bursts of activity, so he went with the flow and kept writing while the inspiration propelled him.

When Sylvia arrived home late on Wednesday afternoon, the town seemed empty without Grace. Grace had only been here for five months, but somehow she'd carved her own special place in the heart of Tarrin's Bay. Come November, Sylvia would see her again. They'd planned to meet at the airport, and stay at Sylvia's parents' house in Sydney the night before the audition. It warmed Sylvia's heart to see Grace pursuing her dreams. Sylvia herself could have quite possibly had a music career, but the urge wasn't as strong compared to pursuing a medical career. But with her idea to play piano at nursing homes and hospitals, she now had an opportunity to combine both. She planned on making some phone calls tomorrow to see what she could arrange.

Sylvia unpacked, filed away her mail, then had the urge to clean. Although it wasn't her scheduled house-cleaning day, she decided to give in to spontaneity and give the house a good vacuum. Once she'd started, she thought she might as well continue, so she cleared out the pantry and wiped down the shelves, washed the tiled floor, then went into the bathroom and did the same. She checked her cosmetics and threw out those that were getting old, replacing them with new ones she had stored away, before adding the items to her shopping list. That way she'd never run out and be left without items she needed every day.

Sylvia was about to close the bathroom cabinet door when she noticed the bottle of Trésor perfume. She picked it up and observed the little that was left, before throwing it in the bin. She hadn't worn it in months, so why keep something she didn't use? She then picked up the bottle of J'Adore and sprayed her neck and wrists, and gave a triumphant nod of her head as she looked at the sparkling results of her cleaning rampage.

Pouring a hot cup of coffee, Sylvia sat in front of the computer and opened her email program. Instead of following the standard email-checking procedure, she clicked on an email that surprised her: 'Nancy Dillinger added you as a friend on Facebook'. Smiling, she thought 'why not?' and clicked the 'confirm' button.

As Sylvia scanned through the news feed of her fifteen friends, a little depressing considering Nancy's eight hundred-odd friends, a small chat window popped up in the corner.

Hi Sylvia, good to see you here! I noticed you arrived home today, how was your trip?

Sylvia typed in a reply.

Hi Nancy, trip went well, thanks. I have no idea what I'm doing on Facebook, I didn't even know you could chat live like this!

I'd be happy to tutor you in social media if you like, I'm quite the expert.

Nancy replied.

Sylvia thought this may be a good way to keep in touch with Grace, although, maybe Grace preferred to use it to communicate with friends, rather than parents. She decided to bring it up casually in conversation next time they spoke.

Sylvia pursed her lips to the side and tapped her fingernails on the table, then typed:

Nancy, how would you like to come over for dinner tonight?

The cursor on the screen blinked as she waited. Nancy was probably considering her pre-planned routine and reconfiguring an alternate plan.

Oh, I don't want to be a bother. You've only just got home.

Sylvia typed:

I've got butter chicken.

What time shall I be there?

Sylvia smiled and told Nancy to come over at six-thirty. She'd picked up the butter chicken at an Indian restaurant on the way home to reheat for dinner, but there was no need to tell Nancy that.

When Sylvia heard the grumbling of the postman's motorbike outside her house on Friday afternoon, she walked out to collect the mail. A couple of bills, a lighting catalogue, and a small parcel had been delivered. She filed the bills away, tossed the catalogue into the recycling bin, and opened the parcel. It was

The Woman in White, the book she'd lent to Grace when they'd first met at the start of the year. A post-it note was attached. '*Sorry, I forgot to give this back to you! I loved the book, thanks. Grace.*' A card was also enclosed, with a photo of a child's hand being held by an adult's hand on the front. Sylvia opened the card and read the handwritten words:

> Dear Sylvia,
>
> I just wanted to send you a little note to say thanks. Thank you, not only for welcoming me into your life this year, but for giving me life in the first place. Although I have faced many challenges in my eighteen years, I wouldn't change a thing. Not even the cancer. Everything has led me to where I am now, and I am so excited about my life and what the future holds.
>
> Although I can't imagine not having had my adoptive parents in my life, I just know that you would have been a great mother, no matter how young you were. And I want you to know that I am one hundred percent at peace with the decision you made, because thanks to you, I am the lucky one. I got to have more than two parents. I was blessed with a loving upbringing, and have many cherished memories of my childhood.
>
> Deciding to find you, and having you accept me into your life, has been the best experience of my life, and I am also incredibly thankful for the musical gift you passed onto me. I'm going to follow my passion with all my heart and soul and do my best to have a successful career.

Keep being you, because you are my inspiration.
Love Grace xoxo

By the time Sylvia had finished reading, silent tears streamed down her face, and she had to sit down to stop the emotion taking her legs from under her. She read the card again, and again. Those words meant so much to her, and she finally knew, after eighteen years, that she did the right thing. Grace was destined to be a part of David and Maria Forrester's life — she'd given them the greatest gift of all, a child to call their own. And she'd given Grace the gift of two parents who loved her.

Sylvia waited... waited for the rebounding guilt to surface as it usually did. But it didn't come. She felt as though she'd rid herself of a chronic condition, and was feeling the relief of wellbeing for the first time in a long while.

Maybe there *was* some sort of magic in the Wishing Fountain after all. Whatever it was, however it happened, by making a wish that day she'd somehow triggered a series of events that had given her the gift of a new kind of life. A life where the past was simply a memory and not a burden. A life where she could be her authentic self without fear or guilt. A life, that like Grace, she was excited about. And just as she'd been given a second chance with Grace, if she were to be given a second chance at bringing another child into this world, she knew without a doubt that she deserved it and that she'd be a damn good mother.

As she put Grace's card on display on top of her bookcase, Sylvia's phone beeped. It was a text message.

Can we talk? If you're free, meet me at Cafe
Lagoon at 4pm. Mark.

So he was back. Sylvia had almost managed to keep him out

of her mind during the past week or so, what with everything going on between her and Grace in Melbourne, but now, she longed to see him. They'd turned a corner last time they were together, but his need to get away was a sign that he hadn't yet been ready to get involved in a relationship. Whether his brief time away had changed anything she wasn't sure, but at least he was ready to talk, whatever the outcome would be.

At a quarter to four, Sylvia checked her appearance in the mirror, and walked down the road towards the main street, and towards the charming, funny, unpredictable and irritating man she was somehow falling in love with.

CHAPTER THIRTY-EIGHT

When Sylvia crossed the road and stepped onto the footpath she almost collided with a woman pushing a large pram. 'Samantha!'

'Hi, Dr Greene!' Samantha Roseford stopped and smiled, though she kept swaying the pram back and forth.

'I see your little munchkins have come into the world, they're gorgeous! How are they?' Sylvia asked.

'Yes, they're finally here. I only got out of hospital two days ago, and they're happiest when they're moving, so I'm getting lots of exercise walking with them, or waddling more like it!' Samantha said. 'I ended up having a natural birth, I can't believe it. When Scarlett came out it was such a relief, but then I had to keep pushing, and Sophia soon followed. Sophia's a little smaller, but they've both been given a clean bill of health.'

'Two girls? How lovely.' Sylvia hadn't been able to tell. They were both dressed in white, with tiny white beanies on their heads, and each wrapped in a thick grey blanket.

'I know. But I reckon they'll send me bankrupt. If they have my genes, they'll be shopaholics by the time they're five.'

Sylvia laughed. 'And how are you going with it all?'

Samantha exhaled. 'I'm exhausted, but loving it. I can't believe how time consuming two little people can be though. I keep trying to tackle my To Do List, but it just gets away from me.'

'Yeah, tackling doesn't always work. I prefer to tie mine up and force it into submission,' Sylvia replied.

Samantha laughed. 'I'll have to give that a try. Something tells me I'll need to sort out a consistent routine if I'm to get anything else done around the house.'

'But just remember, the most important thing, apart from looking after your babies, is to look after yourself. Don't try to be Supermum. Take any offer of help, and don't forget to call me at the clinic if there's anything concerning you.'

'I will, Dr Greene, thanks.'

Sylvia looked at Scarlett's and Sophia's tiny faces and realised how amazing life was. How one baby, let alone two, could live and grow inside another human being was truly remarkable. Medical science had an explanation for everything, but no words could describe the wonderment that was human reproduction, and how each new little person brought their own unique personalities to the world.

As Sylvia watched Samantha cross the road, using all her effort to walk and push the double pram, she realised that not only was Samantha's motherhood just beginning, but hers was too.

Mark stood from behind the table near the window when Sylvia walked into Café Lagoon, and greeted Sylvia with a hug. 'What would you like, a coffee?' he asked, heading to the counter to place their order.

Sylvia was about to say 'yes', but changed her mind. 'Actually, I'll have a dandelion chai.'

Soft arcs formed in Mark's coffee-coloured cheeks as he smiled. He ordered two cups of dandelion chai, and two slices of hummingbird cake. 'I hope you're hungry,' he said as he sat down at the table.

'Starved,' she replied, resting her elbows on the table and clasping her hands together.

Their order was set down on the table by a waiter Sylvia hadn't seen before. He'd probably been hired to replace Jonah, she thought. 'Mmm, this is good,' Sylvia said, sipping her drink. 'I think I may have found myself a new addiction.'

'It's better for you than coffee. Although not many cafés serve it. Café Lagoon is one of a kind,' Mark said, sipping his drink too.

As they devoured their drinks and cake, Sylvia talked about her trip to Melbourne with Grace, and how she'd be returning in November for an audition. Mark told Sylvia how his four day nonstop writing binge had produced a complete first draft of his health book for athletes. Sylvia offered to read it and cast her perfectionist's eye over the draft to edit any mistakes and provide constructive feedback. Mark looked suitably terrified, but agreed anyway.

When they'd both eaten their final mouthful of cake and emptied their mugs of the remaining tea, Mark took Sylvia's hands in his. 'I'm sorry I've messed you around this year. As you know, I've had a few issues to deal with.'

Sylvia's hands melted at his touch, and she tingled all over as his thumbs stroked the back of her hands. 'You're forgiven. And I hope you'll forgive me for my occasional... irrational outbursts,' she replied.

'Occasional?'

'Okay, frequent. But you forgive me, right?'

'I forgive you.'

'And have you... *dealt* with those issues?' Sylvia asked tentatively.

'I won't lie, Cindy's memory will always be a part of me, but I no longer have any regrets. I know that what happened was meant to happen, and it wasn't my fault. The infection was rapid and aggressive, and even if I'd got her to the hospital earlier, there's no guarantee she would have survived.' Mark looked down at their entwined hands, then into Sylvia's eyes. 'I've said my goodbyes, I've made peace with what happened, and now I'm ready to move on. For real this time.'

Mark's eyes spoke the truth. They didn't hold sadness anymore, only hope. And his hands told her what she wanted to hear. That he wanted to be with her. And he was ready to give their relationship a go.

'I'm glad,' Sylvia whispered.

After a moment, a curious curve crawled up the side of Mark's mouth. 'You know, we never did finish that game of scrabble, the night of the blackout.'

'You're right, we didn't.' Sylvia thought back to the inconvenient return of electricity just as he'd been about to kiss her.

'How about we play it tonight, at my place this time?' Mark asked.

Sylvia had never been to Mark's house; he'd never invited her over until now. 'Will it be candlelit scrabble?' she asked with a glint of charm in her eye.

'That can be arranged. I'll even switch off the mains power if that helps make it more authentic.'

'Nah, then we can't have a warm cuppa.'

'True.' Mark nodded.

Sylvia crossed her arms and leaned back in her chair. 'If we're going to play, I think we should mix up the rules a bit this time. That bonus fifty points gave you an unfair advantage.'

'You're just a sore loser.' Mark grinned.

'Am not.'

'Are too.' Mark's grin widened as he leaned over the table. 'Okay, maybe there *should* be a price to pay for getting a bonus. How about, for every triple word score, or triple letter score, we have to remove an item of clothing?'

A jolt surged through Sylvia's body. 'You mean, *strip scrabble?*'

'Shhh,' Mark said as a couple of people looked their way. So much for maintaining a strictly professional image in public at all times. 'Yes, that's exactly what I mean.'

'In that case, you *better* leave the mains power on, we'll need the heater.'

'Oh, I don't think we'll have any problem generating heat tonight.' Mark winked.

Three hours later they were playing scrabble by candlelight on Mark's living room floor. They didn't manage to finish that game either.

CHAPTER THIRTY-NINE

THE FOLLOWING JANUARY

'C'mon, let's line up at the Wishing Fountain.' Mark tugged at Sylvia's hand.

'Nah, I don't need to make a wish.'

'You don't?'

Sylvia shook her head. 'You go ahead though.'

'I will,' he said, walking over to the line.

'Be careful what you wish for, Mark,' Sylvia called out. 'It just might come true.'

'That's what I'm hoping!' he called back, holding up a pair of crossed fingers.

Sylvia smiled as she waited under the cool shelter of a tree, watching the people in line anxiously waiting their turn while the summer sun burned above them. She wondered what each would be wishing for. Recovery from an illness perhaps, a secure financial future, or to find the love of their life, who knew? What she did know, however, was that their wish coming true was certainly possible. *Anything* was possible. Life was always changing, and Sylvia's life had changed into something more amazing and magical than she could ever have imagined. Nineteen years ago she'd given birth to a beautiful baby girl who'd grown up into a beautiful young woman. Now, it was like she was giving birth to a new life of her own, filled with peace, happiness, and excitement. Peace with the past, happiness with the present, and excitement for the future.

After tossing a coin into the fountain and walking around it three times, Mark strutted over to Sylvia with a proud expression on his face. 'I think I'd like to find out now if my wish is going to come true.'

'How do you plan on doing that?'

Mark didn't answer. He bent one knee to the ground, and looking up at Sylvia, produced a black velvet box from his pocket. He flicked it open, and a single diamond glinted in the afternoon sunlight. 'Will you marry me, Sylvia Greene?'

Sylvia's heart skipped a beat. She knelt on the ground and met Mark's eyes. 'You know I will,' she whispered, accepting the ring as he slid it on her finger and engulfed him with her arms.

She *could* have made another wish, done her bit for charity as she'd done last January. She could have wished for a year off to travel to exotic countries, or a three million dollar mansion with a housekeeper and personal chef. But right now, Sylvia was exactly where she wished to be.

EPILOGUE
ELEVEN MONTHS LATER

Sylvia and Mark shuffled sideways into their allocated seats in the auditorium, next to David Forrester and Sylvia's parents. They were in the fourth row and had a perfect view of the stage. The Conservatorium of Music's end-of-year student showcase was sure to be a treat. Sylvia's nerves tickled with anticipation.

Being the first performer for the night, Grace must have a thousand butterflies in her stomach by now, Sylvia thought. She too could feel them. Only they weren't butterflies. Quickly, she grabbed Mark's hand and placed it on the small mound of her belly.

'Can you feel it?'

Her husband sat still as he waited for the subtle rippling sensation. When it came, an expression Sylvia had never seen before graced his face. Love lit up his eyes, but a different kind of love. A fatherly love. While Sylvia had been experiencing firsthand the indescribable sensation of her baby growing inside her, this was his first encounter with their unborn child.

'Wow!' Mark said, as Sylvia's mother reached over in an

effort to join the party. 'She might grow up to be dancer,' he suggested.

'She?' Sylvia raised an eyebrow.

'Or he. I'd have no problem with my son being a dancer either,' Mark said, smiling.

They didn't yet know whether the baby was a boy or girl, and Sylvia didn't mind either way. All that mattered was that early next year she'd be taking this little angel home with her. And Mark would be right by her side.

'What's the name of Grace's composition?' Sylvia's father asked as the lights dimmed and his eyes strained to read the program. 'I forgot to bring my glasses.'

'*A New Beginning*,' Sylvia said proudly, just as the curtains slid open and a spotlight illuminated Grace's red curls, while a sweet melody danced joyously throughout the auditorium and sparkled like the stars in the sky.

THE END

ALSO BY JULIET MADISON

ACKNOWLEDGEMENTS

Thanks to the wonderful association that is Romance Writers of Australia for their support, knowledge, conferences, and professional development. And thanks to the volunteer judges of the RWA competitions I entered who gave up their time to read and provide feedback, which helped me in shaping this novel to prepare it for publication. Thanks also to the judges of the Choc Lit Search for an Australian Star contest who helped this book to become a finalist.

Thank you to Kate Cuthbert for believing in this book, to Betsy Reavley and the Bloodhound Books team for republishing this novel and my Tarrin's Bay series, and to my lovely editor, Belinda Holmes, who has worked with me on many books.

For my parents, thanks for supporting my dreams and leading me to the town I now call home, which is the setting I've based this novel on, and to my late nanna, my mum, and my cousin, Jennie, for reading the first draft of this book and giving me your encouragement.

Thank you to fellow writers and friends, Alli Sinclair and Diane Curran, for always being there to brainstorm and discuss ideas with when needed. And thanks to my writing friends from around the world who make this career choice more sociable!

Thanks again to my son Jayden for being excited along with me and for his advice that I should 'get publishing contracts more often' because of the super-happy mother I am when I get one! Happy to oblige.

And thanks to YOU, the reader for choosing this book. Enjoy!

ABOUT THE AUTHOR

Juliet Madison is a bestselling and award-nominated author of books with humour, heart, and serendipity. Writing both fiction and self-help, she is also an artist and colouring book illustrator, and an intuitive life coach who loves creating online courses for writers and those wanting to live an empowered life.

With her background as a naturopath and a dancer, Juliet is passionate about living a healthy and positive life. She likes to combine her love of words, art, and self-empowerment to create books that entertain and inspire readers to find the magic in everyday life.

Juliet lives on the picturesque south coast of NSW, Australia, where she spends as much time as possible dreaming up new stories, following her passions, being with her family, and as little time as possible doing housework.

You can find out more about Juliet, her books, and her courses at http://www.julietmadison.com and connect with her on social media at Facebook http://www.facebook.com/julietmadisonauthor and Instagram http://www.instagram.com/julietmadisonauthorartist

A NOTE FROM THE PUBLISHER

Thank you for reading this book. If you enjoyed it please do consider leaving a review on Amazon to help others find it too.

We hate typos. All of our books have been rigorously edited and proofread, but sometimes mistakes do slip through. If you have spotted a typo, please do let us know and we can get it amended within hours.

info@bloodhoundbooks.com